Rosco,

Thanks for the love !

Permetrice Milroe Jackson

DUPLICITY:
DOUBLE LIFE DRAMA
Who really lurks behind the mask?

A NOVEL

Permetrice Milroe Jackson

Passion Peach Publishing
Atlanta, Georgia

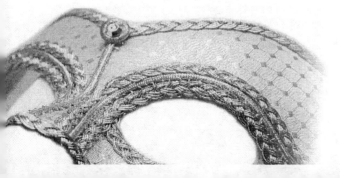

Copyright © 2013 by Permetrice Milroe Jackson

Visit us on the World Wide Web at www.permetrice.com

Library of Congress Control Number 2013908706

Jackson, Permetrice Milroe.
Duplicity: Double Life Drama/by Permetrice Milroe Jackson
1st edition

ISBN 978-1-886815-01-8
1. Suspense—Fiction. 2. Georgia (State)—Fiction 3.Romance—Fiction 4. Adultery—Fiction. 5. Domestic—Fiction.

Cover design by Vivian Fisher

Printed in the United States of America

Passion Peach Publishing
Atlanta, GA

Acknowledgments

I would like to thank my youngest child, Kirsten Janaye Jackson, for being my enthusiastic first reader. My daughter, Jaleese Una' Jackson and Caroline Allen also contributed to the proof-reading process. You will see many of your suggestions included as you read the published book. You encouraged me during the difficult times, knowing that one day I would reap the benefits of my labor. Pursue your dreams!

I have the best editors in the world! They each brought a unique point of view and keen eye for details that I gratefully incorporated into these pages. Mrs. Pamela Benford of Lithonia, Georgia, educator and high school principal extraordinaire; Carolyn Betts Carroll of Chicago, Illinois, retired special education teacher; and Tyran Epps of Ellenwood, Georgia, avid reader and customer service representative. I really appreciate your time, support, and true labor of love for my written words.

Thank you to my family and personal friends who encouraged me as I journeyed to this point in my life. I appreciate your support as I worked to complete this book. May God abundantly bless you!

Dedication

I appreciate the solid foundation of unconditional love from my parents. I would like to dedicate this book to my wonderful mother, Gwendolyn Milroe of Chicago, Illinois. Your love and encouragement helped me survive the storms of life. To the memory of my gentle and affectionate father, Clarence Milroe of South Holland, Illinois; I really miss you and our long and humorous conversations. Daddy, rest in the arms of the Lord.

I also dedicate this book to my three wonderful children. My son, Roger L. Jackson, Jr. always makes me feel loved when I get home. Thank you for your unique sense of humor. My middle child is a girl who I fondly call the Evangelist. Jaleese Una' Jackson, you constantly encourage me by sending me text messages of optimism, special quotes, or wonderful scriptures from the Bible reminding me of my greater purpose. Keep the good words coming Little Jaleese, my miracle baby. Finally, to my youngest child, Kirsten Janaye Jackson—my running buddy. I call you this because I stayed home with you. It was a sacrifice, but placing my career on hold for a season, was worth the investment! I encourage the three of you to continue to develop your skills in the arts because the world is waiting for you!

Duplicity:
Double Life Drama

A Novel

"A double minded man is unstable in all his ways."
James 1:8

Merriam Webster defines duplicity as double in thought, speech, or action, especially the belying of one's true intention by deceptive words or action. The quality or state of being double; hypocrisy; fraudulent or duplicitous representation; acting in bad faith; deception by pretending to entertain one set of intentions while acting under the influence of another; insincerely; a sustained form of deception.

The synonyms listed in Merriam Webster for duplicity include cheating, crookedness, deceitfulness, deception, dishonesty, double-dealing, fraud, guile, and fakery.

Prologue

Confused; that state of being is exactly what Ginger felt as she waited for Keefer to come home. While waiting, she obviously had fallen asleep. Abruptly awakened, she noticed that it was 4:30 a.m. as she sleepily glanced at the digital clock and slowly stretched across her plush California-king bed to find his side empty. She was simply stunned that her husband would have the audacity to stay out all night just months after drawing her back into his crazy world. She thought, *Knowing him and his fragmented mind, he probably thought he was doing me a favor. No thanks. If I wanted to be alone, I could have stayed by myself!*

With the realization that she was home alone, other than her dog Pepper that quietly slept down the hall; the horrible reality of the situation caused her exhausted body to completely wake up, sit up, and get up. Shaking the shock from her spirit, she wrapped her mind around the revelation that Keefer was cheating again. "No the hell this merry-go-round is not going to be my life again with this double-minded, lying man – not this time. The hell you say..."

Chapter 1

Blake Baker kicked the dirt mindlessly as he walked along the ominous trail Elsie Mae Coats had last been seen on. It made no sense how she had vanished, seemingly into thin air, never to be seen again. It had almost been two weeks and there were no new leads according to the newspaper accounts, but you cannot totally trust what is reported by the media. Routinely, the police release only what they want the public to know while the investigation is open.

Surely someone saw her. Somebody knows something in this one-horse town, he thought to himself; then he exclaimed out loud, "These people don't miss anything else! They know everything about everybody's business as long as it's something you don't want them to know!"

He was frustrated about how fast word on any matter got from the poor side of the tracks to the more affluent communities even if it had to be through the mouths of domestic help, talking carelessly to each other while being overheard by their arrogant employers who found time to listen to trivial hearsay from behind closed doors or through sophisticated intercom systems.

Reportedly, Elsie Mae had stopped at a local convenience store to purchase a cold Coke-A-Cola and a pack of Lance cheese crackers before heading home. Her car had been inoperable for some time needing an engine. She had become accustomed to walking to work at the Bennett household located about two miles from her humble, two bedroom shot-gun house. It was called a shot-gun house because you could open the front door and back door, shoot a gun and the bullet could go straight through the house without obstruction; although this was only a hypothetical explanation of her home's design.

The house Elsie Mae lived in may have been small and very plain, but she always kept it neat and clean. It didn't matter if a visitor arrived day or night; she always had something good to eat, either in the oven, on the stove, or she would pull it out of the refrigerator and insist on heating it up.

Certainly, Elsie Mae was considered a Southern Belle. She was polite and lady-like from all outside observations. Her reputation was impeccable and Blake had been secretly in love with her for some time; though he had not openly declared his feelings to her. He had started off very slowly, tipping his hat at her when he would see her at the store or the library. Apparently, they shared a love of reading; two points for her. He had finally mustered up enough nerve to ask her out to the movies. As he reflected on that first and only date with her, he got lost in the bittersweet memories of that night just three weeks ago.

* * *

"Hello Elsie Mae. How are you doing tonight?" He smiled from ear to ear, quickly glancing down at her cute denim dress with the embroidered flowers at the hem. Of course, he noticed her toes painted with pink nail polish. Her big toes were decorated with a colorful butterfly. Her legs and feet were glistening, greased down with Vaseline he supposed.

As he hurriedly brought his eyes back up her tall frame, he noted the curve at her hip and her shapely figure, wondering if she was as innocent as she appeared to be.

"Hi Blake; I'm doing well. How are you?"

Laying on the charm he said, "Much better now that I see you." Smiling, he silently relished in the faint blush in her cheeks.

She shyly returned a smile and quickly locked her door, not bothering to invite him in. As she spun around, she caught the way he looked at her. It was not exactly a lustful look, but one that let her know he admired her.

They slowly walked to his blue Ford Mustang and he opened the door for her as any good gentleman would do. Elsie Mae looked pleased as he glanced back at her while walking around the front end of the car to get in. She thought to herself, *He is one hunk of a man; tall, I guess about six feet, three inches, broad shoulders, blue eyes, sandy-colored hair, a country boy tan, pleasant demeanor, and a smile that makes me melt. I wonder if he's all man as he appears to be. You never know these days...*

After placing the seatbelt around his waist, he looked at her and took in her simple beauty with one quick look. Elsie Mae had an exotic appearance to her, tanned skin, green eyes and auburn hair, and a very shapely body. She seemed shy and wore modest clothes that didn't accentuate her figure. He offered her a smile that she politely returned. For that moment, they were one beaming pair. Even though she had a smile on her face, there was a distant hint of sadness in her eyes that he could not quite identify, but noted nonetheless.

When they arrived at the movie theater he walked to the concession stand and ordered two medium sodas and a large popcorn which he drenched in melted butter from the self-serve machine. After she pulled several napkins from the dispenser, they made their way to the featured film.

While enjoying the movie, Blake resisted the urge to place his arm around her shoulder, not wanting to offend her since this was their first evening out together. *Just take it slow, man, take it slow,* he admonished himself.

After the movie he offered to take her to dinner, but she said she really was not hungry after devouring mounds of buttery popcorn. He persisted and convinced her to at least go to the local Dairy Queen to have a banana split. Elsie Mae finally agreed, but she insisted on sharing the treat with him, much to his chagrin, because he really could eat one all by himself. He ordered it with the 'wet walnuts' in syrup on top.

After a spoonful or two she said; "I'm full and simply can't eat another bite." She yarned and politely pushed the oblong bowl closer to him and rested her spoon on a napkin.

"You're kidding me, right?" Blake felt she may have just been pretending to be full, but the girl still didn't eat anymore when he pressed her to enjoy herself.

"No, seriously; I just wanted to have a taste. I'm watching my figure." She playfully patted her hip when she said this as if she had a real weight problem.

"Okay. But it sure is good, and you know you are welcome to it. Actually, you could have had your own you know." Blake continued to eat the cold treat wondering what it would be like to taste her full lips. As he sat across from her, he admired her big green, oval shaped eyes that were meticulously made up with beautiful eye shadow. He could tell the difference having grown up with four sisters, three of whom used inexpensive products; but his older sister Roxanne only used the best from a boutique in the mall. There was a marked difference in the finished look and Elsie Mae had that polished look. He thought, *She is such a beautiful woman!*

Before he was ready for the evening to end, Elsie Mae started fidgeting in her seat wondering what time it was. Blake had left his cellphone in the car and he had left his watch on purpose. She would not let the issue pass until she found a lady across from them sitting at a booth near the door who had the time. As if 10:00p.m. was a bewitching hour, Elsie Mae insisted she had to immediately go home.

He drove toward her neighborhood wishing that the date could continue, but he reluctantly took her home. She quickly exited the car and almost didn't let him walk her to the door. Although he wanted to steal a kiss, she allowed a quick hug and bounced into the door, which seemed to open on its own. *Didn't I see her lock that door before we left?* Blake felt somewhat uneasy because she offered no explanation about her rush to get home, as if she had a parent waiting with a watchful eye glued to a kitchen clock. As far as he knew, twenty-two year old Elsie Mae lived alone.

* * *

Now that Elsie Mae, the girl of his dreams was officially missing, Blake wondered again how the door to her house came open so easily when he could have sworn the single key was still in her hand, about an inch from the door when it opened. Maybe he was imagining it because he was thrilled to be out with her and didn't want to let her go inside. Perhaps it was nothing; therefore, he didn't bother mentioning it to the police.

Weary with worry, Blake jogged back to his car, fastened his seatbelt, and backed out of the parking space into the road. He had volunteered to help search for Elsie Mae with the organized group which was led by the local police department. There were hardly any clues gathered except a blue bandana found near a dumpster about a mile

5

from the store she had stopped at on her way home. Since the dumpsters had all been checked, it was assumed that she dropped the scarf on her way home. One of the dogs from the police K-9 unit had detected Elsie Mae's scent, identifying the item as hers. Mrs. Cathy Bennett had confirmed that the scarf had been on her head while she cleaned her house earlier that last fateful day.

"Elsie Mae, where are you?" Blake called out to her jadedly while driving home. *God, is Elsie Mae okay? This is not like her to just disappear. I didn't know her well, but she seemed like a nice young lady; and according to everyone that I talked to, she would never disappear on her own. What's really going on?* Blake was perplexed trying to comprehend the disturbing mystery of her disappearance.

Hearing his cell phone ring, he reached into its holder, pulled it out saying, "Hi, Mom. Yes, I just left the search team, but we didn't find anything other than her scarf. It is so frustrating Mom. I feel like she is still alive, but why would she stay away so many days without at least getting in touch with her relatives?"

"Dear, I just don't know....it makes no sense at all to me. They say she didn't appear to be the type to up-and-go-at-the- drop-of-a-hat, so to speak."

"No; she's a good girl. She's a lady for sure. Some people have fooled me, but I know she is as innocent as the freshly fallen snow. Mom, she is a good girl; the kind you want to bring home." Blake reached up and combed his fingers through his hair, letting his hand rest at the nape of his neck.

"Now son, I wouldn't say all of that. Innocent, I doubt that! Fresh fallen snow – that's a stretch. You know son, some people just have a slick way of hiding their misdeeds. We used to call them 'undercover saints!' – always acting the part like they are so holy, but they really live a different life!" Maryann Baker kept washing down her stove top while talking to her youngest and very much, idealistic son who had recently turned twenty-three. Mrs. Baker was a middle-aged, high school secretary who old folks would have called plump. She also had blue eyes and a curly brown permanent in her hair.

"Mother, why do you always have to think the worst of people? There are some people out there who truly live above reproach, just like the good book says to live. I actually think Elsie Mae was-I mean is, one of those people. I just wish I could have gotten to know her better before all of this happened."

"Baby, I just don't want you to be naïve about life. Everything is not what it seems and everybody is not who they appear to be. Trust me on that one! You can bet your sweet bottom dollar that more people fool you with their fake face, than reveal their true identity with their words!"

"Mother, why do you have to be so negative? I can assure you; you're wrong on this one." Blake retorted.

"Baby, I may not know what happened, but that girl had plenty of skeletons in her closet. I know it in my heart to be so." She touched her chest with her hand as she emphasized her point. Continuing, she said, "And, stop referring to her as 'was' and 'used to be.' It ain't been confirmed that she is dead yet!" She paused to place her hand on her hip. She had already noted Blake's switch from calling her Mom to Mother. It was a telling sign that he had gotten a little annoyed with her.

"Now, you've got a point on that, Mom. I've got to hold on to the faith that she'll return again real soon. It's hard though, because the officer I talked to said chances get slimmer and slimmer that she'll be found alive with every passing day." Blake usually was upbeat and positive, but the strain of the events of late, were really stressing him out.

I guess he's not mad anymore since now I'm Mom again, she reflected before answering him. "Blake, do what you can to help, but that girl may be on the other side of the world, on a beach sipping a mixed drink, not thinking about any of us!" She laughed at her statement.

"I told you before that she didn't even drink alcohol! I'll talk to you later, Mother."

Hell, this boy is flipping from mad to glad on me every other second, over a girl he really doesn't know anything about. "Son, how many dates did you say you'd had with 'Miss holier than thou'? One whole date wasn't it? You can't really know a person with one encounter, sweetheart." *For crying-out-loud; did I keep this man-child too sheltered to recognize a possible undercover hoochie momma?*

"You'd be surprised at what I know. I'm not a baby anymore, Mother! Elsie Mae is good people, I tell you!"

"Whatever you say, son; just don't be surprised if what I said turns out to be the truth. And, stop raising your voice at me!"

"I'm Sorry. I'll talk to you later, Mother."

"Well, I love you son even if you do have strange friends."

"I love you too Mother, but I don't appreciate your last remark about Elsie Mae."

"Did I say Elsie Mae? Anyway, if and when I'm proven wrong, I'll apologize. Time will tell baby boy. Time will tell." Mrs. Baker heard the sound of the dial tone in her ear and hung up the phone. She made a mental note to discuss his rudeness with her husband once he got home from work.

Curious and thoughtful, she continued her daily routine working around her ranch-style brick home, pausing to switch the channel to CNN. Finally, as a story caught her attention, she hung the dish towel over the faucet, grabbed a soda pop from the refrigerator, walked to the family room, flopped down on the comfy brown leather sofa and released the recliner button to elevate her legs. "I don't know where that girl is, but I know one thing, I'm about to have a Coke and a smile." And she did just that.

Once Mrs. Baker tired of watching the news on CNN, her favorite soaps, and an investigative forensics program, she walked to the door leading to the deck and went outside. Descending the five steps, she lazily walked through her Japanese garden admiring the beauty of the flowers and bushes. After taking in some deep breaths of the fresh country air mixed with floral scents, she sat on the fancy leaf-swirled, wrought iron bench in the middle of the oasis of flowing waterfalls, under a Bloodgood Japanese Maple tree and closed her eyes. Sighing heavily, she thought about the naivety of her son, Blake and his unbelievable blind trust of people. Slowly shaking her head she reflected on recent chitchat she had overheard in the beauty shop. *I heard some things about that woman. I don't know how true they are, but eventually the truth always comes out. The good book says, 'What's done in the dark comes to the light.' Elsie Mae, you don't have me fooled by your plain dress and phony piety. There're probably plenty of stories to tell about your under-cover life; sneaky woman. I feel it in my heart. Lord, I know you'll show me after a while.*

Suddenly she said, "Elsie Mae, you may be missing now, but if you return and hurt my son, you'll have me to deal with! You'll wish you had really moved on. Now run and tell that." There was a humming bird resting on a tree limb that briskly flew away as if it had stories to tell and appointments to keep. Could it simply have been the sternness of her voice that alerted it to move on? Who knew? Sometimes truth is stranger than fiction.

Chapter 2

Pauline Howard decided to hurry to the daycare center that her twin daughters attended by five-thirty, to beat the six o'clock rush. Her plan was to meet Joseph, (her loving husband of six years) at home, leave the kids, and keep it moving.

Pauline's sister, Elsie Mae, was missing and she was determined to join the search crew again that evening. These days, her heart raced every time her cell phone rang with an unrecognized number registering in the caller ID screen. Pauline always tried to keep things positive, but with every passing day, her sister's whereabouts became a greater unfathomable, unsolved mystery.

Deep in thought, she jumped when the phone's chirping sound rang while easing into the evening traffic on Interstate 285, the circular expressway that entirely looped around the city of Atlanta and the surrounding areas called Metro-Atlanta. She was heading to the southern town of Tyrone, Georgia, which she called home, while styling in her champagne colored Lexus SUV. Picking up her Blackberry cell phone she said, "Hello...Yes, this is Pauline Howard. How can I help you?"

"Yes, Mrs. Howard, I'm Detective Ian Irving of the Griffin City Police Department. We have some new information on the Elsie Mae Coats' case. I read from the file that you are the representative for the family. Is this correct?"

Momentarily, her breath caught in her throat and prevented her from answering him. She took a deep breath to calm her nerves which were raging out of control.

"Mrs. Howard, are you still there?" Detective Irving drummed his fingers on his dashboard while waiting for a reply from the obviously distraught family member of the missing woman.

Pauline collected her composure before answering him. She stammered, "Uh, yes...that's correct. I am the spokesperson for the family. Have you found my sister?" Her voice quivered as she spoke. She tried to brace herself for any possible bad news the detective was about to share with her.

"Well, Mrs. Howard, I'm not at liberty to talk over the telephone, but could you meet me this evening at, let's say seven o'clock? I have some important updates for you and your family."

"Yes, of course. I was supposed to meet with the search and rescue crew today to explore the forest preserves again, just outside of town, but I'll meet you. Hold on while I pull over and grab a pen and something to write on." As she ended her statement, she exited the expressway turned right, and pulled into a parking lot off the main road. Quickly seizing her Gucci tote bag from the rear floor, she dug through it to find a pen and a piece of scrap paper to scribble down the address as he rattled it off to her. "Is that where your office is located?"

"No Mrs. Howard, but it's an excellent new coffee shop called Perk You Up on Tara Boulevard-Highway19/41. Have you been there?" Detective Irving glanced at his watch to check the time.

"I passed by it a couple of times when it was being built. It looks pretty fancy from the outside, but I haven't been there yet." She sighed now and briefly closed her eyes.

"Well, good; how soon can you get here?" He glanced at the folder that contained Elsie Mae Coats' information with a gut feeling that deceit and betrayal were at the bottom of this bazaar case.

"It will take me at least ninety minutes to get there because I'm in Gwinnett County and I have the rush hour traffic to get through. Will that be too late to meet with you?" While talking, Pauline once again entered the expressway to fight the long commute home.

"Of course not, Mrs. Howard; I'm here to serve you. I'll see you when you get here." He clipped the city issued fountain pen to the folder and proceeded to exit his black, unmarked Ford Crown Victoria.

"Sir, are you sure that you can't give me some kind of clue to what you have to tell me?" She closed her eyes in despair, wondering what the news could be.

"I'm sorry, but as you know, your regular cell phone is not secure, and this information is sensitive. You also know our investigation is on-going; so, we can't be too careful. I hope you can understand that our procedures are based on regulation, proper protocol and confidentiality. Please understand that we have your best interest in mind. We'll talk when you get here."

"Okay, Detective Irving; I'll be there as quickly as I can. Bye." With that, she slipped her phone back in its case with her free hand while continuing to drive. She was now more nervous than she was when the search and rescue group was her destination. *I wonder what they have found out. I'm under so much stress. I can't take much more. It's too much.*

* * *

Strangely, after talking to the detective, Pauline felt nervous driving. Reaching for her phone she thought about calling her actress cousin Georgia to tell her about Elsie Mae; however, she called Joseph.

On the second ring, Joseph answered his phone. "Yes love, how are you holding up this evening?"

"Honey, I feel horrible. I just received a phone call from a Detective Irving. I guess he's new on the case. He wants to meet at seven tonight. Would you please meet me at the house to get the children? I'm on my way to pick them up now." She silently hoped his schedule would permit the help she needed.

"Of course, baby. I'll see you at home. Pauline, try not to worry. Elsie Mae is a country girl with a lot of street sense. I really believe she is going to be found alive and well. I feel it deep in my heart." He silently prayed that he was not giving Pauline false hope, but he really felt that there had to be an explanation, no matter how bizarre, as to where Elsie Mae was.

"Joseph, I hope you are right. I don't know though. When I asked what the meeting was about, he said he couldn't say. That could only mean bad news…right?"

"Not necessarily sugar. Don't think the worse. Keep the faith, darling, and I'll see you in a New York minute!"

"Ok. Hey, Joseph…" She paused as tears now welled in her eyes.

"Yes, baby."

"I really do love you; and, I'm so happy you're in my life." Her voice was caught in her throat, as the flood gate of tears broke, making a gurgling noise as she tried to smother the sound of her weeping.

"Baby, I know. I love you too. If you weren't my wife, I would be out in the corn fields looking for you right now!"

Through her sniffing, she started laughing out loud and said, "Man, I never worked in corn fields! And, who are you talking around? They'll think you're married to some sort of country bumpkin!"

"You may not have worked in corn fields, but you worked in cotton fields, bean fields, tomato and hot pepper fields! What difference does it make the type of fields I mentioned? You're a country gal and you're mine! And sweetness, I wouldn't trade you in for the finest model on a European runway. Besides, most of those skinny women probably don't even know how to cook! A man would starve to death foolin' with them. And, I'm being polite because I'm still in the office!"

"Well, I guarantee you that I would trade my size 14 with their size 2 any day of the week! But, I really appreciate you making me feel sexy and beautiful all of the time. How did I get so blessed to have you?"

"I am quite the prize, aren't I?" He was smiling now, trying to bring some cheer to his beautiful wife, at a stressful time for her and her entire family. "But baby, never forget what I told you. Who would be comfortable sleeping with their arm wrapped around a broom stick? I'd rather have a pillow with some padding any day! In other words, I'd rather have my voluptuous Pauline." As he laughed, she could almost see the sparkle in his blue eyes against his tanned face, which was lined by auburn hair with sprinkles of grey along his hairline.

"Yes, you are the prize, honey. I don't know what I would do without you in my life. You have been so supportive through the years, and especially now."

"Pauline, 'for better or worst' was not just a phrase to me. This is a difficult time for you; hell, for all of us. But, I'm committed to you and to our children. Nothing and nobody will ever come between us. Whatever I can do to lighten your load is what I want to do. Okay?"

"Okay honey; and you know I feel the same way. How soon can you leave work?"

"I'll be pulling out in about twenty minutes, love."

"Okay Joseph, I'll see you later."

"Bye baby." He placed his cell phone back in the holder clipped to his waist and turned his attention back to his computer screen to close out the two accounts he was working on. He took a few seconds to reflect; *where could Elsie Mae be?* Once, he had heard a scandalous rumor about his sister-n-law, but nothing was ever confirmed. Out of respect, he hadn't addressed it with his wife or any other member of the family dismissing the shocking story as fictitious and malicious gossip. Now he wondered whether the account had any validity to it. He thought, *Could it be true that Elsie Mae is a loose tramp and not as innocent as she appeared to be? I just don't know…That wouldn't make any sense.*

Joseph snapped out of his thoughts when his office phone rang. After taking the call, he shut down his office computer, secured his laptop in its case and gathered his keys to head home.

* * *

Pauline was not sure why, but she held on to the telephone for a few minutes after he hung up as if expecting another call. She continued to drive on the expressway until she reached Highway 74, the exit she needed to take in order to reach the daycare center and her home.

"This has been a long day. I can't wait to see my babies." she exclaimed. Pauline drove along the highway with the flow of traffic when she started thinking about the issue at hand.

With Elsie Mae missing, I feel like I'm in a hellish nightmare that just won't end. How could this happen in Griffin, Georgia? There has got to be an explanation. This is crazy. I'm going to get to the bottom of this fiasco. I just know she is still alive! I will not let my mind accept anything else. She is alive, and I just hope I can say, 'alive and well'. That's all I can ask for right now. Lord, just let Elsie Mae return to us alive. Tears rolled down her face as sudden thoughts and images about negative, alternative scenarios hit her mind like tactical missiles. *This is horrible. I wouldn't want my worst enemy to experience this kind of torment.*

As she collected her thoughts, she had entered a day-dreaming state of mind and unfortunately, took her eyes off of the road missing a flashing red light. Instead of stopping, Pauline plowed right into a turning, grey Chevy Tahoe.

All of a sudden, Pauline snapped out of her daze, as she saw a sea of grey immediately in front of her eyes. She heard herself faintly whisper, "What have I done?" as her car violently crashed. She heard breaking glass, crumbing metal, screeching tires and screams from the Tahoe's occupants. Like looking at a dream with your own image performing a starring role, she could faintly hear the ominous sound of her own scream, while fear gripped her heart. *Am I going to die?*

Within seconds she could only see blurred images of psychedelic proportions. Most of the cars behind her vehicle swerved to avoid becoming part of the collision, but the first car, whose driver had been tailgating hers for a mile, didn't' make it, plowing into the rear of her vehicle as if propelled like a rocket. Driving without her seatbelt fastened, the unknown woman was thrown from her vehicle dying on impact. The nearby witnesses wondered how neither driver noticed the flashing red light which indicated a stop was mandated.

Pauline felt the sudden violent jolt from behind reminding her of an amusement park, bumper-car ride, gone bad. Her blurred vision turned hazier until everything went abstract. Imaginary objects floated just pass her grasps as she stretched her arms forward to catch something - anything, to stabilize the swimming in her head, before she totally blacked out.

Several pedestrians were either hollering, "Call an ambulance!" or "Call 911!" Others could be seen taking out their cell phones to report the horrible accident to the police.

Two brave young men, who had been walking, immediately ran up to Pauline's side of the car to ask if she was okay. They found her slumped over the steering wheel and apparently, unconscious. Bits of glass from her window were wedged into her face as blood dripped down from the wounds, staining her clothes.

Glancing in the rear of the vehicle, they noticed the two booster seats implying that the woman had two toddlers who fortunately, were not in the car.

"Wow, Jacob, she's got little kids. It's good they weren't in the car when the wreck happened."

"Yeah Chris, you're right. It's five forty-five. She probably was on her way to the daycare center or wherever they stay because kids usually have to be picked up by six o'clock. I wonder should we pull her out of the car."

"I'm not sure if we should move her. We probably need to wait. I would hate to move her when we don't really know what we're doing. See if she's still breathing?"

While leaning into the partially opened window, Jacob placed his two fore-fingers on the side of her neck to check for a pulse. Chris moved closer and tried to open the driver's side door, only to find out that it was jammed.

"Jacob, the door won't open!" As people started to crowd around the twisted wreckage, the distant sound of police and ambulance sirens could be heard with increasing volume as they got closer to the scene.

Once the police and ambulances arrived, the policemen moved the pedestrians back from their front-row view and directed the flow of traffic to one side of the road.

The driver of the Chevy Tahoe was a tall, slender, red-haired woman who was obviously shaken. She slowly paced back and forth from the front of her truck to the back of it, on the driver's side, which had not sustained much damage however; her rear end and passenger side were ruined. She was practically screaming into her cell phone in near hysteria, asking her boyfriend to come to the scene.

Pauline's accident had caused significant damage to the passenger's side of the Tahoe as she had plowed through the intersection like a bat out of hell. The redheaded driver was apparently not physically injured, but it was a different scenario for her passengers. A female senior citizen, also a redhead and a teenager were both pulled from the SUV, placed on separate gurneys and rolled toward two ambulances for quick on-site treatment. Minutes later, both of the emergency vehicles roared away in the direction of two different hospitals, leaving their distraught looking driver rubbing her head and neck, still talking on her phone. The teenager was the driver's niece. Her first call had been to her sister, who was driving to meet the ambulance at the children's hospital.

One of the officers radioed for a fire truck with equipment to cut Pauline from her SUV. In the meantime, the emergency medical service workers painstakingly extracted the numerous pieces of glass from Pauline's face, neck and forearms while she was still in the driver's seat.

18

Fortunately, her window was rolled down enough for them to start administering care to her after taking her faint pulse.

Once the car door was severed, Pauline was carefully removed from the blood-soaked seat and placed on a gurney. The EMS workers earnestly worked to stabilize her and placed her into the ambulance. As soon as the door closed, the emergency vehicle made its rush to the hospital, siren blaring. Pauline looked like a dead person, drained of color, her face void of expression. What a difference a few minutes can make. One minute she was talking to her wonderful husband and the next, she was unconscious.

Chapter 3

Ginger Davis Graham woke up abruptly to the faint sound of the television airing an infomercial about some miracle pill that claimed to enable you to drop two dress sizes in thirty days or "your money back."

"Yeah, right!" Ginger sarcastically exclaimed at the television screen. Her irritation was not toward the actors for pushing a product they knew didn't work; but at herself because she had gained thirty plus pounds since starting her retail clothing store.

Ginger focused on the bedside clock/radio to discover it was 2:30a.m. She reached over to the nightstand, grabbed her designer eyeglasses and quickly put them on. A yawn barely escaped her lips before she swung her legs over the side of the bed and eased her freshly pedicured feet into plush, Daniel Green house shoes and stood up. She took a few sips from the glass of water that was no longer iced, but none-the-less enjoyed the needed liquid.

Ginger walked across her fabulous master bedroom suite and reached the bathroom in time to release what was apparently overdue. She had started another diet in an effort to shed the unwanted burden of excess weight realizing the time frame of her latest efforts was fighting against her. She had always been able to drop ten pounds in a couple of

20

weeks with little effort, but since turning thirty-five, fat cells claimed her as a best friend clinging for dear life.

In just about four hours she would be getting up to start her day; but a wee-hour bathroom break was needed since she now was drinking at least sixty-four ounces of water per day.

After returning to bed, she lay awake thinking about Cameron, the new manager in the restaurant next door to her retail clothing store. Cameron had caramel colored skin, alluring hazel eyes, stood at least six-feet, two inches, sported a smooth bald head, had biceps to die for and a warm friendly smile. They had met the day before when they mutually arrived at the entrance to their prospective businesses to open up. He had introduced himself holding her soft manicured hand longer than necessary looking deeply into her eyes as if sizing up her character in one easy sweep.

"It's nice to meet you." She had exclaimed.

"The pleasure is mine." Cameron had answered her smiling, his southern accent very apparent. He had touched his hat and bided her farewell. It left an indelible impression on her almost as impressive as the expensive cologne he wore.

His scent was so inviting that Ginger had casually stepped over to his door to get another whiff of it before reluctantly opening her door.

She had quickly walked over to the security control panel, turned off the alarm and flicked on the fluorescent lights in one easy flow, ready to start her day. No matter who came in her store to shop that day, she periodically thought of the handsome manager who conveniently worked next door to her.

Now lying in her bed, she wondered if he was like most eligible men in this small town, already spoken for. He was

21

not wearing a wedding band, but that didn't necessarily mean a thing. Some married men don't wear a ring as if to imply they are single, available and ready to go home with the next admirer. Conversely, others wear a ring but based on their wild undisciplined life styles, the ring, nor the marriage it represents, mean much to them. Why marry if you are not ready to commit? Is it enough simply to have a live in sex partner, cook, maid, therapist and cheerleader who emotionally gets nothing in return from the union? *I think not.*

Ginger shivered as if cold, from the thoughts that suddenly flooded her mind. Keefer, her estranged husband, had pulled a fast one so-to-speak, leading a double life right before her eyes.

* * *

Keefer was fourteen years Ginger's senior and he had wined and dined her. Nothing was too good for her in his eyes. He would shower her with gifts of flowers, candy, perfume, unique gift baskets, jewelry, clothes and wonderful trips. After a year of exclusively dating Ginger, he proposed and presented her with a platinum, 3-caret diamond solitary, pear-shaped engagement ring. She accepted his proposal, beaming with joy, as he slipped the brilliant rock on her finger.

After six months of engagement, and much hurried planning for a modest wedding, the guest list grew and grew and the modest planning changed to elaborate arrangements. Whatever Ginger wanted, she got; and Keefer smiled and wrote the checks or swiped the credit card, seemingly unconcerned about the increase of budget for the special nuptials. He literally seemed "too good to be true."

Their special day arrived and Ginger was indeed beautiful with a stunning up hairdo. Her wedding gown was an ivory colored Vera Wang original with a spaghetti-strap and fitted pearl-beaded bodice. The bottom of the dress flowed outward in the back, creating a swishing sound as she sashayed down the aisle in the Saint Peter's Cathedral, holding her father's arm. She carried a beautiful ivory and peach orchard bouquet.

The wedding party of four attendants, adorned in beautiful, peach colored gowns with similar features of the bridal gown, each looked on with joy and anticipation for the new couple. Ginger had suffered enough grief with her first serious relationship that had not ended in marriage; however, she ended up with a son, Justin, to bring up by herself.

Justin's father, Benson, had been a selfish brute who picked the occasion of her pregnancy to skip town. What a deadbeat! Who needed him, Ginger had exclaimed, but she was smart enough to hunt him down with court-ordered papers for generous child support payments which were automatically taken out of his paycheck from the neighboring county's payroll after he became gainfully employed as a fireman. Fortunately, Justin was a well-adjusted, fourteen year old, who missed having a father, but appeared to mature normally, acting as though he was the man of the house. Although he had scrutinized and disapproved of Ginger's other male interests, he surprisingly took to Keefer. He had accepted the new man in his mother's life and was even in the wedding as a junior groomsman, escorting his new stepsister Candace, from Keefer's first marriage, down the aisle.

The lavish reception followed at a hotel downtown, complete with a pre-reception in the majestic gardens. At the main reception, the waiters served mixed salad greens and warm bread with portions of butter shaped like flower buds.

After the salad, the guests were served a plated dinner of stuffed chicken breast, green beans almandine and rice pilaf with more assorted dinner rolls. The cake was filled with a rich creamy mousse made of real strawberries. It was a grand affair to say the least. The after party was held at a local hot spot for all of the mid-thirty plus crowd who were not afraid to let their hair down. They partied until times got better. Finally, Keefer whispered in her ear that it was time to sneak away.

They were driven to the Ritz Carlton hotel in a white stretch Lincoln Navigator, fully stocked with all of Keefer's favorite drinks. Ginger was not a drinker, but made the special occasion an exception and enjoyed some champagne.

Arriving at the hotel, Ginger asked to be taken to the nearby lake, which the chauffeur happily obliged, silently acknowledging that the couple actually had over an hour left on their chartered vehicle. He swiftly got back into his seat and took off to the lake only twenty minutes away. Once there, the chauffeur assisted her exit from the luxury automobile and she and Keefer immediately took a lazy walk along the lake's bank holding hands. Keefer stopped and held her tightly, while looking deep into her eyes, kissing her forehead, neck and lips.

"Your perfume makes me crazy. Girl, I can't wait to get you back to the honeymoon suite." Turning her to him, he hugged her, making her frame press against his body. His aroused nature was apparent and his breathing had become heavy.

"Okay big boy, let's go back to the hotel." Ginger was more than ready to show him the time of his life in the elaborate suite. She thought about the sexy nightgown she had purchased from Vivian's Secret Closet and the oils she had packed to massage her new husband.

24

The ride back to the hotel was filled with romantic words and sweet kisses. Keefer signed the credit card form that the chauffer handed him on a fancy clipboard, carefully including a generous tip. Keefer then exited the limousine, reaching back to extend his hand to his beautiful bride. He admired her long, slender legs down to the French pedicure that adorned her toes making a mental note to massage her feet once in the suite. The driver retrieved their luggage from the trunk and carried it to the hotel's bellman stand. "Sir, would you like me to carry these inside for you?" The driver was very professional, dressed in a standard black suit and tie, with a crisp, white shirt.

"Yes please, and thank you for everything. I'll have to personally ask for you when I need Grey's Limousine service again. Another car was scheduled to pick them up in two days to carry them to the airport for their honeymoon. They were bound for the United States Virgin Islands with both St. Thomas and St. Croix awaiting their special visit. It appeared to be the start of an awesome life together; however, appearances rarely reflect the real plot of a good mystery.

* * *

Ginger and Keefer enjoyed wedded bliss for months until little red flags in his behavior started popping up. At the beginning of their marriage, Keefer would call Ginger several times during the day; abruptly, his calls to her were noticeably more sporadic. He also started leaving his phone off which didn't make any sense. Ginger thought at first that he was just busy when he stopped calling as much, but when he was too busy to return his wife's calls, it became one of the straws that broke the camel's back, so-to-speak.

Keefer started coming home late from work about three days out of the week and once home; he didn't want to talk to her. He would come in and start an argument with her over the smallest little things. The biggest red flag was when he would finally arrive home and they would go to bed, he didn't have an interest in making love to her. If Ginger approached him for romance, he would shockingly say he was 'not in the mood.'

Not in the mood? What's really going on? Since when, was Mr. 'Eveready' not in the mood? Ginger may not have graduated in the top ten percent of her class and maybe some things went right over her head, but she had sense enough to know something was really wrong with the relationship. She knew all too well from past experiences that it must have been another woman influencing her husband.

One night after Ginger finally drifted off to sleep alone in her king-sized bed, she had a disturbing dream. She dreamed that she was in her OB/GYN's office crying over a piece of paper she had been given. She peered at the report with blurred vision from her tears, as she heard the doctor say, 'I'm so sorry Mrs. Graham, but you've got to protect yourself.'

Ginger looked back at the doctor in stunned disbelief as if shell-shocked from a major military battle. Who in the devil would think about wearing a condom with their 'devoted' husband? She had suddenly felt weak and hot and was thankful that a seat held up her weight because had she been standing, she was sure her legs would have become like putty, unable to hold up her frame.

'Well, it is such a shock. I need time to process all of this.' Ginger had spoken in the dream with quivering lips and a shaking hand.

'Time! You don't have time to think!' The doctor shrugged her shoulders and grunted. The thin woman stood suddenly and pointed a crooked, arthritic finger at Ginger, shouting, 'Your time has run out!' There was a cold stare in her eyes as a smirk crossed her face. With a menacing chuckle, the doctor sat back down, leaned backward and then forward again rudely pointing her index finger at Ginger. With an evil snarl she said, 'You-don't-have-time-to-waste!'

With that final rant of FYI, barked out without compassion, Ginger abruptly woke up, sitting straight up, wildly shaking her head from side to side. Beads of sweat were cascading down her face and her gown was wet at her lower back. She struggled to wake up and focus her eyes. The nightmare was all too real, but did it have a deeper meaning? She wondered, and she was very concerned.

Glancing over to her left, she noticed Keefer sound asleep. *I wonder what time he made it home,* she thought to herself. She leaned over to rest her head on his chest. He moved slightly from her touch and then circled her body with his arm. She usually loved his embrace, but this time she got a faint whiff of liquor emanating from him and knew he had been out drinking, and God knows what else, again.

She started caressing his chest and private parts hoping to arouse him because it had been a while since they had made love. At first he lay motionless, but gradually he moaned and moved toward her as if he was feeling her.

Out of the blue, his eyes opened wide as if controlled by someone or something else and he pushed her off.

"No Ginger. I can't do this now." Keefer spoke, but there was a hazed-over look in his eyes as if he was not really speaking to her. It was as though someone else was in his body. The voice was his, but it was not his spirit, if that makes any sense. She didn't understand what he was talking about.

"What do you mean? You can't do this now! Who or what is stopping you? It has never been a problem before.

Who are you messing with? Do you have a girlfriend on the side? Talk to me Keefer Gregory Graham! Talk to me!" Ginger was exasperated by the time she finished her surge of questions.

He simply responded, "I just can't. I'm not in the mood." Keefer then turned his back to her, hoping she would drop the subject.

"Keefer, don't turn your back to me. We need to talk! I'm over here ready to make love and you tell me nonchalantly, 'I'm not in the mood.' Have you lost your mind? It has been too long already, Keefer!"

He ignored her questions and plea to talk and within minutes she could hear the measured sound of him snoring. Hearing his even breathing, she roughly shook him to wake him up. It was useless because he kept right on sleeping. "I don't believe this crap! What's really going on with you?" Begrudgingly, she turned over in the bed unfulfilled and angry enough for tears to flow down her cheeks feeling rejected and needy.

The next morning Keefer got up complaining about a headache, playing on her sympathy, but Ginger acted like she didn't hear him, making herself busy preparing a high-protein shake for her breakfast. After he passed her in the kitchen, she rolled her eyes to the ceiling in irritation thinking about 'Mr. I'm not in the mood' and his excuse for not touching her. *What's really going on?* She wondered.

After scooping up the powder mixture she added it to the soymilk already in the blender, throwing in some fresh fruit and flaxseed oil to make it even healthier and pressed the blend button. As the appliance buzzed while mixing her meal, the dream she had the night before suddenly flooded her mind.

Oh yeah. That dream had to mean something. I wish Big Momma were still living because she had a gift of

28

interpreting dreams if they were from God. Oh well. Maybe it is a sign or perhaps it doesn't mean a thing. Let me take my power walk and when I come back in, I'm going to call the doctor's office and make an appointment for a Pap smear. I dread a pap smear like the shot of Novocain from a dentist; but it is one of those necessary evils that you endure because the effects without it can be worse than the fear of enduring it.

After downing the protein mixture, savoring every drop as if it was a milkshake from the local Baskin Robins/31 Flavors; Ginger walked to her room and sat on the bed to put her sneakers on. As she leaned over the side of the bed, the image of the doctor from the dream pointing her twisted finger at Ginger made her feel anxious about calling for an appointment. "Girl, grow up and when you come back in, make the call!" She firmly spoke out loud like there was another person in the room. Instead, it was the voice of reason from the attic of her own mind, telling her to be a big girl and deal with it; whatever 'it' might be.

Ginger took her usual power walk around her private lake, enjoying the picturesque view. Birds were chirping and squirrels were running to and fro in search of nature's goodies. A family of deer stopped briefly to check her out as she paused momentarily to behold their beauty. Noting that she meant them no harm, they gracefully sprinted away into the woods beyond the lake quickly hiding in the thickness of the trees.

After exercising, Ginger was drenched with perspiration rolling down her face, neck and back. She returned to the house to take a bath. Once out of the tub, she dried off and applied lotion and oil until her skin glistened. She casually eased into her hunter green velvet bathrobe while reaching for the telephone. She grabbed the business card for the doctor's office from her purse to make the appointment while walking to her home office.

"Good morning, Dr. Melody Gonzalez's office, Mary Cunningham speaking. How can I help you?" The ever-efficient receptionist cheerfully greeted her.

"Yes Ms. Cunningham, this is Ginger Graham and I need to make an appointment for a Pap smear. What is your earliest available appointment?" Ginger nervously waited for the lady to look for an opening on the computer.

"Yes Mrs. Graham, there has been a cancellation for the 24th. Would that work for you?" Ms. Cunningham straitened her skirt as she waited for a reply from Ginger.

"I'm pleasantly surprised to get an appointment so soon. Let's see here..." Ginger flipped in her day planner to the day in question and noted the time would be okay. "Yes that will be fine. Thank you, Ms. Cunningham and have a great day." Her appointment was set for the following week and she could hardly wait, needing to know, though not wanting to hear, if there was indeed something wrong concerning her health.

* * *

Unexpectedly nervous, Ginger sat in the waiting room glancing at the other women before picking up two magazines. Several women were obviously pregnant and others were probably there for routine appointments. Trying to calm her nerves, Ginger flipped through a Fitness magazine, reading an article on a new high protein, low carbohydrate plan for weight loss and another story about a woman who lost ninety pounds by power walking and eating five small meals per day. *Five meals a day! How could that possibly work? Lord, I'd be big as a house eating that many times a day. Humph. Well, it does say small meals. Maybe*

I'll give it a try. Any pointers and encouragement I can get will help in this battle of the bulge. From the looks of these patients, I need to share this article. Ginger smiled as she amused herself with humorous private thoughts.

Her cell phone rang and she noticed that it was her son Justin calling. "Hey Justin, what's going on?"

"Mom, remember the field trip I mentioned to you for the Fernbank Museum of Natural History?"

"Yes I do. When is the trip?" Ginger looped her finger around a lock of curly hair.

"The trip is next Friday, but both the permission slip and the money are due today. Mom, will you please bring them up to the school? I left the form on my chest-of-drawers." He waited, ready to hear her fussy reply. To his surprise, she didn't complain too much.

"Boy, what am I going to do with you? I'm at the doctor's office now, but when I leave here, I'll run by the house, pick up the form and bring the money to you. You owe me big time! Are you on some kind of break right now at school?"

"No. I asked to go to the restroom so that I could call you. Mom, thank you soooo much!" He was now smiling knowing he would not have to miss the trip. He thought to himself, *What would I do without Mom?*

"Okay baby; see you soon. Get back to class before you get caught on the phone."

"Okay Mom; see you in a minute." Justin whistled softly as he put his phone back in his pocket and rushed back to class.

Once Ginger was finally in the examination room, she scanned the small area and picked up a brochure on breast cancer and monthly breast examinations reminding her that she had missed doing hers for the last couple of months. *I'd better get serious and do it diligently every month. I just get*

31

so busy caring for everybody else, I forget to think about myself, she reflected.

Finally the doctor, accompanied by a nurse, came into the room and proceeded to conduct the exam. Ginger stared at the picture on the ceiling of a timid cartoon character: the caption underneath admonishing the patient to relax. *Easier said than done! Whoever designed that poster does not understand how that cold instrument feels probing my insides. It was probably a male artist!* Ginger thought sarcastically.

"Mrs. Graham, it has been over a year since I last saw you. Now you know when you are on the pill, I need to see you every six months." The doctor lifted her head from Ginger's chart and eyed her from under her glasses. "You are still on the pill aren't you?" She clicked her pen top several times as she waited for Ginger to answer.

"Well 'Doc, Keefer doesn't want any more children so we talked about it and he recently had a vasectomy. So we're covered in that area." Ginger spoke matter-of-factly and threw her hand toward the doctor for emphasis like she was talking about eating a chicken sandwich or some other casual affair.

"I see. How long ago was his procedure?"

"Actually, it was about five months ago and everything still works the same." Ginger threw her hand again and laughed this time, amused at her own frankness. *I wish it was more often I might add, but I won't let her into my business like that,* she thought to herself.

"Well, you can get dressed now. We are going to send the sample to the lab and you'll only hear from us if there's a problem. Otherwise, keep enjoying your husband. However, I do see that you are due for a mammogram screening. I'll have Patricia print out the form and I'll sign it before you leave. Do you have any further questions for me?"

"No. I hope everything comes back normal." Ginger was apprehensive, especially since Keefer was treating her so coldly. She couldn't get her recent dream out of her mind.

"Hopefully it will. Have a wonderful day Mrs. Graham."

"Thanks, 'Doc. You have a good day too."

Ginger redressed and left the doctor's office. As promised, she stopped by her house to pick up the permission slip for Justin and took it to the school along with the field trip money. She then drove to work feeling a little worried, her recent dream about a health scare still burning in her mind. She was so preoccupied that she nearly ran a stop sign, screeching brakes as she realized her error. Checking her rear-view mirror and the screen from the back-up camera, she moved back to realign her car with the corner while shaking her head. She thought to herself, *I hope my medical report is normal.*

Arriving at work, Ginger parked her car in her reserved space in front of the store and walked to the door, stopping only once to watch a cute set of Caucasian twins being rolled in a fancy European styled stroller by an older woman of Asian descent, presumably the nanny. One of the infants was fast asleep while the other one pulled on her sweater with one hand and held on to a pacifier with the other hand. *They are precious at that age,* Ginger thought to herself as she smiled at the woman, who returned the gesture.

Chapter 4

Stretching at his desk, Keefer looked like an ordinary business executive. His office was lavishly furnished and it had the standard pictures on the credenza; one of his wife, who was looking radiant and one of the entire family beaming like they enjoyed Christmas morning every day of the year. He glanced at Ginger's picture, admiring her and despising her, two very conflicting emotions, all at the same time. He walked over to his private restroom located at the rear of his office and handled his business. While washing his hands, he grabbed some extra paper towels and ran water on them. Gathering them as to prevent the water from dripping, he muttered to himself, "These cleaning services are not worth the money I'm paying! Why do I constantly have to clean and wipe off these pictures when I am paying them for the extra detail service, not the basic, disinfect the restrooms and empty the trash cans? I'll call the representative in the morning and complain."

His office phone rang and he briskly walked over to the desk to answer it on the first ring if the caller ID would cooperate and reveal his side, sweetheart's number. "Now, Beverly Jacobs has it going on." he said. Beverly was 5 foot 9 inches without heels and she didn't mind using every toned muscle in her body to please him. Keefer had leased a

Buckhead townhome to insure he could see her either at lunch or after work without prompting any suspicion from Ginger. Beverly didn't mind playing second fiddle as long as her bank account stayed packed and her credit cards that he secured for her had high enough lines of credit to satisfy her want-to-feel-rich taste. Frankly, her salary from her job didn't support her living status; but sugar daddy Keefer did.

Catching the phone on ring number two, Keefer said his normal, after-hours sexy greeting, "Graham Industries, may I help you?" His voice changed depending on if the call was from his wife Ginger or one of his lady "friends."

"Hey Hon; how's my hunk-of-love?" Beverly rubbed her lace camisole as she spoke to him.

"I'm better now that you've called Sugar-Lump. Are you feeling like company tonight?"

"I wouldn't have it any other way."

* * *

Keefer pulled into Beverly's garage after pressing the numbers on the automatic pad, while glancing toward her nosey neighbor's house.

As if she knew his schedule, the woman glanced his way through the slightly cracked curtain as if he would not be able to see her looking. Annoyed, he thought to himself, *Why don't you take a picture lady? She must be awfully lonely to spend her nights looking out the window, all in my business!*

He closed the overhead door and sprayed some peppermint mouth freshener on his tongue. He exited the vehicle feeling good and full of pride, knowing he had an exciting woman waiting for him upstairs and his wife waiting at home. *You're a bad boy Keefer. Well, a man has got to be a man.* He smiled as he thought about all his father had told him, and shown him, about being a man.

Keefer's father was well respected in their community, a pillar in the church, on the city council and perceived to be a great family man. However, Keefer remembered many nights hearing his mother cry, when the "good pillar" remained in the streets, womanizing and drinking, sometimes even gambling away his check before stumbling home to his waiting family. Although Keefer's father had died relatively young from cirrhosis of the liver, his mother, Betty Graham, lives in her home with the aid of a nurse, enjoying her money from his hefty insurance policy, savoring her senior years. She plays Bingo twice a week and travels on a regular basis.

A hint of guilt nagged Keefer as he climbed the stairs. He could almost hear his mother's words of advice to him as a young man... *Keefer, I've been through a lot of trials in my life, but God has been with me. My biggest hardship was your father's playing around with the town whores, and the fact that everybody knew it. Please don't treat any woman the way he treated me. The Lord sees and knows everything. The wages of sin is death. Don't gamble with your soul, son. Get you a good wife and make Momma proud.*

As a boy, Keefer had quickly assured his mother that he would never do what his father did. Nevertheless, as a man, Keefer had broken every one of his promises and had become a carbon copy of his two-timing, drunken father minus the gambling habit.

Pulling the key out from a hidden compartment in his wallet, Keefer opened the door that led to the kitchen of their shared haven. Immediately, he could smell the aroma from the oven full of anticipation, thinking about her good cooking and good loving. Closing the door, he turned around to admire her seductive beauty as she sashayed into the kitchen from the hallway.

"Hey Baby, you look delicious. How was your day?"

36

"Keefer, it was okay, but it's definitely better now that you are here. Are you hungry? I made some filet' mignon and baked potato with tossed salad. Sit down Keefer, and I'll get you a drink." Beverly motioned for him to sit in his favorite chair. He sat down, but before he sat back in the deep chair, he grabbed her around her waist and held her momentarily, taking in her scent. His mind was reeling with conflicting thoughts; part of him wanted to be in this townhome across the city from home and a part of him knew he couldn't continue to neglect Ginger whom he knew loved him unconditionally. Feeling drunk with emotions, before drinking one drop of liquor, he stood again taking her into his arms. Turning, he led her to the bedroom.

"But the food will be cold Keefer..." She felt her legs grow weak as she walked close behind him, her voice trailing into a whisper.

"Right now, I'm only hungry for you." He replied.

* * *

South of Atlanta in a town called Peachtree City, Ginger rose from the sofa in her family room, lonely after watching a movie by herself. Tears welled in her eyes as she wondered where Keefer could be. It was now three hours past his time to be home and she had not received so much as a courtesy call from him.

Ginger quickly wiped her eyes and reached for the remote to turn off the television. She then retreated to her bedroom. Glancing in the mirror, she admired her new hairdo with the fancy highlights. She was looking extra cute with a husband missing in action. Sighing heavily, Ginger removed her robe to take a shower. She normally relished the feel of the pulsating shower heads, but tonight while standing facing the wall, she barely noticed, so preoccupied with worry and an awful feeling of dread over the possibilities of his escapades.

Unexpectedly, tears started rolling down her face as she started heaving with emotion. *Why, God? Why does my life have to be filled with so much pain? I'm a good person. I don't deserve this. Where is Keefer?* Her thoughts trailed off as she grieved the apparent breach in their relationship. On the one hand, she was livid that he would dare do the unthinkable and be unfaithful. On the other hand, Ginger loved him more than the law allowed, and wanted to give him the benefit of the doubt.

Ginger wondered if Keefer had been in an accident. *Don't be a fool, girl. This man may say he's not involved with anyone else, but you know better!* "If I catch him, he'll have hell to pay! Wait a minute. Did I say 'If,' I catch him? I know what's going on and when I get the evidence I need, all hell is going to break lose! Wipe your tears girl, and get ready for battle!" She roughly wiped her eyes with her wash cloth.

With that last bit of proclamation, Ginger exited the shower and dried off. She quickly applied her peach scented lotion all over her body and reached in her dresser drawer to grab a night gown. She chose a black lacey number that Keefer seemed to love, when he was home to notice it. It had slits up either side revealing her moisturized skin. She applied his favorite perfume behind her ears, on her neck, wrists and on her ankles, resolving in her mind to just wait the evening out watching television until her husband made it home.

She flipped on the television and the first program that was staring at her was "Cheaters," a program where a suspecting spouse can have the show's detectives follow the other spouse to determine if suspicions of infidelity are indeed accurate. *Is this a sign? Maybe, I shouldn't watch this*

38

program tonight. It may make me feel worse about the situation. Although she wanted to turn immediately, her finger seemed frozen, unable to change the channel. She subsequently watched the episode; however by the end of it, she was weeping like someone had literally beaten her.

"This can't be my life! What have I done to deserve this? Maybe I should go out and get me somebody else – someone who appreciates me for me." Shaking her head in disgust, she exclaimed, "What am I saying? Am I losing my mind too? We both can't be crazy, can we? There must be a logical explanation why he isn't home yet. Girl, who are you fooling? You know your man is out there somewhere having a party and you weren't invited. I don't believe this! Two can play this game! The problem is, I don't want anyone else but him."

After the episode of "Cheaters" was over, she walked to her bedroom and crawled into her plush pillow-top, quilted mattress cover bed, 800-thread-count sheets and a down-feathered comforter. "Hmm," she sighed. "This is wonderful. What man wouldn't want to come home to me and this plush bed?"

Ginger reached across her pillow to retrieve her facial mask, placing it over her eyes. Before long, she was drifting off to sleep, deliriously tired, wondering where the love had gone. Her last thought was wondering where Keefer was. *Where is he? Girl, sometimes you have to just do you, and let other people take care of themselves.*

As a tear formed in the corner of her eye, she wiped it away, not wanting to cry again. Regardless of her efforts to control her emotions, the sadness she felt overwhelmed her and a floodgate of water escaped her eyes moistening her pillowcase. As her shoulders heaved in misery, she sat up and reached for her phone. Frantically, she dialed Keefer's cell number. Instead of ringing, his voice mail immediately came on, indicating that his phone was turned off. She left a message anyway, saying, "Keefer, this is Ginger. Please call me." She spoke in her best non-crying voice not wanting to sound distressed, and hung up the phone. Dropping the phone on her bed, she burst out into a howl of regret and sorrow wondering whose body her husband's arms were wrapped around this time.

Chapter 5

The Chief of Police, Bruce Spurring, looked up from a manila folder when he heard his secretary/investigative assistant Maritza A. Martinez, approach his desk. "Yes, Maritza; what do you have?"

"Well, I received a strange phone call, followed by a text message from a man who said Elsie Mae was not as innocent as she's being portrayed in the media. What worries me is that this so-called-informant has my cell number. I don't know who he is." She looked perplexed as she leaned to one side with her hand on her hip, while waiting for him to reply. Maritza was Hispanic, relatively short, slightly overweight, dressed in business attire and wore stylist eye glasses over her brown eyes. For work, she kept her brown hair pulled back into a bun, ponytail, or up in a French roll. During her leisure time on the weekends, she let her hair hang down to compliment her relaxed, amiable personality.

"Did you ask the man his name and he refused to give it to you?" Chief Spurring picked up his coffee mug and momentarily stared into the miniature sea of mocha swirl.

"Sir, I asked his name, but he just hung up the phone in my face!" Maritza wasn't tickled. Annoyed, she shook her head.

"Maritza, what about the phone the text message came from? We should be able to determine that."

"Chief, I'm already one step ahead; I asked Beverly to order a trace only to find out that the phone call and the text message came from a prepaid cell phone which has already been destroyed. There is no way to find out who made the call. It's a dead end; but at least it gives us a lead to further investigate the missing woman's character." Beverly was an investigative assistant who worked primarily with the detectives. Ironically, she had skeletons in her own closet because she was dating a married man – Keefer G. Graham.

"Thanks Maritza. I wouldn't worry too much about the person knowing your cell number. Today, just about anything can be found on the internet."

"You've got a point, Chief. It's almost scary what perfect strangers can find out about you by simply pressing a few keys and moving a computer mouse. Big Brother is watching us." She motioned with her hands to simulate quotation marks.

"Thank you for the information. Remind me to give you a raise." He smiled as he said this.

She knew he was kidding and almost let a curse word escape her lips given the absurdly low salary she survived on. But, she loved the headache of her job more than the peace of staying home with absolutely no money. So, she put up with his smart mouth, quick wit, and her tip at the end of every two weeks.

Maritza turned and walked back to her cubicle to make some calls from her desk phone. As if the caller knew she had returned to her little office space, her telephone rang. "Hello, Griffin Police Station, Maritza Martinez speaking; may I help you?"

"Are you an idiot, Maritza? I told you in my text message that the missing woman named Elsie Mae Coats is

42

not innocent as her neighbors stated in the news story. She is a tramp! Either you hold a press conference telling the public what she's really like or you'll be sorry. She might even die tonight!"

Because his statement was so serious, Maritza chose to ignore his insult of calling her an idiot and remained professional. "Sir, please calm down. Would you like to talk with Chief Spurring? While talking to the unknown man, she was frantically waving her free arm to get the chief's attention. She was afraid that if she put the man on hold he would hang up. She continued to talk to the man asking probing questions to keep him engaged in conversation. So far, it seemed like it was working. From his conversation, she noted that he talked as if he relished her attention.

Chief Spurring was on the telephone and his back was partially turned from her so he didn't see her flinging limb. Finally, Officer Bill Minor, who had just come back into the station noticed her arm about to fall off, and threw up his finger to her around the partition to acknowledge her need. He then briskly walked to Chief's office doorway.

"Hey Chief, Maritza is trying to get your attention." Officer Minor motioned with his hand in the direction of Maritza's cubicle.

The chief threw up his hand to acknowledge the announcement and concluded his conversation. "Okay, Dale, if you find out anything further, you know my number. Thanks; out."

"Thanks, Minor." He quickly walked to Maritza's cubicle to see the distressed look on her face. Without a word passed between them, he reached for the telephone, and said, "Hello, Chief Spurring here, how can I help you."

"Didn't your sorry help give you my message? The woman you are portraying as a nice young lady is anything but. She's a whore!"

43

"Well, she might be a whore, but I still want to find her. By the way, is she a good whore?" Chief didn't have a bit of sense.

"You and Maritza are both idiots. Have the press conference, you son-of-a...."

"Now, now, you don't have to go there do you? You sound like a smart man with a desire to assist in this case. If you have some information that would help us solve this mystery, I would love to meet with you to discuss it. To be perfectly frank with you, we don't have any leads." Chief lied. They didn't have much, but to say they didn't have any leads was a stretch.

"Do you really think I could help you, Chief Spurring?" The man seemed to be contemplating the thought of being a help to the situation.

"Yes, I could even make you an honorary deputy for a day if you would like. Can you come to the station or would you like for me to meet you somewhere?"

"Meet me somewhere public and come alone. Now, you are not trying to trick me are you Chief?"

"Of course not; I'll even bring a badge with me to deputize you. Why don't we meet in town at the Crosby Diner? It'll be my treat. Do you know where that is?

He replied, "Sure. Everyone in Griffin knows where the Crosby Diner is."

"One more thing, what's your name?" Chief Spurring reached for a pen on Maritza's desk to write down some notes.

"Just call me Ben," he said.

"Okay Ben; what do you look like?"

"Don't worry about what I look like; I know who you are."

Does Ben have a little attitude? Noting the firmness in Ben's voice, Chief Spurring dismissed the importance of his

44

description and proceeded to give him the time for them to meet and soon hung up the phone. While rolling his eyes, he said to Maritza, "I think this is another nut case, but I can't ignore any lead. This young woman seems to have vanished into thin air. We'll get to the bottom of it. There has to be an explanation."

* * *

Chief Spurring pulled his patrol car into the eatery's parking lot. To an uninformed observer, he was seemingly alone; however, he was no fool. Six plain-clothed officers were on the property with him. Approximately ten minutes after the officers had arrived at the diner, they were in their respective places nibbling on salads when the Chief arrived. A burly male officer and a petite policewoman were told to act like a couple. They rode in a white Ford Mustang. Two tall, male officers were in a blue Ford Jeep Cherokee making small talk to look like regular customers that had stopped by for a bite to eat. The final two muscular men were in a black Chevy Trail Blazer positioned in the parking lot to guard against a surprise attack from outside the business. The couple had arrived first and took seats in a booth on the far side of the dining room. When the two male officers, one being Officer Minor, arrived minutes later, they sat down at a table near the restaurant's entrance. All of their seats were strategically chosen so that they would form a perimeter to surround the possible perpetrator as well as provide safety for the customers as well as protection for the Chief. Unfortunately, they were all at a disadvantage because no one had a description of Ben. As they discreetly looked over all of the many guests, they wondered was he already in the restaurant eating. Without a description, it was hard to determine a perpetrator in the crowd. One thing was for sure, everyone inside the restaurant appeared to be busy enjoying the delicious Southern cuisine.

While exiting his squad car, Chief Spurring quickly scanned the area looking for "Ben." *I wonder if that's his real name; probably not.* Acting like he was stretching, Chief indiscernibly reached behind him and touched at the small of his back, verifying that he had his extra service revolver. Check. His trusty 9mm was in its holster; he could feel its weight against part of his chest and side. He affectionately called it Gabriel after the Arch Angel in the Bible. Under his breath he whispered, "Okay, Gabriel, don't fail me now. We may have to do battle." With a smirk that tugged at his lips, and his back to the patrons so he wouldn't gross them out, he spit on the pavement and then stepped up on the curb that led to the side walk and the entrance of the restaurant. While pulling open the front door, he heard Ben's eerie voice behind him.

"Hey Chief Spurring, I'm Ben. Slowly step away from the door." As the police chief released the door, he caught the glance of Officer Minor who was already in place facing the entrance. Seeing the chief signal him with a wink of his left eye which was not visible to Ben, Officer Minor resisted the urge to immediately bust a move on Ben.

With professional ease the two officers that were in the Chevy Trail Brazier had exited the truck and were crouched beside the vehicle's two side doors, guns drawn, but lowered at their sides, respectively, ready to spring into action. They quietly tipped to the sidewalk without making any noise and waited. They could hear Chief Spurring speaking to the man.

"It's good to meet you Ben. What information do you have for me?"

"You think you are so smart don't you Chief Spurring?" His voice was laced with sarcasm. "You and your backward staff didn't even know the chick's a hooker." He shook his head as if disgusted with the idea.

"Well, I don't know that to be a fact. It may be true; however, as despicable a life that she may have lived, she is still somebody's daughter, and somebody's sister. We need to find her. Do you have any information that may help us, Ben?" Inconspicuously, Chief Spurring slightly raised his fingers on one hand that was near his leg, to make sure the police knew to stand down and be at ease.

"All I know is that your police report on the news described Elsie Mae as a good woman, but I know the truth about her. You need to tell what was really going on with her!"

"I agree that our report should be accurate. We'll check into what you are saying. Now, my assistant Maritza told me that you threatened the safety of the woman. Do you know where she is?"

"Hell, no; I wouldn't keep up with the likes of a tramp! What do you take me for? But, I may be able to take you to the general area where she works. Get in my car!" Suddenly, Ben produced a 38 caliber pistol from his pocket and motioned for the Chief to walk toward his beat up jalopy.

Cool as a cucumber, Chief Spurring said, "Well, Ben is this any way to greet your boss? A weapon pointed at me is not the best way to start a career as a deputy." Chief Spurring wanted to keep the mentally ill man engaged in conversation, but distracted at the same time so that the officers near the truck could take him down. He also wanted a chance to calm the man down to determine if he in fact had some credible information to share. Doubting the latter, he motioned a signal to the outside officers by touching his hat, alerting them to respond with appropriate force. He had trained them to only use deadly force on the rare occasions when no other method was adequate.

The revelation of an armed perpetrator changed everything. Chief Spurring cocked his head to the side and shook his head and said, "I won't be able to do that, Ben. And, you've just blown your chances of becoming an honorary deputy." With the Chief's utterance, the officers behind Ben swiftly came toward him and effortlessly, took him to the ground before he knew what hit him. Within seconds, the other officers positioned inside the restaurant were out in the parking lot, guns drawn like a scene from a movie. As they took Ben down, his gun hit the pavement and dislodged striking him in the leg.

Ben shouted, "Oh! My leg, my leg, my leg! What are you idiots doing?" Ben was in obvious agony.

"Ben, or whatever your name is, don't you ever aim your weapon at me again. The next time, it won't be your leg." Chief Spurring then looked at his officers and said, "Book him guys. And remember, the Word says to comfort the feeble minded." He chucked as he turned to assure the patrons that everything was under control. Officer Minor read the suspect his Miranda rights.

Blood flowed from Ben's leg as a siren from an ambulance was heard in close proximity. One of the officers applied pressure to the wound with a clean, white cloth from the diner. Once the emergency vehicle arrived, he was loaded into the back accompanied by EMS and an officer. Shortly afterwards, the squared vehicle exited the parking lot heading through the city to a local hospital. The unstable man could have easily and justifiably, been shot for pointing the weapon at Chief Spurring; however, killing folks, even perpetrators was not what the Chief wanted to do. If it was at all possible, the Chief preferred to take down a suspect without deadly force. Clearly, the man had a psychological problem; though it may have been undiagnosed. Confusion was clearly written all over Ben's face.

The chief went to his car and called his assistant Maritza. "Another nut bites the dust. But, we'll have to investigate the validly of whether Ms. Coats was, or is a prostitute."

"Yuck, Chief Spurring! You know how to pick a victim." She shook her head and took notes from the Chief of calls to make and errands to run as he rattled them off to her. When she hung up the phone, Maritza found herself thinking, *another day in the life of a small town police department; surveillance, hookers, and feeble minded informants, just to name a few.*

Chapter 6

Mrs. Cathy Bennett and her husband William were laughing and talking over dinner at the new Southern Specialties Restaurant. "Bill, this food is simply delicious! We'll have to come here again real soon."

"Honey, I'm glad you're enjoying it. We'll be back, that's for sure." He picked up his warm bread, spread a thick portion of butter on it, watched it melt and took a big bite.

"Bill, I wonder what happened to Elsie Mae. It's mighty strange for her to miss work days without calling. I just can't imagine what's keeping her away. I wonder if her absence is of her own free will. This makes no sense. I just hope she's still alive! What do you think?"

"Honey, I have no idea. There was some talk down at the barber shop about her being a loose woman. I don't know if it's true. She didn't strike me as a bad girl, so I just kept my comments to myself."

"Bill, I heard folks at the beauty shop discussing horrible rumors, saying Elsie Mae might have been a hooker! I don't believe it! Do you hear me? I wouldn't have a nasty girl in my home, cleaning nor doing anything else! There must be an explanation that's logical. I miss the work she used to do. I'm not able to get the house immaculate like I used to when I was younger." She sipped her sweet iced tea.

"I know Cathy. If she's not found soon, we'll just have to hire somebody else. It's a shame because you'll have to train a new girl to make sure everything is done how you want it." He commented and then cut a piece of his steak.

"Hopefully, she'll turn up and have a good explanation for us. She's welcome back to our home as long as it's a legitimate reason for her missing these work days." As a manager approached them, Mrs. Bennett addressed him.

"Sir, I just want to tell you how glad we are that you opened this wonderful restaurant in the area. We shop here, and now we have a great Southern cooking spot to eat in after we work up a good appetite." Mrs. Bennett was speaking to Cameron Castleton, according to his name tag.

"Thank you. We are delighted that you came in to dine with us today. Please tell all of your friends about us. Y'all come back now. Have a great day!"

"Oh yes, we'll be back!" Mrs. Bennett happily stated.

Cameron walked to the next table to inquire whether the guests had been satisfied with their meal and service. "Are you finding everything all right?" Cameron spoke to the couple, looking directly into their eyes with a genuinely concerned expression.

"Yes. Everything was fabulous indeed." The portly man and his equally plump companion were all smiles at the friendly manager as they continued to eat their steak, loaded baked potato and asparagus spears with warm pumpernickel bread and butter. Although they hardily drank the Boston tea, he noticed that they also had an expensive bottle of wine on their table.

Cameron could almost hear the cash register sing equating to a very impressive bottom line of profit for the night. The restaurant had been well received in the area. Since he was not only the manager, making a nice salary, he was also part owner; therefore, he had a vested interest in its success.

Cameron noticed that a cutie in the far right corner kept eyeing him. He finally made his way over to her table. "Madam, I hope everything is okay." Her big bedroom eyes, high cheekbones and pleasant smile intrigued him. As he paused at her table, she extended her hand to shake his. When he took her slender hand, he was surprised to feel the business card that she pressed into his. Looking down, he silently read her name and title; Carla Mathews, CPA. According to the card, her office was located on Peachtree Street near Underground Atlanta, a unique development of restaurants, clubs and various shops designed with tourists in mind.

Shamelessly, she flirted with her eyes looking him up and down, nodding her head affirmatively. "Mr. Cameron Castleton...Yes, everything has been great! I'm waiting on my desert now. The cheesecake with strawberry topping was calling my name. I know I shouldn't, but tonight I can't resist. I'm not on this side of town often so when I come this way, I'll make sure to stop here again." Carla spoke knowing full well that if she didn't come back for the food, it would definitely be for the manager in charge. *Look at this hunk of love standing here asking me if everything is okay. Doesn't he know that it was simply okay before he came over here, now it is off the chain, so-to-speak! I wonder if he's married or already committed to anyone. Lord, have mercy! That is one fine brother!* Carla was grateful to have all of these private thoughts knowing she had at least a few more days this week to work her magic on him. *Mr. Castleton will get used to seeing me since I will be in the area this week. Fortunately, I've got to work on this Brock & Torrance project. Yes, yes, this is going to be a good week.* Her assignment was in the office building directly across the street from the restaurant.

Maybe I can find a way to squeeze a couple of extra days into the schedule to get to know Mr. Castleton. I told those jerks back at the office that I would need to sort through the mess that the other CPA created. The IRS is breathing down the company's neck, so they probably will not notice that I'm over the budgeted days to complete the job. She was busy brainstorming on strategies to trap the handsome hunk of love. Carla had heard 'through the grapevine' that he was also part owner of the business. As the words from a Kanye West song says, "I ain't saying she's a gold digger, but she ain't messing with a broke..."

"Well, just enjoy yourself. Worry about the diet another time. I see by your card that you are a CPA. I believe the owners already have one on staff, but I'll keep this for future reference." Cameron spoke guarded because she could have been one of the spotters that had been hired to ensure that all of the employees conducted themselves in compliance with the company rules. The spotters were independent contracted workers who went around to various restaurants and adult dinner clubs to rate them according to food quality, customer service, facility cleanliness, décor, and ambience. One thing that their corporate office stressed was professionalism, and they frowned upon employees fraternizing with the patrons.

As she waved her hand in the air for dramatic emphasis she said, "Frankly, you have all of your food, service and ambience together, but I was hoping to get a lunch date away from the place when you get some time." Carla never held her tongue if it was something she wanted badly enough. She didn't care about being perceived as a lady or not; nor did she care to wait for the man to ask her out first. Some of her best friends were by themselves following that philosophy.

"Oh, I see. Well, maybe we can talk about it the next time you come in." Cameron was extra careful in answering her direct request for a date, not wanting to insult her, but also realizing the need to remain professional.

Keith would have my head in a locked down position for days if he even suspected that I was trying to take a guest out to lunch. Well, actually she asked me to go out with her. He tossed the idea around in his head and arrived at the same conclusion. *No. No. No. Man, you cannot start seeing the customers. Stay professional no matter how good the honeys look to you. Besides, Bridget down the hall from you is the best thing that has ever happened to you. What more could you ask for? Somebody new, that's what! Do I have a problem? Diane said I needed my head examined. Maybe I do. This is absolutely crazy! Man, get a grip. Grow up!* The voice of reason and also the sound of his ex-wife's parting words resounded in his ears.

"Do you promise?" Carla tilted her head while looking at him, patiently waiting for his reply.

"I promise to be pleasant and greet you with a smile the next time you come. Unfortunately, we are not allowed to date our customers." Cameron hoped that would satisfy the would-be admirer, but she was persistent.

"Are you saying that I would have to pick another restaurant to dine at, in order to eat out with you when I love your restaurant?" Carla now stretched out her legs knowing full well that they were her best assets.

Sister girl is not taking "no" for an answer. If she is a paid spotter, she is really earning her pay tonight. How can I let her down nicely? Cameron was a little perplexed by her insistent manner of pursuit. At the same time, he found it hard to take his eyes off of her Tina Turner look-alike legs.

"Ms. Matthews, I am indeed flattered, but I really cannot go out with you. Thank you for the offer anyway; and like I

54

mentioned, I'll save your card for future reference. Who knows? We may need your services one day – that is your professional services." Cameron was quick to clarify what he almost inadvertently left as a come-on line. He didn't want any misunderstanding with the customer.

"Whatever. Will you tell my waiter that I am ready for my check?" Carla Matthews was clearly offended by his flat refusal to oblige her. She was not used to being turned down. If he could have only seen the invisible twist of her mouth that she was too grandiose to display, although a curse word was on the tip of her tongue.

"Yes madam. I'll get him right away. Thank you for coming and have a good evening." Cameron was glad to leave her table feeling somewhat awkward by her bold forwardness. He beckoned for her waiter who quickly came to bring her the check.

Who does he think he is turning me down? He doesn't know what he's passing up! Whatever! He probably could not afford me anyway! Carla snatched up her oversized, Dooney and Bourke leather handbag from the side of the chair, with clenched jaw muscles feeling embarrassed by the rejection from the manager, but she didn't want to let her inward feelings show. She quickly marched to the exit door, but paused when she didn't see the valet driver at his station. A couple of minutes had passed before he returned. He noticed that her countenance looked solemn whereas she appeared jubilant when she arrived.

As Carla approached the valet attendant's post she was fuming inside. Without uttering a word, she handed him the ticket, not realizing the irritated look pasted on her face.

"Was everything okay in the restaurant?" His words were laced with concern.

"My food was just fantastic! Why do you ask?" Carla was curt, making no apologies for her rude demeanor.

"I'm sorry, it, uh, it just looked like someone had upset you. Excuse me, because I didn't mean any harm. Let me get your vehicle." He quickly left her to retrieve her grey classic Ford Mustang from the upper deck. Once inside the car, he thought to himself, *One day I'm going to own a ride like this! This baby is beautiful! I'd do this job for free just to drive in all of these wonderful wheels! Nope, who am I kidding? I wouldn't park them for free because that wouldn't pay the rent!* He smiled now as he brought the car to a smooth stop directly in front of the door where the annoyed patron was waiting. He wondered what really happened in the restaurant. Usually, every guest came out full and happy. The staff was trained to make the dining experience enjoyable from start to finish. As he looked at the woman now, he noted the sad look in her made-up eyes.

"Have a good night and please come again." He handed her the keys to his dream car and noted how she snatched them from him.

Carla instantly felt a hint of guilt at how she had rudely taken the keys from the attendant so she paused before leaving, placing the dollar bill in her hand back in her wallet. "Young man, come here. It's not you. Thank you so much." Placing a five dollar bill in his hand instead, she was pleased at the smile that tugged at the corners of his mouth.

"I appreciate that. Again, enjoy your day!"

Carla forced a rigid smile, suppressing an impatient sigh. She was truly irritated at her failure to secure a date with the handsome manager and business owner.

When Cameron's shift was almost over, he walked back to his office to do some paperwork and run reports to have them ready for review by the accounting department in the morning. Of all the guests that had patronized the restaurant that night, the one that stuck out in his mind the most was none other than, Carla Matthews, CPA.

I wonder what made her so interested in me. Could she have been a spotter sent from corporate? She is a beautiful woman. If she would have the sense to keep things quiet, maybe I could date her. No man, leave it alone. Cameron spoke to himself as if to convince somebody else that a certain person was not good for him; but who knows you better than yourself?

He took out her card again and nervously twirled it over and over between his first two fingers and his thumb as if he was a male majorette practicing for an upcoming parade. The only procession he was rehearsing was the, I'm-a-man-who-is-never-satisfied club.

As if she could read his thoughts, feel his lust and see his nervous flip of the woman's card routine, his girlfriend Bridget called his cellular phone at that precise moment. Recognizing her number from the caller ID, he answered his phone.

"Hello, Sugar. How are you today?" The master player was working his charm.

"Hey, Baby. What 'cha doing?" She had just climbed out of her wonderful bath and was spraying on Guilty by Gucci in all the right places, in anticipation of his visit.

"Sweetness, I was just sitting here thinking about you as a matter of fact." He lied right through his teeth. She was the furthest thing from his mind. She sucked it right up as he knew she would.

"Cameron, you are so sweet to me. What time are you coming over tonight?" She leaned over toward the dresser mirror and applied her lipstick, winking at her own image.

"You deserve the best baby doll. I'll probably be there around nine. If it will be any later, I'll call you, okay?"

"That sounds like a plan. I have some new tricks to try when you get here. Don't keep Momma waiting!" Bridget purred like a cat as she dropped the receiver in its cradle.

Walking to the kitchen, she opened the refrigerator door checking the bowl with the ripe strawberries covered with clear wrap and the whip cream next to it, wine bottle on deck, and desire in her heart. She closed the fridge door quickly, pleased with her plan of attack for her man.

Cameron hung up the telephone and then checked his watch. *Good, I'll spend a little time with Bridget and then I'll tell her some kind of line in order to go see Ms. Brownie-Baby. Now, that is one sweet piece of pie. I wonder if she's working tonight. What an evening I'll have; Bridget, then Brownie Baby. You are one smooth player Cameron. Life can't get any better than this.* Unfortunately, his arrogance and promiscuous ways would soon catch up with him.

Cameron was one selfish and deceitful man. Based on what he told Bridget, she thought he was monogamous and truly all hers. Little did she know it, he was living a duplicitous lifestyle. He was saying one thing to her and pretending to be faithful, while he was sleeping with others on the side — unprotected! His reckless behavior had the potential to land them all in a health crisis. What was done in the dark shadows of night would soon come to the light!

* * *

After spending time will Bridget, Cameron made an excuse about his need to go home. Bridget kissed him goodbye and he left; however he wasn't headed home.

As Cameron pulled to the corner of Hellborn and Lost to indulge in one of the street women, he noticed all new faces. This should have been a sign; however his lust blinded him. Eyeing a beautiful woman, he stopped and invited her over to his car saying, "Hi sweetie, how much for everything?"

"Hey, so you want a date tonight?" He nodded yes.

After she gave him the price, he invited her to get into the car, drove to the back alley, and reached into his wallet producing the money.

She took the money and winked at him. Giving him the directions to her hotel room, they exited the car and started walking toward the building.

When they got to the entrance, he opened the door to let her go inside. She looked back and winked again letting her extra-long false eye lashes momentarily mesmerize him.

"I've never seen you here before. Where do you usually work?" He asked.

"You've never seen me?" She asked.

"No, but it doesn't matter. We're going to have a good time sweetie!" Suddenly, he heard the sound of cars coming to an abrupt halt and the tapping of shoes running on the pavement.

"Stop! Police! You're under arrest for solicitation!"

"What! That's entrapment - man please! I was just kidding with that woman."

"Tell it to the judge. Now, turn around." Cameron looked shocked and devastated as he turned around and was cuffed and read his Miranda rights.

* * *

Once he was allowed to make his one phone call, he phoned Bridget believing he could lie and sweet talk his way out of the situation. She bailed him out with his promise of repayment; however, she made her own promise. She emphatically told him that she would never see him again.

He went back to work, but his personal life was in shambles. Unfortunately, the love of his life was lost forever. His unbridled lust made him lose his lovely woman. His duplicitous ways had been unmasked!

Chapter 7

Jeff King and Jenna Jones enjoyed each other's company as they playfully and skillfully competed in a friendly bowling match. So far, Jeff was leading by fourteen pins.

"Girl, you can't handle me. Let the pro show you how it's done." Jeff threw a kiss to her as he expertly thrust the bowling ball down the polished lane to precisely knock down all ten pins.

"Wow, Jeff! That was beautiful, but don't count me out so fast. I'm not too far behind you." Jenna retrieved her fuchsia colored ball from the trough and steadied it in her hand before eyeing the targeted pins. She focused her attention between the marks on the floor and the white bowling pins, started walking slowly to the lined border and skillfully released the ball as graceful as a ballerina. As the ball sailed majestically down the lane, she silently hoped to hit a strike, wanting to catch up with Jeff. Thrown with the force of a pro, the ball crashed into the targeted pins and she happily observed all ten of them come tumbling down.

"Yes! That's the way to do it Jenna!" She spoke out loud to herself as she walked back to the curved table where Jeff was sitting. His hand was outstretched; palm outward to extend her a "high-five."

"There you go, baby. I knew watching me was going to pay off eventually." He winked at her as she slid beside him, planting a kiss on his cheek.

"You would like to think you taught me everything I know, but who are you kidding? Give me a few frames to warm up and that's all I need to spank that ..." She glanced around to see who was near her, spotting children, she decided to keep her comments clean..."rump."

"Girl, stop." He reached for his beer, took a large gulp, wiped his mouth with his napkin and stood to take his turn.

"Go baby." She gave him a shout out just before he let the ball flow from his hand. One, two, three...nine pins went down, not the strike he was aiming for.

"Tenth frame for me, love. Watch a pro in action." She picked up her ball and then sat it back down. Stopping to dust her hand, she glanced across the broad room and noticed Mr. Graham from Graham Industries bowling about eight lanes from where they were. The shocker was that he was not bowling with Mrs. Graham, but a woman that Jenna didn't recognize.

"Jeff, look over at lane seventeen. I thought my eyes were playing tricks on me, but that's my boss over there bowling with some floozy. He is the owner of the company. Can you believe this? His wife would have a fit if she knew. He is a bold somebody! I guess he didn't think he would run into anyone he knew on this side of town, but you never know who you will run into. Why take the chance?" Jenna was simply outdone by the blatant disrespect that Mr. Graham was showing his wife, being in public with another woman.

"Jenna, don't jump to conclusions. You really don't know who that is with him." Jeff wanted to simply dismiss the accusation as wrong and unimportant.

"I may not know who she is, but I definitely know who she's not. That is not Mrs. Graham! I like Mrs. Graham and she does not deserve this!" Jenna loathed an adulterer more than anything. She had grown up watching her mother suffer because of a stepfather that refused to be content with her mother who was petite, fun-loving, and smart. She was also a great mother and an awesome cook. He just had to have women on the side and it almost drove her mother insane.

"Honey, just stay out of it, it could be his niece or something like that." Jeff got back up to take his last frame of the bowling game.

"It's his niece all right!" Her sarcastic comment was confirmed when suddenly, Mr. Graham glanced quickly around the room as if to double check his obscurity, and then he leaned over the table where the woman was seated and planted a kiss on her mouth.

"See Jeff!" she whispered. "Who kisses his niece romantically on the lips? This is some bull. I'm going over there." Jenna turned red with anger and contempt. She had known the Grahams for about ten years and knew that they were still married. *What a blow. I wonder would Jeff ever cheat on me like that. I thought Mr. Graham was a good man, so smart and business minded. He even goes to my church. Who would ever believe he is a cheater?*

As the woman stood to take her turn, Mr. Graham surrounded her waist with his arm while smiling like he was supposed to be there with her.

"Jenna, that is kind of deep; but, I really think you should just leave it alone." Jeff was also surprised by Mr. Graham's actions.

"I'll be right back." Jenna quickly got up to approach the couple.

Touching her arm he said, "What are you going to say?" He took in a deep breath knowing that when Jenna set her mind to do something, it was no talking her out of it.

"I don't know what I'll say, but I want him to know that I see him. I really can't believe my eyes. This is so sad to me. He parades his family around the office like he is so happy with them. How hypocritical. This is a mess! Look at him." Jenna shook her head as she was totally disgusted with the images of him hugging the woman and caressing her arm.

As Jenna walked on the path that led to the concession stand, she acted surprised to see them and said, "Hello Mr. Graham, how are you?" As she spoke, she glanced from him to the woman in a look that said, 'Who is this?'

Mr. Graham turned to see who in the world was greeting him is this remote bowling alley. When he saw Jenna, his surprised face told the story. The slick grin immediately dropped from his face. Although he was usually demure, now he looked totally embarrassed, but he tried to recover. Fortunately for him, he didn't even try to lie about the woman's identity. He just acted like she was invisible, not bothering to acknowledge her presence.

"Hello Jenna. What brings you out here?" he asked.

"Actually, I come here quite often." Jenna didn't crack a smile, but looked disappointed in him. It was hard not to show her emotion because she knew the family so well. She looked from him to his companion and back to him, raising her eyebrow as if to speak, 'And, who is this?' Of course, she didn't verbalize what her face quietly conveyed.

Ignoring her unspoken question, he said, "Well, enjoy your game." Mr. Graham icily turned toward the woman, dismissing Jenna because apparently he had nothing else to say.

Jenna didn't make a reply. She walked over to the refreshment stand and ordered a deep dish, Chicago style pepperoni, sausage, bell pepper, and onion pizza, a Coke for herself and another beer for Jeff. As she waited for her order, her cell phone rang. Glancing at the caller ID, she noticed it was Jeff.

"Man, what do you want? I'm over here getting some food." Her tone was playful, but sarcastic.

"Hey, what did he say?" Jeff really wished that she would have stayed out of it, but Mr. Graham opened up this can of worms himself by being out in public with the woman.

"Look, what could he say? He didn't make any excuses because he knows he's wrong. I'm through with him. I wonder what kind of lies he's going to tell Monday when he sees me at work. He may avoid me all together. Anyway, our food will be ready in about eight more minutes."

"Okay; what did you order Jenna?"

"The usual deep dish pizza; and it smells delicious!" She rubbed her stomach just thinking about it.

"That sounds tasty. Babe, don't let that mess with your boss ruin your evening. I know it's a blow when you thought he was a family man. You know, some people never change. Maybe that's the way he has always been. I'll see you when you get back over here." Jeff absentmindedly rubbed his head while thinking about Mr. Graham. *That guy has got to be crazy. He has so much to lose! He has a beautiful family, a successful business, rental properties, investments and no pre-nuptial agreement! Or so Jenna says; although I don't know how she knows all of his business like that. What a mess.*

While waiting for the food to be prepared, Jenna stepped into the restroom and washed her hands. Once their food was ready, Jenna balanced the tray with one hand and carried

Jeff's beer with her other hand. The beer was too expensive to spill it on the tray. She thought to herself, *Jeff will have a cow if I spill his rich brew. I had better carry it carefully. I guess he is worth it though.* She smiled as she approached him.

"Alright Jeff, help me out." She placed the tray on the table, lifted up her Coke and placed it in the recessed cup holder, and she put his beer in the other fluted slot. Jeff simultaneously slid the pizza onto the table.

"Hey, this looks like a delicious pizza. Let me go to the restroom and wash my hands so I can get my grub on. I'll be right back."

"Okay. Jeff, will you carry the tray back for me?"

"No problem, Sweetie." When he stood up, he kissed her cheek and slid something into her shirt pocket.

As Jeff walked away, Jenna reached into her pocket to find enough money to more than cover the cost of the food and drinks. Opening her small wallet, to put the money inside, she then placed the strap of her Coach purse on the back of her chair. *Mr. Graham has really got a lot of nerve being out here with that woman. It's going to be awkward looking at him on Monday.* As she thought about her possible encounter with her boss on the following week, she looked over to the bowling lane where the couple had been. They were now gone. Homeboy had gotten the hell out of dodge.

Chapter 8

Keefer walked his girlfriend Beverly out to her car and whirled her around to give her a parting kiss. "Girl you smell so good. I'll come see you later tonight."

"Okay baby, but why did we have to leave the bowling alley in the middle of the game? I probably would have won! When have you seen me get three strikes in a row? You have to admit I was on a roll – no pun intended. Why did we have to rush out the door?"

"Bev, I'll make it up to you. I just had to leave. I have something I need to do back at my office." He easily lied again.

"I know you better than you think I do. You didn't want that nosey woman named Jenna to see us having a good time. Who is she anyway?" She took a sip from her strawberry and banana smoothie while looking expectantly at him.

"Jenna is one of my employees and she also knows my wife very well. I'm sorry honey. I literally freaked out when I saw her. I drove out this way to avoid the work crowd, but I see we are better off staying home and ordering in." He spoke to her as if staying hidden was a great idea.

"Baby, to be completely honest with you, I'm getting sick and tired of simply being the other woman. You said you'd made a mistake marrying her and that if I would just wait for one year, you would do right by me. It's been three years. Keefer, you promised to divorce her and marry me. What happened to that plan?"

"It's not that simple, honey. She has a son that I've grown close to and I don't want to hurt her by dropping a bomb on her all of sudden. I do have a conscience, even though my heart really belongs to you–to us, you know. Girl, you know I love you!" He lied right through his teeth. He didn't love her. He really just liked what she did for him in the bedroom. In fact, sometimes he didn't think he really loved anyone. *Silly woman: What's love got to do with it?* He wanted to laugh at her naivety and concluded that Beverly easily believed anything he told her. "You're my girl! Come here." He gently hugged her.

"I don't know anything anymore. You act like you're ashamed of me. We never go to the fancy restaurants that I see on television. We only pick up food and go back to our place. That's not enough for me."

"I know, you deserve better than that. How about I take you to Vegas soon? I'll show you the time of your life and we'll have a long talk and work everything out. You'll see."

"Okay Keefer. I don't know why I let myself be charmed by you. Will we really go to Vegas? Is this a promise that you're going to keep?"

"Of course dear, don't I always take good care of you?" He reached for his wallet and withdrew a Visa gift card. "Now, I was saving this for a special occasion, but take this and have a good time at the mall on me. It should make up for tonight."

Flipping over the envelope, she saw the gift amount of five hundred dollars and beamed with joy. "For me? Thank you, baby." She reached up to give him a tight hug when they heard a man's voice close behind them.

"Keefer Graham, my man. How have you been?" It was his neighbor, Mr. Milton Straight.

If Keefer could have melted, he would have. What's the likelihood of running into two people that you know when you've driven thirty-five miles away from home to be in an obscure place?

"Mr. Straight, how are you? Oh, umm... this is my niece Deborah who is visiting from D.C." He stammered. "How is your lovely wife?"

"She's good; you can speak to her yourself. She's right there in the car waiting on me."

Keefer turned around in the direction that his neighbor was pointing to see their vehicle which was parked two cars from his. Mrs. Betty Straight was looking right at him frowning and hesitantly waving. He put up his hand in an awkward wave to her and then proceeded to quickly move away from Beverly.

"Okay...Just tell her that I said hello. I'll talk to you soon."

"Hey now, what's your hurry? Come say hello and introduce your niece to Betty." Mr. Straight was grinning as he placed his hand on Keefer's shoulder and proceeded to lead him to their car. The man was oblivious to the fact that Keefer was caught up in drama and lying about the woman's identity. *What can I do now?* Keefer wondered.

Mrs. Straight pressed the automated button and as the window went down, Keefer thought of something general to say while eyeing Beverly in hopes that she would play along, and cover for him.

"Hello Mrs. Straight. How are you tonight?"

"I'm doing tolerably well, thank you for asking. I saw Ginger at the homeowners' association meeting last week. I asked about you, but she said you were extremely busy these days." She thought to herself, *busy doing what I might ask. I*

68

saw how that girl was hugged up with him. These days, men are a mess!

"Yes, I've been working late quite often, but I took off early today to pick up my niece for a fun afternoon before she has to go to the airport later tonight. Mrs. Straight, this is my niece Deborah, Deborah, this is my neighbor and friend Mrs. Betty Straight."

"Hello, nice to meet you. I'll have to tell Ginger that I met you." She had a knowing smirk on her face because she knew that this woman, who had just placed a bear hug around his neck while holding some kind of card, was not his niece. She thought to herself, *Momma didn't raise a fool. I know that's some bimbo he's all excited about. Men!*

"Hi. It's good to meet you too." Beverly was seething mad now. It was one thing to be rushed out of the date because of an employee; now she had to pretend that she was her man's niece! This mistress business was beginning to get on her nerves. She loved the man, but deep in her heart she knew that she wanted to have him permanently. Seeing him once or twice a week was not going to be enough anymore.

"I'll talk to you later Uncle Keefer. Thanks for the gift card. I'll think of you when I go shopping."

Do I detect an attitude in Beverly? He thought. "Okay Deborah, call me when you get home."

"Sure. Bye." Beverly dryly answered as she quickly got in her car and started it while trying to hold back her tears. She backed her car out of the space and proceeded to make her way through the parking lot. Before she pulled out into the traffic, the floodgate of tears rushed down.

I'm tired of living like this. We have been dating and sleeping together for three years now and I am really no closer to becoming Mrs. Keefer Graham than I was the day this relationship started. He promised to marry me! Now I know he'll never leave Ginger – not for me anyway. He loves her despite what he tells me. I'm going to spend this gift card that he gave me because I deserve it, but it does not make up for how empty I feel. My parents raised me better than this. Sometimes I feel just like a dirty worm grinding in the dirt messing with this married man. Nothing good will ever come out of this mess. I deserve to be loved by a man that is willing to put a ring on my finger and get a license to tell the world that I am his and he is mine. I love Keefer and I don't want anyone else. The sad thing is that he doesn't love me. Or, does he? He says he does when he comes over, but is that just because of what I let him do to me? Life sucks sometimes. She heaved as the tears flowed like a fountain. The driver's horn behind her stirred her out of her dazed state. She noticed that the light had turned green and she was just sitting there staring into space. Beverly then drove her car out into the flow of traffic, rigorously wiping her eyes.

When Beverly had driven about three miles away from the bowling alley, her cell phone started ringing. Grabbing it, she noticed it was Keefer. She allowed it to ring until it apparently went to voice mail. She said, "I'm just tired of Keefer's lies. I can't stomach his hypocrisy another minute. Maybe I'll talk to him later." She thought, *I need to get myself together. He's good to me, but who wants to continue to be with someone who feels he has to hide you when out in public? This is a sick life and I just can't believe it's mine.* Disgusted, she tossed her phone down on the seat, and turned her attention to the radio, adjusting the dial to some soothing jazz music.

* * *

While driving away from the bowling alley, Keefer was surprised when Beverly didn't answer her phone. She never ignored his calls. *I've messed up now. It doesn't matter; all I have to do is sweet talk her the next time I go over there for some loving. She is 'easy like a Sunday morning.'* Keefer was stuck in his pride and arrogance. His habit of disrespecting women continued. "Well, I guess I'll go home now and see what I can get into with Ginger.

Instead of going straight home, Keefer decided to take in a movie. He figured Ginger would still be awake and he didn't want to hear her complain about him being late. *After the movie, she'll be asleep and I can slip in the bed next to her. She'll never know exactly what time I came home.*

After the movie Keeper drove home. He pulled into their driveway feeling guilty for being caught with Beverly – twice! His employee saw him out bowling all hugged up with his other woman, and his neighbors, Mr. and Mrs. Straight were parked in the shopping plaza lot adjacent to the bowling alley where he had also parked. *I wonder will Mrs. Straight really mention my 'niece Deborah' who allegedly was here from D.C. That would be a big mess because Ginger knows I don't have any family from that area! Well, I'll deal with that when I have to.*

Keefer quietly opened the basement door and pulled off his shoes so that he wouldn't make any noise. Walking up the hardwood steps, he felt ashamed that he needed to sneak into his home like a common criminal. "This is ridiculous. I'm getting too old to live like this!" He whispered.

When he reached their bedroom door, it was locked. He positioned his key, but suddenly dropped the massive bunch of keys on the floor, loudly bumping the door. That was all the noise needed to wake Ginger up.

He eased the door open, but Ginger was sitting straight up in the bed looking at him with rage in her eyes.

"Midnight Keefer, you've got to be kidding me! Where have you been?" Ginger was absolutely livid.

71

"Before you jump to conclusions, I needed to clear my head, so I went to a movie. I have the stub to prove it."

"That just proves that you bought a ticket! Besides, your business closed hours ago. I'm fed up with your foolishness! Why don't you save your lies for somebody who cares?" She paused at first waiting for an answer. She then moved over to the far end of the massive bed – communicating nonverbally, but clearly, don't-touch-me-or-talk-to-me! Case closed.

Keefer didn't say a word. There was nothing to say that would make her feel better. Midnight was too late to come home to your wife; even Keefer had to silently admit that. Before going to sleep, he admonished himself; *I better get myself together before I lose my wife. I love her, but I also want Beverly. What am I going to do?*

* * *

The next morning felt like the inside of a freezer in the Graham home. Keefer attempted to make small talk, but Ginger didn't want to talk, only answering his questions with one-word responses. She kept busy and went to work wondering where the love had gone.

Keefer brushed Ginger's icy demeanor off as if it would only be a temporary thing. He was overly confident of his ability to sweet-talk himself into her good graces. Keefer obviously didn't realize that even the most patient person, has a breaking point – a place that could erupt at the most inopportune time. Had Keefer forgotten there was a cable television show called Snapped? The lifestyle he was living and the trauma that he was inflicting on Ginger could be the very circumstances that would make his wife emotionally break down and do the unthinkable! Could the seven letter word 'snapped' qualify the Graham marriage for an episode?

* * *

On Monday, Jenna saw her boss from a distance down the hall before he left early for the day. Actually, she was glad it was not an up close and personal, face-to-face meeting. She felt extremely awkward, armed with the knowledge that he was seeing another woman on the side. She was still in shock, although she didn't understand why because she realized that many men cheat; she just had no idea it would be someone that she knew – or thought she knew. *I don't have the same respect for him that I used to have! I can appreciate his accomplishments in business, but now I see he doesn't have the personal integrity that I assumed he had. He attends my church and looks and acts the part of a good family man, but he's perpetrating, fooling everyone. The church members and his employees all think he's a good Christian man, but he's deceitful; that's so scary to me. Hey, he's leading a double-life like it's the normal thing to do. His lovely wife Ginger doesn't deserve this betrayal! I wonder does she know. Well, I've always heard that a woman has a sixth sense about these things. I hope Jeff isn't unfaithful. I believe I would feel the breach in our relationship because we are so close – or are we? That's horrible that I even feel the need to question my wonderful boyfriend's loyalty. I hope I'll never have to worry about him straying away from me and breaking the bond that we share. Sometimes he even mentions marriage although he hasn't officially proposed. Maybe we'll be one of those fortunate couples that go through some things-that's life; but the scandalous secret life that Mr. Graham is living is too much to process! It's affecting me and I'm not in the family! You never know who is watching you...Well, that's enough daydreaming, back to work kiddo.* She turned back to her computer screen and continued working on her reports.

Chapter 9

Chief Spurring looked at his clock that hung on the wall across from his desk and noted the time was half past six. He and Detective Irving were scheduled to meet with Mrs. Pauline Howard at seven. *I had better hurry up so that I'm not late. I wonder what Mrs. Howard will think about this new information that I've found out. She probably won't believe it. Most family members are in denial about stuff like this. It isn't pleasant to think about your loved one doing something illegal. I know firsthand, because Robbie, bless her addicted heart, could have been helped sooner if Sandy had not insisted on keeping her head in the sand. I told her that Robbie was using drugs. The signs were all there. It's tough to believe the kid you put all of your heart and soul into is living such a destructive lifestyle. How do you wrap your mind around an addict for a daughter? I know first-hand the pain and disappointment. It's almost unbearable.*

"Hey, Chief Spurring. Chief; oh, Chief; back to earth Chief." Maritza was standing at his doorway attempting to get his attention. She didn't like to enter it until he gave the okay.

Chief Spurring suddenly snapped out of his trance-like state and looked at Maritza waving her hand at him. "Chief, after the fiasco at the diner, I know you don't feel like

74

dealing with another crazy person, but this lady on the phone says she has some information for you." Maritza simulated quotation marks as she said it.

"Who is it this time?" Chief Spurring waded through papers on his desk while waiting to hear who the latest nutcase was.

"Well, she said she wants to meet you at the infamous 'red light district' after ten this evening to talk over things. I suggest you take back-up with you Chief Spurring. You know that's not the best area in town."

"Back-up, Maritza? Of course, but thanks for the reminder, you know I like to play lone-ranger sometimes. What's the woman's name?"

"She says her street name is Slick Baby. Go figure."

Maritza left the doorway shaking her head, fussing under her breath in Spanish.

"Wait Maritza, what's her real name? I don't want to go there asking for Slick Baby: I would rather know her real name, if possible." Chief Spurring sighed heavily as he considered the task at hand wondering if he would finally get some credible information to help them find the missing woman. The local newspapers were begging for another interview. Fortunately, the local television news stations were keeping her picture in the public's view and generating leads, even if some of the leads led to unbalanced people with insatiable desires to be heard. Though nerve wrecking, routine police work mandated that officers had to work through all leads; including weird people. Eventually, the goal was to get some useful information to help solve cases.

"Chief, you know I asked her name. She would only give me the name Slick Baby. Now you know that's not the real deal."

"Maritza, nothing would surprise me at this point in my career, absolutely nothing." He placed Elsie Mae's file back into the folder, stood and walked to the hallway in order to hear Maritza better as she walked away.

"I know. Let me put her alias in the database to see if she has any prior arrests. Maybe I'll be able to cross-reference her street name with her real name." Maritza rushed over to her computer and pulled up the National Crime Information Center software that she needed to run the check.

"Okay Maritza, you do that. Remind me to submit your paperwork for a fat bonus check at the end of the fiscal year. You deserve the best, Chick-a-Dee." He smiled and wondered what he would do without her patience and persistence.

"Yeah, yeah, I've heard it all before." She said, but she thought, *these jokers would miss me if I really do resign. Girl, who are you fooling? Resign and do what? I would crumple up and wither away if I didn't have Chief and the other guys to harass me from time to time. Maybe I need my head examined thinking that this is paradise!* Maritza had to smile to herself thinking about the absolute crazy, but necessary headaches she put up with daily in this small town, police precinct. The real truth is, she wouldn't have it any other way.

* * *

Chief Spurring went back into his office to go over what he knew so far. Elsie Mae Coats had been missing for about ten days. On the last day she had been seen, she worked as a housekeeper in a private home, left work, stopped by a local convenience store, and while walking home, she disappeared without a trace. The crime scene technicians, with the help of police dogs found her blue, bandanna scarf about a mile from her cleaning job. The home owner testified that the scarf covered Elsie Mae's head earlier that day while she vacuumed and dusted her home. One lead from a lunatic claimed that Elsie Mae was a tramp, not an everyday, sweet girl-next-door type as reported on the news. *How much credence can you put in the testimony of a screwball who actually believed that I would deputize him for a day? Not much. I've got to look into it though. Now, I've got to meet a hooker in the red light district! I need a regular nine to five. Who am I kidding? I wouldn't survive in a normal job two weeks. I would crave the streets of this good town. These roads and hills run through my veins. It's the reason I get up in the mornings. That means I've got to get a life! But lately, work is the only pleasure I have. I'm starting to sound like my father. Maybe it's time to retire.*

"Chief Spurring, I got a hit!" Her name is Claire Underwood, known on the streets as Slick Baby. She has arrests dating back ten years, but they were in North and South Carolina. I guess she decided to move a little west to start a new life of crime, Georgia style." Maritza was quite proud of herself for expeditiously finding the information.

"What would I do without you, Maritza? I guess I'd be looking for you, interviewing until the cows came home. Thanks, and why don't you take the rest of the day off, you've earned it!" Chief leaned back in his chair and folded his hands behind his head while smiling. He seemed quite pleased with being a boss who could make decisions.

Maritza had become so engrossed in working and in her search for information that for a second she thought he was actually giving her something. She smiled and glanced down at her watch. Her smile faded when she realized that she had already worked forty-five minutes past her off time. Chief was at it again; quick wit at her expense.

"Thanks for nothing, Chief. I'm out of here. You get too much of my time anyway." She grumbled. Faking irritation, she stomped over to her desk in her cubical.

"You're not fooling me. You wouldn't have it any other way." Chief closed his door so he didn't hear the sarcastic comment she hurled his way.

Rolling her eyes, she gathered her purse, slipped on her walking shoes and flew out the door. "Move out of her way before you get knocked down! It's almost seven o'clock, for the love of Pete!" Officer Minor commented.

"Whatever, Officer Minor; what does that mean? Who the heck is Pete?"

"Good question; I really don't know. It's just a figure of speech. Have a good night Maritza."

"Yeah, yeah," was her only reply as the door closed behind her.

Chapter 10

Chief Spurring pulled into the parking lot of the Perk You Up, coffee shop at five minutes before seven. Out of habit he glanced around the lot to check out his surroundings. All was clear. Five minutes later, he noticed Detective Irving drive inconspicuously into the lot in a silver colored Ford Crown Victoria. The Crown Vic model had been in the Griffin Police Department fleet for years, but this vehicle was new and Detective Irving's baby. It was shining like a new silver dollar, freshly waxed and ready to roll.

After parking the Vic, Detective Irving turned off his radio and eyed the parking lot to ensure he had a clean perimeter. Check. He stepped out of the car looking cool in dark shades. Slightly lowering his sun glasses, he spotted Chief Spurring and waved at him.

Chief Spurring waved back and watched the detective walk toward him. When Irving reached Spurring he leaned on his patrol car. Looking around to make sure there were no apparent listeners, he said, "Hey Chief, let me get in your car for a minute."

"Sure. What do you have? We can compare notes." Chief Spurring reached over in the passenger seat to grab the file on Elsie Mae Coats.

"Chief, I've gotten at least six calls about Ms. Coats and they are not pretty. Even though the people in town love her and think the world of her, she seems to have a shady past. Allegedly, she is leading a criminal life now. I've got at least four men who say she is anything but the good girl next door. They say she was doing tricks at one hundred dollars for half an hour. The strange thing is that, even her regular clients have not seen her in ten days."

"Who are they? Are they from Griffin?" Chief Spurring was ready to solve this case. Even if she was a whore, she was a person that he wanted back with her family.

"Well, it's kind of sticky because these men will not come forward willingly. They are all married and three of them have children from teens to toddlers. They all say the same thing, they don't want their reputations ruined and that they really do 'love' their wives." He motioned air quotes with his fingers when he said love.

"I don't get it Chief. Why would they risk losing their marriage, family, and maybe their health for a quick thrill? I guess I'll never understand it. My Angel says if she ever catches me cheating, it's over, and I believe her. Besides, one good woman is enough for me. And with a hooker; that's too much mileage on that! No thanks."

"You're right, Irving. You make a lot of sense. I never stepped out on Sandy, but she thought I did. We are separated now because I spent so many hours working cases. She said she couldn't take it anymore. I'm not sure what we're going to do. I love her, but I love my career too. The job doesn't help on long cold nights. It's no fun snuggling up with a few files, a laptop and brain-storming notepads. I've got to make some decisions soon. Do I want my marriage or do I want my job. It's sad that I have to make a choice." He looked crushed as he poured out his soul to his long time buddy.

"Look Chief, it doesn't have to be a choice. You have to prioritize your life. I know you know how to do that. You taught me everything I know. Sandy is too good a woman to be left alone all night, three and four nights a week. Any lady would think you are out with another woman. Chief, you have a great staff, trust us to do our jobs and go home at a decent hour. Don't lose your wife over this crap. In the end, it's your family that truly counts. Isn't that what you used to tell me?"

"Yeah, Irving, it is. You're giving me back my words and you are absolutely right. I'll give her a call later tonight to see if we can go out this weekend to talk, and work things out. Maybe she'll give me another chance."

"Sir, if you don't mind me asking, how long have you been separated?" Detective Irving had heard the rumor that they had parted ways, but he had refused to believe it. Chief and Sandy made a great couple and he didn't want to trust the water-cooler talk.

"It's only been five months, but it feels like a year. I miss her. Our home on the lake is nothing without her in it. I would have moved if she would have warned me. She was disgusted and jumped up and moved."

"Well make it happen, Chief. You'll be glad you did."

"Back to business, Irving; what do you have?" Chief Spurring had spoken; therefore, he and Detective Irving sat in the car for a while trading notes and conversing on the case. After about twenty minutes, Detective Irving glanced at his watch; it was twelve minutes after seven. Mrs. Howard was late.

"Mrs. Howard is late. I'm not surprised. Sometimes civilians have no concept about time management. You know, I'm a Marine man. We believe in being early for most appointments and on time for the rest. I really want to see the sister's reaction to this new information. Do you think she'll

81

be in denial like most family members?" Detective Irving ran his fingers through his straight auburn hair with his right hand. Irving stood six feet, two inches tall, he had tanned skin, large brown eyes, and thanks to a rigorous exercise routine, he had well defined chest and abdominal muscles. He was a family man, always proud to show the pictures of his three year old son and nine month old daughter. His wife Sally, who he called Angel, was the love of his life.

"Yes, she is late. Maybe she won't be too much longer. We have plenty that we can catch up on in the meantime." And so they did. After discussing all of the details of the Elsie Mae Coats' case that they knew of, they talked about other open cases, procedural information, current events, gasoline prices, financial investments, sports, and dream travel destinations.

* * *

After forty-five minutes had passed, they had caught-up on all of the latest news, issues, and even some office gossip. Detective Irving looked at his watch again and it was almost eight o'clock. He pulled out his cell phone and called Mrs. Howard's number. After the fifth ring, it went into voice mail.

"Chief, she must not be coming. She seemed interested in what I had to share; she even wanted me to tell her over the phone, but you know I couldn't do that. Let me look through my notes and get her home number." He found the number and dialed it.

Joseph had placed the cordless phone on the table. Hearing the ring, he checked the simmering rice that he was cooking, and then answered the call.

"Hello." Joseph had a deep, but pleasant voice.

"Hello, is this Mr. Howard?"

82

Joseph had placed teriyaki chicken wings in the oven to serve for dinner. He had already put together a salad with romaine lettuce, chopped boiled eggs, shredded cheese, tomatoes, cucumber, French's fried onions, and bacon bits. He thought to himself, *I guess the twins will eat tonight. They are such picky eaters. I wonder where Pauline and the girls are. Maybe she made another stop.*

"Yes, it is." Satisfied that the salad looked fine and would taste delicious, he placed the salad dressing on the kitchen island and focused on the telephone conversation. Pulling out a bar stool, he sat down.

"Yes. I'm Detective Ian Irving of the Griffin City Police Department. I'm here at the Perk You Up coffee shop in town waiting for Mrs. Howard. Chief Bruce Spurring is also with me. Your wife seemed sincere about meeting with me; however, she hasn't shown up. Do you know if she plans to come to the meeting?"

"That's strange. I spoke with my wife earlier and she mentioned your meeting. She is definitely planning to come. I'm home now waiting for her to drop off our twins, so that she can meet you. I kind of lost track of the time while preparing dinner. I didn't realize it had gotten this late. Let me call her and I'll call you right back. Your number showed up as private. Can you give it to me?"

"Of course I can. Please call me once you talk to her. Thank you and we'll be waiting to hear from you." Detective Irving gave him the number then hung up the phone. He then shrugged his shoulders at the chief and told him what Mr. Howard had said.

Once Joseph hung up the landline, he looked at his cell phone and noticed that he had four missed calls – all from the daycare center. *That's strange. I wonder what's going on.* He quickly dialed the daycare center trying not to worry, because they never called his number. He had it listed in his phone's contact list in case of an emergency, so the number showed up four times as missed calls.

"Hello, Tyrone's Christian Daycare Center, Mrs. Carter speaking. How may I help you?" She was the director of the center. Mrs. Carter glanced at the last two children in the center hoping that this was their parent calling because the caller ID read 'unknown.' It was past the normal time to go home.

"Yes, Mrs. Carter. This is Mr. Howard. My wife was supposed to pick up our twins, but she has not made it home. I just noticed the missed calls from you. Did she pick them up yet?"

"No. Your babies are here with me. Everyone else is gone. I called you several times and left messages. Didn't you get any of them?"

"No, I'm sorry I didn't. I just saw the missed calls and called you back. Something is definitely wrong. Pauline would never pick the kids up late. I'll be right there."

"Sir, I hope it's nothing too serious. We'll be here waiting for you." Mrs. Carter then picked up one of the twins. The other one was asleep in a soft chair.

"Thank you and I'll see you in a minute."

"I'll be right here waiting for you." She repeated. "Bye." While gently rocking the toddler, she whispered, "Your dad is on his way."

He quickly hung up the phone and called Pauline's cell number. He got the voice mail too, just like the detective. While walking past the oven, he turned it off, walked over to grab his suit jacket, retrieved his keys from the counter, and literally ran out of the house. As he started up his late model Volvo and backed out of the driveway, he heard the sound of a police siren very close by. By the time he had almost reached the edge of their sprawling property, a Tyrone City Police car carefully pulled into the end of the driveway. A young, relatively short, thin officer got out of the car, leaving his door open.

Removing his hat and wiping the sweat from his brow, he said, "Sir, are you Mr. Howard?"

"Yes, I am. What's the problem?" Joseph had no idea what to expect.

"Sir, there's been an accident. Unfortunately, your wife has been injured. My boss, Sergeant Gains told me to come get you and drive you to the Piedmont Fayette Hospital. He said y'all are friends." That was a unique small town officer, friendly and considerate thing to do.

"My God, is she okay?" He was now very worried.

"I'm sorry. I don't know her condition. Please Mr. Howard, let's go."

"Of course," he replied. Joseph reluctantly got out of his car and into the patrol car while trying to calm down his nerves. While the police car sped away with the siren blaring, Joseph called his older sister, relayed the situation to her and asked her to pick up the twins from the center. He called Pauline's parents so that they could meet him at the hospital. Finally, Joseph called Detective Irving to inform him about his wife's accident. While talking, he had mentioned what hospital she was in.

Laying his head back on the headrest, Joseph closed his eyes and continued to pray, not even giving his mind a chance to think anything negative. *My God, please don't let me lose Pauline. She has to make it. I can't bear the thought of losing her.* Sighing heavily, he shook his head and anxiously, but quietly rode to the Piedmont Fayette Hospital.

* * *

Joseph didn't know it, but Chief Spurring and Detective Irving had decided to meet him at the hospital. Chief

Spurring had called his office and had spoken to an officer who he delegated to ascertain the details of the car wreck in Tyrone, Georgia. Chief also wanted updated information on the woman's condition. He and Irving were driving to the facility with the hopes of interviewing Mrs. Howard.

When Chief Spurring's cell phone rang, he immediately answered. The officer said, "Chief, Mrs. Howard is listed as critical and she is in a coma. I guess if she could speak, she would say 'I have no comment, at this time.' I guess you'll have to wait on that interview boss. Also, she caused the accident, hitting a gray Tahoe."

"Thanks, out." Chief said and then turned his attention to Detective Irving.

"Mrs. Howard is listed as critical and she's in a coma. I'll have to wait for an interview. Let's go anyway. We may get lucky and meet a witness that knows something about her missing sister. That's a lot for one family to deal with; one sister missing and the other one listed as critical in the hospital."

"You're right, Chief Spurring. That's a lot to cope with at the same time. I wouldn't want to trade places with that family for anything." Detective Irving agreed.

* * *

Later that night Chief Spurring went to the 'red light district' to interview Slick Baby. Apparently, the woman had a change of heart about being an informant. She also had warned everyone that the police were coming and the area was totally empty. The women of the night were not available for the cruising clients.

86

Chapter 11

The officer who was transporting Joseph Howard still had his siren blaring as he pulled the police car into the circular driveway for the emergency room at Piedmont Fayette Hospital. Joseph could hardly wait until the car stopped before he was opening up his door. Briefly, he looked over his shoulder and said, "Thanks officer."

"You're welcome. I hope your wife's okay."

Joseph nodded his head as he rushed inside toward the desk to inquire about his wife's condition and location.

"Excuse me, my wife, Pauline Howard was in an accident and brought here. How is she? Where is she?"

"May I see your identification?" She turned to the flat computer screen and went to a display that enabled her to track a patient's general information. It was the same information that could be given when someone called in and made the same type of inquiry in person.

"Yes of course, I have ID." He reached into his back pocket, retrieved his wallet and handed the woman his driver's license.

"Okay, your wife is in emergency surgery on the third floor. This is the ground level. Take the elevators down the hall on the left to the third floor, turn right and follow the hall until you see the signs for ICU - Surgery."

87

"What does it say about her condition?" Feeling nervous, a sweat abruptly broke out on his forehead.

"Sir, I'm sorry, but she's listed as critical." The woman noted the distressed look on his face and offered, "She's in good hands."

"I hope so. Thank you." Joseph quickly pivoted around and jogged to the elevator bay, pressed the up button and anxiously waited for the elevator to arrive. Within minutes, other people gathered in the area. Finally, as the doors opened, a few people exited the crammed space and the people already in the elevator moved further inside to make room for the new riders. Each one eyed the slowly changing numbers as they ascended to the various floors. When they reached the third floor, he briskly walked to the nurse's station.

"Yes, may I help you?" The older, thin nurse had one hand tracing a column in a spiral notebook and the other held an ink pen.

"My wife, Pauline Howard is in emergency surgery. Would you please tell me where she is?"

"I'm sorry, what's her name again." The woman rolled her chair over to a computer to check the patient list.

Irritated about having to repeat himself, he said, "Her name is Pauline Howard."

"Let's see, Howard, Pauline…She is in ICU surgery, R, 307. Take a right at the end of this hall. There's a waiting room on the left. The doctor will be with you as soon as possible."

"Thank you." Rushing for no apparent reason, he walked to the crowded waiting area. Taking a seat near a window, he dropped his head into his hands, totally drained mentally. He thought to himself, *You never know what a day will bring. Pauline was just fine this morning and now this! I'm glad we always part for the day with a hug, a kiss and pleasant conversation. She looked beautiful as we ate breakfast and drank coffee together. She is such a great wife and a wonderful mother! What would I do without her? 'Lord, please guide the surgeon's hands and let my wife survive. I love her and I need her. You've given us precious twin girls who definitely need their mom. Work a miracle God, in Jesus' name, Amen.'*

After a few minutes, he reached into his pocket, pulled out his hankie and wiped the perspiration from his forehead and neck. He then detached his cell phone from its holder and called his sister.

"Hello Joseph, how is Pauline?" She absentmindedly reached over to pick up the spoon that one of the twins had dropped, took it over to the dishwasher and placed it into the silverware holder. Pushing the appliance door closed, she turned, walked to the kitchen table and sat in a chair to give him her undivided attention.

"Gail, she's listed in critical condition, but that's all I know. She's in surgery and I can't see her yet. The doctors are still working on her. What more does our family have to endure? Her sister is missing and now this! I wonder what happened."

"Oh my God, Joseph, can it get any worse? We will just have to pray that she pulls through. She just has to! Call me later with some good news. I'm lifting her up to the Lord. You and these babies need her. In fact, we all love Pauline and depend on her. She's going to be fine, Joseph; do you hear me? She's got to pull through! Be encouraged baby brother, I feel like she's going to be just fine."

"Okay Gail, I'll call you later. Call anyone that you know who can get a prayer through. Pauline has got to be okay."

"That's the spirit! We'll all pray for a miracle. Stay strong Joseph and know that I love you."

"I love you too. I'll talk to you later." He placed his phone it its holder and momentarily closed his eyes.

"Whew." He anxiously blew his breath. Exasperated because he didn't know for sure that she would actually live; he took out his wallet and found her picture, removing it to get a closer look at her. Kissing her image, he whispered, "Baby, you've got to make it!" As a tear formed in the corner of his eye, he grabbed his hankie again from his back pocket, quickly wiped his eye and turned to focus on a television news report. *Man, crying in public isn't cool,* he chided himself.

Ten minutes into the news program, his cell phone buzzed. It was his brother Brent. "Hey Joseph, I heard from Gail about Pauline's accident. How is she doing now?" His conversation was laced with concern for his favorite sister-in-law. Brent lived in Los Angeles, California and worked as a pilot for a major package shipping company. When he exited his last flight, he had listened to a message from Gail, called her back and was simply shocked by the news.

"Well, she's listed in critical condition right now and she's still in emergency surgery. Man, I can't lose Pauline. I love her and I can't imagine my life without her."

"Joseph, let's believe that she's going to be okay. Do you know what happened? Was it the other driver's fault?" Brent was in his car, but he stopped backing out of his reserved parking place to listen to his brother.

"At this point, I really don't know anything other than she's in surgery; but we all know how strong she is. I have to believe she'll be okay. I can't let myself think of anything else, but her being well and coming home as soon as possible." Joseph positioned his head in one hand as he supported the phone with his other hand.

"That's it brother, just think positive thoughts and let me know as soon as she gets out of surgery."

"Will do, talk to you later." Joseph returned his phone to its leather holder and continued to watch the television. He and the others in the waiting room listened intently when a report came on about the missing, Elsie Mae Coats.

One woman nudged her friend and whispered, "It's a shame that girl is missing. I hope the things folks have been saying about her at the beauty shop aren't true." Her voice went even lower, but Joseph could still hear her. She continued by saying, "I hear she's a nasty girl! I don't know if the rumors are true; I'm just saying!"

The other woman said, "I heard those rumors too; but either way, I know her family is sick over her being missing. Lord, have mercy is all I've got to say." The woman then took out a hankie and wiped perspiration from her forehead.

Even though the women didn't know he was related to Elsie Mae, he suddenly felt embarrassed as he silently reflected on his missing sister-in-law and his injured wife. *If those rumors about Elsie Mae are true, it may kill her parents. They are such respectable and proud people. Their youngest daughter is still missing and now Pauline's in critical condition. What a load to bear.*

As Joseph was thinking, he looked up in time to see Pauline's parents walk through the entrance. Her mother's eyes were bloodshot and her father's face was strained. They all embraced and took seats. Worried sick about her daughters, Mrs. Coats cried and leaned her head on her husband's shoulder. They agreed to pray and believe God to work miracles for Elsie Mae and Pauline.

* * *

Down the hall, three doctors worked earnestly on Pauline. There were a host of nurses and other medical staff busy assisting the doctors. Pauline's blood pressure was

91

dropping, she had suffered a concussion, had numerous lacerations, and her pelvis was broken as well as several bones in her left leg. Broken bits of glass had pierced her skin and veins and she had lost a tremendous amount of blood. She had arrived at the hospital unconscious. The goal was to stabilize her so that she could be transferred to an intensive care unit. Unfortunately, one very distracted driver moment has the potential to negatively alter your entire life.

Chapter 12

"Georgia, it's great to see you! How long has it been? I don't believe you girl. You look like you haven't aged a year, much less twenty years. Whatever you are doing to look so fabulous, you need to just keep it up." Leah, whom everyone called Twigs, threw her hand toward Georgia to emphasize her flattering points. She finished by placing her hands on her hips to wait for Georgia's reply.

"Well, all I have to say is we must be going to the same stylist because you are looking mighty good yourself." Georgia was happy to see her old friend.

Leah tilted her head and said, "Child, flattery will get you everywhere! What brings you to Tyrone, Georgia? I had heard that you are jet-setting all over Europe when you aren't in Hollywood. What's up? And what brings you back to our hometown Tyrone?

"First of all, don't believe everything you hear and definitely don't trust what you read in the tabloids. Most of that garbage is to ensure that the trash papers sell. Very little of it is real. You should know that by now." Was there a hint of irritation in Georgia's tone?

"SHhhhh. Stop the madness! What else is a girl to think? I call you and never get a return call, as if you've gotten too good for the home folk. I've tried through the years not to take things too personally, but seriously girl, I've missed you." Leah's lying behind sounded authentic for a change.

"Thanks Leah. I've missed you too. It's funny how living with the very rich and famous of the world has a way of making you forget your roots for a minute. I apologize. I'd like to blame it on my public relations people but really, I have no one to blame but myself. I didn't have to listen to them."

"No, the hell you didn't have to. You and I were the best of friends in college until you dropped out. I was disappointed about that. You know how much my mother stressed education. Everyone thought you were doing a foolish thing following your dreams. To be honest with you, I was scared for you too knowing how competitive the movie industry can be, but you proved everybody wrong. You went out west and made a name for yourself. I'm so proud of you!" Leah beamed with joy.

"Thanks. Now that's enough about me. What have you been up to? Right after college, I remember you writing about a daughter. Did you get the gifts I sent her through the years?"

"Yes, every one of them! I sent thank you cards to your management company. Are you telling me that you didn't get them?"

"No I didn't, but that's pretty common out there. That's okay. We'll make up for it while I'm home for this break." Georgia touched Leah on her shoulder.

"You can believe that! Now, let's go get a refill." Leah turned to walk back to the bar, but before she could get there, one of the servers had sashayed to her and placed a fresh drink in her hand, carefully removing the used glass.

Service; now that's what I'm talking about. They don't know it, but I really don't deserve to be here. Good I know

Georgia! Leah was happy to be there with the wealthy residents who had sponsored the charity event to welcome Georgia home. *It pays to know the right folk!* Leah smiled as she continued to mingle with the well-to-do folk just south of Atlanta.

* * *

When Georgia got back to her hotel, she started checking her E-mail and her voice messages. She had an urgent message from her mother who had heard from the relatives in Griffin and Tyrone that her cousins were both in a crisis situation.

The message said, 'Georgia, this is your Mom; call me child. There is an emergency down South. Call me as soon as you get this message. Love you baby. Bye.'

Georgia called her mother and the older woman immediately filled her in on the grim details.

"Hey Georgia baby, Elsie Mae is missing!" She sounded out of breath as she said the horrible news.

Georgia gasped and said, "Missing! You mean as in gone. They don't know what's happened to her? You've got to be kidding me!"

"Child, you know I wouldn't play about something like that. It's so sad. We just hope she's alive somewhere, but if she's alive, why doesn't she call home?"

"That's true, if she is okay, why not call home? That's the million dollar question."

"Georgia, the news reporter said that her disappearance has just baffled the authorities so far."

"Mother, so I assume since they have not found a body, there is a possibility that she may be alive, somewhere – doing what, I don't know."

95

"And if that was not enough, her sister Pauline had been on her way to the search party to help look for Elsie Mae when she hit a car. She's listed in serious condition at a hospital. Hold on while I find out which hospital it is." After a brief pause, she came back to the phone. "It's called Piedmont Fayette Hospital. Please check on your cousins and get back to me and let me know what's what. Okay?"

"Mom, that's horrible. I'll see what I can do. Thank you for calling me."

* * *

After making some calls to Joseph and his sister Gail, Georgia was able to confirm that what her mother had heard was accurate. She called her mother and assured her that she would keep her posted about Pauline's condition.

She thought to herself, *I call myself coming here to get away from drama and problems only to find my own family is in crisis. Well, I'll stay as long as I can and be supportive before returning to work.*

Chapter 13

Ginger was closing the shop worn out from the busy day she had. On the one hand, she wasn't complaining because the busier the boutique was the better she lived. On the other hand her feet and legs were aching. *I feel so drained today.* Where's my energy? *What's wrong with me?*

The gentle buzzing of her cell phone alerted her to an incoming call. It was Justin, her fourteen year old son.

"Mom, Candace called to remind us about her dance recital. Can we go? It's tomorrow night, and starts at eight. You can't get in if you're late. So Mom, we're going right? I hear it's going to be great!" Justin played his game system while waiting for Ginger to answer his question.

"Justin, why am I just hearing about this recital? I've mentioned to Candace before that I need more notice. I have always enjoyed her performances, but I would like some lead time to put it on my calendar so that I don't have a scheduling conflict." Ginger was irritated now, plus very tired.

"Mom, I knew you were going to wonder why she's just telling us about it. When I asked her she said she told Keefer over two weeks ago and he was supposed to tell you. The tickets are twenty dollars and he told her that all of us would be there. Mom, we can't disappoint her." Justin hoped his

97

persistent pleading would be enough to convince his mother. Candace was his step-sister whom he had grown to love.

"Justin, I'm walking to the car and I'm exhausted. Let me get home, relax in my favorite chair, and check my calendar. I never make a quick decision without seeing how it will affect other plans. You know that. I've told Candace to notify *me* when something is coming up. Keefer seems too preoccupied with other things these days to be concerned with his 'family.' Hey, did you walk Pepper?" Pepper was their Labrador Retriever.

"Mom, I know the drill by now; when I get home from school, I take Pepper outside. She's been walked. Now Mom, can we go to the recital?"

"I'll let you know son. See you when I get home."

"Okay. Bye Mom." Justin continued to play his game.

Pepper was stretched out on the wool rug in the center of the den. "Pepper, you better get off that rug and get over to your bed. Mom would have a fit if she saw you." Pepper looked at Justin like he had spoken in Russian or some other language she didn't understand. She just turned her head, looked at him and then turned right back around, as if to say, 'leave me alone.'

"Pepper, did you hear me? Go, girl." Justin pointed to the fuchsia colored princess bed that stood on curved, iron legs about six inches off the ground. It looked very comfortable and it was for her use - not the wool rugs. Pepper reluctantly gave up her spot on the rug and strutted over to her bed. She loved it too, but sometimes she wanted to use the rugs. When she made it to her bed, she stepped up into it, circled several times, for what, Justin didn't understand, and then she finally lay down. After getting comfortable, she blew her breath like she was simply exhausted with all of her directions to lie here, not there, poop here and not there. Humans, who needed them anyway?

"Good girl Pepper; act like you've been trained!" *I can't believe it; I'm starting to sound just like Mom.* He became engrossed in his video game and missed hearing the chime of the alarm, alerting him that the outside door had been opened. When Ginger walked into the den, he was startled and jumped.

"Why'd you walk up on me like that?" he asked.

"Son, the chime rings every time an outside door is opened. Don't have your gaming system up so loud because it makes it difficult to hear someone coming in."

Pepper had bothered to get off her royal resting spot to greet Ginger, her tail wagging a hundred-miles-a-minute. Ginger smiled and said, "I get more of a welcome from Pepper than any man in this house! Hey baby girl, are you enjoying your new bed?" Pepper looked over at Justin as if to say 'Don't you dare tell her that I wanted to sleep on the wool rug.'

Justin winked at Pepper as if that gesture would ensure that the dog would know that their secret was secure. When he looked over at her, her ears went up. *Big Momma always said that dogs can do everything but speak words; they communicate right on even though you can't hear them talk; they get their point across. Just like when there's no food in the dog dish, Pepper will look at you and lick her lips as if to say, 'I would like to eat before I die of starvation.'* Justin smiled at her human-like ways.

"Yeah Mom, she loves it. Didn't you see that's where she was snoozing before you came in, right on her royal princess bed?" Pepper looked at him again for good measure. He called her then and said, "Come here Pepper, everything is going to be alright." He patted her head.

"Well of course it is silly boy." said Ginger.

"What's for dinner?" he asked. "How about pizza and wings, you know I'll eat pizza any time." He said while grinning from ear to ear.

"Pizza it is, because I don't feel up to cooking anything." She sighed and walked over to the desktop computer on her desk to get the number to order the food. After placing the call, she mentioned that the meal, Greek salad, pizza and hot wings, was on the way.

"Baby, take this money to pay the delivery man when he comes. If I fall asleep, wake me up because not only am I tired, I am definitely hungry. Good pick son, tonight's dinner will be quick and delicious. Keefer may not be big on pizza and wings, but he can just eat the salad if he wants. I can't do anything else but lie down and go to sleep as soon as I eat. Don't bother me unless you are bleeding or dying. You know the drill."

"Okay Mom, go on and rest for a minute. I'll try not to eat everything up from you." Justin started laughing.

"You had better not eat a whole extra-large pizza and twenty wings! If I wake up and it's all gone, it will not be pretty up in this house; I'm here to tell you."

"Yes Miss food police. I'll save you a bone or two."

"Those bones had better have some meat on them, and the pizza better be full of toppings. Do you remember when you were five years old – old enough to know better, you told me that Mother had called me. By the time I got back to the table my pizza looked like it had been picked over by a rat or something. You little rascal, I know how you will eat until nothing is left and think it's alright. Boy, do you have a conscious? Better yet, does your stomach have a bottom to it?" She walked away mumbling, "I need an extra job just to feed this child."

"That's right, get another job just to feed me. Then I could eat every last one of those wings and every slice of pizza!" He was laughing as he saw her walk over to the stairs that lead to her spacious master bedroom. She gave him a funny look and turned her back to him and walked up the stairs.

Ginger went into the double-door entrance of her master suite. The first room had a triple tray ceiling with extra crown molding in each row. There were custom blinds in the windows along with designer swags. The bedspread matched the window treatments and there were Oriental wool rugs over the floor of wall-to-wall Berber carpet. The second room was a sitting room large enough for a sofa, two chairs, a stone and glass coffee table, two Oriental cabinets, and a fifty-five inch television mounted on the wall. The master bathroom suite was big enough that ten people could stand up in it and they would not feel the least bit crowded. There was a winding two sink vanity with six feet of beautiful black and cream granite separating the sinks. The shower was built for two, and had nickel, Delta jets that would message your body like a private masseuse. Finally, the tub was a two person, heaven on earth oasis. Every time she got out of that tub with its awesome Jacuzzi jets, she felt like she had just left the spa. The over-sized double-pane window was as big and long as the tub. My, my; it was a bedroom and bath suite suitable for royalty.

Ginger stepped into the shower with all of its atomizers, buttons and gadgets letting the rotating jets sooth her muscles. After her shower she dried off and grabbed a peach-colored gown from her dresser. Before putting it on, she applied lotion and got ready for bed.

While resting across her bed, she flipped through her planner and realized that they could attend Candace's dance recital. *Justin will be happy to hear that. He really is a sweet kid, both of them are. I'm blessed; if only Keefer would cooperate, I'd really feel like a rich woman- rich with love, instead of depressed and lonely.* She heard the doorbell indicating that the food had arrived. Justin rushed to pay the guy and turned around all proud like he had made the dinner himself. He walked over to the intercom system and pressed the button to call Ginger. "COME EAT MOM!"

Ginger shook her head at how loud he was talking, while she pressed the 'talk' button to respond. "Son, you don't have to yell. Lower your voice when speaking into the microphone. I'm coming down right now." She released the button and slipped on her house shoes. *I sure didn't want to turn that bed a loose,* she thought as she smiled and walked downstairs. "Justin, I checked my calendar, and yes, we can go support Candace. I'll give her a call later and remind her about giving me some notice next time."

"Yes! Even though I would go just to see Candace, there's a girl I'd like to get to know in her troop. Maybe Candace can introduce me to her after the performance." Justin exclaimed.

"I should have known you had an ulterior motive. Boy, you are a mess! Do you want some old-fashioned butter popcorn?"

"You know I do Mom. How about watching a movie with me?"

The look in his eyes suggested that he really wanted company; so, Ginger glanced down at the items in her hand and chose to spend some time with her son.

"Pick a good one on HBO and I'll go make the popcorn." Ginger turned and walked toward the guest restroom, washed her hands, then she went into the kitchen for the pot, lid, popcorn, oil, and butter. She poured just enough liquid oil to cover the bottom of the pot, let it get hot and then added the kernels. Ginger gently shook the pot back and forth over the flames of the gas stove top. As the corn popped, she thought about her life that appeared to be spiraling out of control. She thought to herself, *I feel like one of these kernels must feel, in a hot, horrible situation being stung and tossed emotionally around and haphazardly, left to explode!* After the batch was finished, she melted butter in a cup in the microwave oven. Retrieving the melted butter, she happily poured it over the snack, adding salt to taste. Ginger and Justin watched a good movie together and they were engaged enough to discuss the scenes after the movie.

* * *

It was eight-thirty at night and Keefer had not come home from work. *I wonder where he is.* Ginger thought.

She and Justin sat across from each other eating pizza and dipping wings in the ranch dressing.

"Mom, we can have this all the time, this is delicious!" Justin acted like she had cooked a feast suitable for a Thanksgiving meal.

"Son, I'm glad you are so happy with our meal, however, we can't eat like this all of the time. We need various vegetables and truly balanced meals. This is okay sometimes, but normally I would cook dinner. Hey, how about I teach you some simple meals and then you'll be able to prepare dinner sometimes."

"That sounds like a winner to me Mom. Like you always say, I need to be able to feed myself if nothing else. That's cool. I want to learn how to prepare good food. I hear that girls love guys who cook!"

Ginger playfully rolled her eyes and said, "That would make you an even better husband one day. Remember, you'll also need to be faithful, supportive, kind, attentive and a great communicator. *I'm not ready for him to date! I do want to plant the seeds of knowledge for him to be a good boyfriend and eventually a wonderful husband.*

103

After devouring numerous wings, Justin chewed his fifth slice of pizza, licked his lips, finally finished, and wiped his mouth. "Mom, I'm full!" He pulled gristle from one of the chicken bones and tossed it to Pepper. She lapped it up immediately, wagging her tail looking from Justin to Ginger as if to say, 'I'll take another one, please.'

"Boy, that's enough for her. I didn't say anything at first. You probably thought I didn't see you sliding her table food. You're going to have her so spoiled." Ginger drifted off now wondering what time Keefer was going to find his way home. *I'm sick of this. Keefer is so disrespectful. When will this nightmare end?*

As if he could read her thoughts, Justin said, "Mom, where is Keefer?" He walked over to the remote control, changed the channel and sat down looking her way for a response.

She sighed heavily before responding to him. "He probably had to work late again." She didn't believe that herself, but she didn't want Justin to be worried about grown folks' business.

"He sure is working late a lot these days. I kind of miss him Mom. I think I'll call him." Justin pulled out his cell phone from his pants pocket and dialed Keefer's number. After five rings, Keefer's voice mail came on. "Hey Keefer, I was wondering if we could play my X-Box or watch a movie when you get home. Hit me back, and I'll see you when you get here." He placed his phone back in his pocket and turned toward Ginger. "Mom, I hardly get to see him anymore." Justin momentarily looked sad.

"I know; I miss him too." A wave of disappointment flooded over her. *This is really bad when it starts to affect your child. Why can't he see that whatever he is doing in the streets has a negative effect on me and my son? Keefer said he wanted to help me raise Justin. If I had known he would flip the script on me, I would have stayed by myself and waited on a man that wanted to be a real family man. This is really a sad, hot mess. I am fed up with his games. I should have stayed single, if I would wind up alone most of the time anyway. I can't take this anymore. I feel like I'm going to snap.* She could never remember feeling so miserable, hopeless, and frustrated all rolled into one ball of gut-retching confusion. She just knew she was ready for some changes in her life.

Suddenly, her cell phone rang; it was her gynecologist calling. This was the late night for the office and the doctor would usually make all calls after seeing her patients.

"Hello." Ginger got up from her seat in the kitchen nook to walk into the living room away from Justin.

"Mrs. Graham, this is Dr. Gonzalez. How are you tonight?"

"Well, I've been kind of stressed and very tired lately. Other than that, I'm okay; however, if you are calling me, it can't be good news." Ginger felt a wave of dizziness contemplating what Dr. Gonzalez was going to say.

"Are you sitting down, Mrs. Graham?"

"No, I'm not; should I sit down?" Her voice quivered and her legs suddenly felt like noodles under her frame.

"Please, sit down Mrs. Graham. I have disturbing news; fortunately, not life threatening, but upsetting none the less."

"Just spit it out, Doctor. What is it?" Ginger thought to herself, *Can my situation get any worse?*

"You said you had been feeling very tired. I now know why. Apparently, your husband has given you a sexually transmitted disease; gonorrhea. Before you panic, I want you to know that this is totally treatable. I need you to come into my office tomorrow for treatment, and he will need to go see an urologist."

"What? There must be some kind of a mistake? I..." She stammered, not sure how to respond. She sighed heavily and shifted in her chair. As she did this, she inadvertently spilled the pop from her glass onto her nightgown. It was soaked and she would have to change. *This can't be real, an STD? I've never had an STD in my life! My God, it feels like a bomb has been dropped in my lap.* Suddenly, she felt woozy, like waves of nausea in her head. She finally recovered and said, "Thank you doctor; however, he's not only going to need an urologist, but a psychiatrist, a psychologist, and an internist when I get through with him. Are you sure it couldn't be some kind of error?" Ginger was devastated and furious, to say the least.

"Mrs. Graham, I understand your question, but there's no mistake. Thankfully, this is treatable. Would you like information on an excellent marriage therapist that I could recommend?"

"No thank you, Dr. Gonzalez. I've got his therapy. Wait till he gets home!" Disgusted, she shook her head and closed her eyes.

"Mrs. Graham, try not to worry. I know you are going to be just fine. For tonight, find a way to relax and take care of yourself. Can you come into the office for nine in the morning?"

"I'll be there doc. Thank you for calling."

"Mrs. Graham, it's going to be okay." Dr. Gonzalez said. What else could she say?

Ginger replied, "You're right, one way or another, it's all going to be just fine. See you tomorrow."

"Yes, I'll see you then." Dr. Gonzalez said.

The news from her doctor hit Ginger like a ton of bricks. She had never had an STD in her life and to get one from her husband was shocking. Hurt and irate she sat in her living room for about three hours. It was hard to wrap her mind around having an STD. She periodically got up from the sofa to glance out of the window to see if Keefer's car was in the driveway. Feeling like it was getting late; she walked into the den to tell Justin to go to bed because he had school the next day. She also didn't want him awake when she confronted Keefer.

Justin had tried to wait up for Keefer, but he had fallen asleep on the sofa. Instead of bothering him, Ginger covered her son up with a blanket and dejectedly went back upstairs.

Reaching her bedroom, she flopped down on the bench at the foot of her bed and dialed Keefer's number. As it so often did these days, his phone rang five times and then went into voice mail. Livid, she left a stirring message, "Keefer, where are you? Justin tried to wait up, but he fell asleep again. I'm tired of you disappointing my son. And, I'm tired of you betraying me. Your lies have caught up with you. When I see you, we've got something serious to discuss. You might want to hurry and come home while your key still fits the damn lock!" Angrily, she hung up the phone and threw it on the bed.

"He's a lunatic! Who needs him, and now this? I know one thing, I'm not waiting up tonight. I can't believe this…he's going to stay out late again? This man is pushing me to my limits. I can't even wrap my mind around him cheating on me again after all we've been through. He's hanging out with trash…an STD? Are you kidding me? One person can only take so much! You're going to have to help me Jesus, before I help myself and hurt that man. Wait a minute, what am I saying? I can't do jail. I'm claustrophobic; I'd go crazy in a cell." Suddenly, she blinked her eyes and shook her head. "No, I'm not going to let him drive me insane. He can be crazy by himself!" She then walked over to the bathroom suite, washed her face and stripped out of her soda-soaked nightgown.

107

Ginger had spoken out loud like someone was in the room with her. She hardly recognized her own tone or her words. *Who am I becoming-a mad woman?* Depressed and angry, she undressed and stretched out across the bed naked, too weary to even make another sleep wear selection. She was solemn in her spirit, felt crazy as hell, and angry enough to cut Keefer.

Before going to sleep, Ginger could almost hear Big Momma's advice in the back of her mind telling her, 'Child, when you find yourself in a personal storm, you've got to pray, and pray some more until you get your breakthrough!'

"Okay Big Momma, here goes." She took a deep breath and said, "God, please heal me from this STD and deliver me from this situation. And by the way, your boy Keefer may need some extra protection tonight." Despite her dilemma, she had thrown in a little humor in her sleepy, criminal-minded prayer.

Ginger then said, "Lord, I think I'm going crazy because I really want to hurt this cheating man." She nodded her head knowing her thought pattern right now was totally out of character. She was having serious violent thoughts that she just might act on. Knowing that her husband had infected her with a foul STD was over the top–way too much to process! *And to think, I'm not even the cheater and I've got to go see the doctor. This ain't right!* She was motionless on the bed, emotionally in shock. Finally, pulling a sheet over her naked body, she drifted off to sleep.

Chapter 14

About an hour after falling asleep, Ginger woke up enjoying the comfort of her bed. Looking for Keefer, she got up, slipped on a robe and went across the hall to glance out of a front bedroom window to see if his car was in the driveway. She went downstairs, checked the garage and only her cars were inside. Ginger didn't know it, but Keefer was in a sleazy part of town on the verge of engaging in scandalous acts.

Excited, Keefer sat in his car scanning the parade of women who worked the corner of Hellborn and Lost. Yes, they literally worked the beat. They were women of the night; strutting their wares in the red light district. He thought to himself, *Do I want Miss Daisy Dukes over there in those sexy shorts that are barely covering her goodies? Or, do I want my normal treat, Miss Bee-Bee Sweet? Where is she? Ah, I see her in that pink mini dress looking like a yummy piece of candy!* As the scantily clad women enticed would-be customers to have a "date" with them, Keefer tried to remain calm. Beads of sweat cascaded down his temples as he tried to make up his mind. Miss jean skirt with the purple midriff bent over into the window of a luxury vehicle. As she briefly solicited the driver, her micro-mini skirt revealed a tip of butt cheeks; that was just enough to cause

Keefer elation. He could hardly contain himself. His mind contemplated; *pink mini dress doll or blue jean queen; blue jean queen or pink mini on my mind? Man, make a decision!* He chided himself, torn with irrational indecision.

Suddenly, blue jean queen stood up and threw her hand at the air toward the would-be client with attitude as if to say, 'Forget you.' As the car sped off from the shadows, Keefer could see that it was a silver colored Lexus. The driver apparently had a change of heart. *He must have chickened out, punk!* Keefer scorned the apparent moral decision of the driver for not partaking of the prostitute's services. He drove his car closer, but remained across the street.

The butt cheek flashing, hot momma turned toward his car, winked her false eyelash and started walking his way. She was about fifty-five feet from him, and with her every step he got more excited.

That's the one for me tonight! I like her aggression. She had not waited until he pulled to her side of the street; she made the effort and walked toward him. Keefer had made a decision; his illicit, sexual addiction clearly ruling over his sound thinking. He was a greedy man. He already had a beautiful wife at home, a girlfriend waiting across town, and still, he indulged in street women of ill-repute. There was no shame in his game. He wanted them all. As twisted as his thinking was, he considered himself perfectly normal.

Abruptly, his cell phone started ringing. Glancing down he noticed it was Ginger. Sighing, he quickly picked it up and lifted up his index finger indicating that he needed the hooker to wait a moment. Rolling his eyes, he answered the phone, "Hey baby, how are you tonight?" He had a talent of turning on the charm for his wife even while in the midst of contemplating cheating on her with a cheap whore. He was a reckless playboy with a propensity to flip personalities at a moment's notice.

"I'm not okay! I was wondering... should I wait up for you tonight?" She said sarcastically, before continuing. "Lately, you claim you've been working long hours. What time are you coming home? We need to talk! Besides, Justin wanted to spend some time with you too." She stroked her wrist where she had just removed a tight bracelet, while waiting for his reply.

"No honey, I'm working late again tonight. Don't bother waiting up for me because I have no idea what time I'll be home. We can just talk tomorrow." He lustfully winked at the prostitute who returned the gesture.

"What? What kind of work are you supposedly doing? No idea what time...Keefer, what's really going on?"

"Nothing, I've got to go now." He pressed his phone to hang up on her, however, before his phone was completely disconnected, Ginger faintly overheard a distant female voice say, "Hey, sugar...want..."

"But..." Ginger gasped as she tried in vain to catch him, but he had hung up. Highly insulted, Ginger re-dialed his number, but the voice mail immediately came on indicating that Keefer had turned off his cell phone. *Who was that woman in the background? Was she possibly talking to my man? Surely not....*

Furious at her husband, Ginger glanced at Justin, who was waking up. He must have felt her gaze because he looked up and smiled. She smiled back not wanting to alert him that she was upset. "Get up and go to bed."

"Ok. Good night Mom." Justin said as he walked away.

Emotionally devastated, a tear eased out of her eye as she seethed and mourned simultaneously. She reflected, *I don't know what Keefer's into, but he constantly lies. It doesn't seem like he even has a conscience anymore. Just as sure as my name is Ginger Davis Graham, I'm going to find out what's going on!* "Lies flow from Keefer's mouth as smooth as melting butter." She said under her breath while shaking her head. Feeling angry, hurt, confused, and bitterly rejected, Ginger snatched up her leather portfolio and purse. *He knows good and well that he's not working – not at his business anyway!*

Remembering some candy that she had purchased a couple of days earlier, Ginger stopped and dropped the black, rawhide folder on the kitchen island. Opening her handbag, she looked through it to locate the giant Snickers bar. It had become slightly smashed, but it didn't matter; she needed to sooth herself by any means necessary. She reasoned within herself, *eating these extra calories would be better than going upside his lying head when he finally makes it home!*

While Ginger nursed her hurt feelings with chocolate and later a glass of wine, Keefer was across town doing the unthinkable.

* * *

Keefer was aroused and turned to the pretty young thing that was his for the asking. "Hello Doll, what's your name?"

"I'm Brownie-Baby. What's your name lover boy, and what are you looking for tonight?" As she talked while leaning into his car, she licked her lips and looked him up and down while raising her accentuated, arched eyebrows.

"Just call me Dr. Feel-good honey. How much for everything?" They discussed the pricing and decided on the deluxe works. He pulled his car around to the back of an abandoned building and quickly exited the car. Placing his arm around her slender waist, he let her lead him to the entrance of the old hotel that was next door to the vacant structure. When they got to her room on the second floor, he asked her to perform without using a condom. For fifty dollars more, it was a done deal. They had sex. When it was all over, he took her back to her corner where she adjusted her clothes and started motioning cruisers, trying to entice her next customer. Nasty girl...

Momentarily, he watched her walk up and down the street; he then drove a block away to another corner that was void of people and parked his car while leaving it running. He relaxed for about five minutes thinking about what Brownie-Baby had done to him. Abruptly he shook himself as if cold and then swiftly pulled away from the area. Suddenly, the rendezvous he just had, hit him in another way.

As Keefer had experienced numerous times before after indulging in this type of extra marital, illegally purchased activity, the pattern was unfortunately, the same. He went from the rush and excitement of the partner selection, then the pleasure of the unbridled sex to the overwhelming burden of guilt and shame. His ugly reality was a script that he couldn't seem to stop rehearsing. He was trapped in a web of corrupted, risky behavior; excitement, indulgence and then ignominy.

Keefer's total lack of regard for Ginger, Beverly and the other women left him and all involved vulnerable to sexually transmitted diseases, thanks to his bankrupted morals. Unfortunately, neither of the women he had a relationship with had a clue of how entangled he was. While Ginger assumed that he was cheating with someone, she had no idea that he was addicted to a life of multiple, twisted connections. Beverly was the other woman, but she thought her only competition was his wife. The master player had them both deceived!

* * *

Even though he should have gone home and cleaned up, he couldn't face Ginger right now. Though he felt guilt about committing adultery, he refused to stop doing it. *I love Ginger and I don't want to lose her. I don't know why she is not enough for me. Man, this doesn't make any sense, not even to me. What's really wrong with me? What are you doing with your life, man?* He sighed heavily and exclaimed, "Well, I don't want to see Ginger right now because she may figure out I was with Brownie-Baby. Beverly isn't taking my calls....So, I think I'll go see Tracie. Yes, I've had my main meal already. Tracie will be my sweet desert. These women are so gullible and easy to use." He chuckled, sprayed his mouth with peppermint favored freshener and turned his phone back on in order to call Tracie.

"Hey Tracie, this is Keefer. Want some company tonight?" He asked, while another side of him knew this night was becoming crazier by the hour. He could faintly hear in the recesses of his mind a recent sermon that his pastor had preached on what it means to be faithful. Pushing the message notes out of his conscience, he turned his focus back to the issue at hand – another woman from his electronic "black book," his cell phone's contact list, Tracie Hardy.

"Keefer, it's been awhile. Where have you been?"

"Is that a yes or a no, Miss Tracie? I'm not far from your house. I know it's been a long time, but I thought about you tonight and know how good we could make each other feel. I couldn't resist you another night." He had been reminded of her because Tracie used to walk the streets as a prostitute, but she had given it up once she had a son with a boyfriend. Seeing Brownie-Baby tonight had made him think about his old fling.

"Well, it has been a while for me. Come on by and make Sugar happy, if only for one night."

"I'll be right there." He said. "See you shortly." Once he hung up the telephone he started talking to himself. "These women are so easy. You don't even have to take them out to dinner or call them periodically. You can wait months before you touch base with them and they still will say yes to the booty call. Man, this is too easy! And, I don't have to commit to them or make any promises. I really should have stayed single, but a man wants to have a comfortable home base; a good woman at home waiting up for you, cooking, cleaning, and earning money too! Everybody wants somebody to grow old with. These whores are just my playmates. Ginger is my wife, and this is the good life!" Keefer smiled at the distorted thoughts that flowed from his twisted mind.

* * *

Keefer arrived and was well received by the lonely Tracie. After his rendezvous with her, he had planned to shower and go home, but his activities for the night had left him extremely exhausted. It was a physical toll as well as a psychological drain. Deep down, he knew this was a risky way to live, running from woman to woman having unprotected sex. Keefer believed this was a dangerous lifestyle, but he couldn't seem to stop himself. The reality was that he really didn't want to stop his extra marital liaisons.

As he drifted off to sleep, his last thought was, *What am I doing here?*

* * *

Before Keefer knew it, he had fallen asleep next to Tracie and when he awoke, it was the next morning. He whispered, "I've messed up now! What will I say to Ginger?"

Tracie started waking up and she said, "What did you say Big Boy?"

"Nothing important, I'd better go. Thanks for last night." He quickly got up and grabbed his pants and undershirt. Pausing, he took out his wallet from his pocket and placed two one hundred dollar bills in her hand.

"What is this, Keefer? I'm not a hooker anymore. Is that all this was for you? After all that romantic crap you talked last night – I thought maybe..., perhaps..., we could have something special. I should have known better. Get out! And, take your money with you!" Frustrated, she threw the money toward him.

"I didn't mean it that way. I know you are not tricking anymore and that you are now a good parent. I just know that you're a single mother and I thought you may have needed some extra cash. I have it and I just wanted to give you a little something. At least, spend it on your son. Children always need something." He picked up the money and placed it on the end of her dresser.

"I have money Keefer, I want you." Abruptly, she started to cry.

"Girl, don't do that. You even said last night, 'Come on over if only for one night.' I've never tried to mislead you. I am married and I want to stay married. But, one woman is not enough for me. I like coming to see you. I didn't mean to hurt you though. I'm really sorry Tracie."

"Keefer, don't call me again. I'm through being your playmate. I deserve better." She then took the money, shook her head in disgust, and put the bills in her purse.

Keefer left without saying another word. He was not going to stress about it because he already knew that the next time he called her, he could say a few words differently and she would welcome his company again, 'if only for one night.'

It was sad that Tracie played herself for a cheap thrill with no commitment or future benefits.

Chapter 15

When Ginger woke up the next morning, she felt refreshed despite her predicament; she had taken some herbal tea and prescription medication to get some rest. She noticed that Keefer had apparently gotten up earlier than her because he was not in bed. That alone was strange because he usually slept later than her. *Man, I must have been mighty tired that I didn't hear him when he came home.* It was still dark because it was only five in the morning. She was wide awake. *Well, I should get up and get my day started.* Stretching and bending in her large sitting room, she prepared to exercise. After her warm-up routine, she got on the floor and did some crunches, sit-ups, and leg lifts. Feeling like she had stretched enough, she went to the bathroom, brushed her teeth and washed her face. As she washed her face, the dream she'd had about a health scare flooded her mind. She had dreamed of a negative report at an evil doctor's office and at the time, she felt that it had something to do with Keefer. "Oh, my God, the dream was a warning."

She then walked to her enormous room-sized master closet, retrieved her jogging suit and shoes and momentarily, reflected on her life. Sitting down on the bench inside the spacious area, she laced up her shoes. She didn't hear any noises to indicate that Keefer was making breakfast or coffee this early. *Besides, that would be strange because this man does not get up, rattling pots, pans or anything else this early. I wonder what he's doing.* She walked down the hall and peeked in at Justin, a ritual that she always did since he was a baby. The only difference now was that she didn't have to check to make sure he was still breathing as she had done when he was an infant. As she suspected, he was still asleep, looking like an angel. *Don't get it twisted, he is no angel; he may not be an angel, but he is my big baby!*

Ginger then walked down the winding steps to go into the gourmet kitchen which looked like it was the model for a magazine spread. The main feature of the kitchen was the spacious granite counter tops with deep, dropped in stainless steel sinks. There were forty washed oak, stained cabinet doors ensuring that everything had its place, a huge pantry and sixteen drawers around the kitchen. Her stainless steel, Jenn-Air appliances were a cook's dream including a built-in-the-wall conventional oven and micro-wave above it. There was a commercial sized stove top, a grill, bread warmer, and of course, an upgraded dish washer. The huge island in the center of the kitchen was the size of a standard dining room table. It had a granite top with overhang and they had barstools around it. There was also a breakfast nook area that sat adjacent to a bay window. She reached into the cabinet where she kept the vitamins and other supplements and took her tablets with bottled water. She then went to the refrigerator and took out the fresh squeezed carrot juice to give her body some kind of nutrients to start the morning out right. *I'll eat a little breakfast when I get back.* By now it was 5:45 a.m. and she planned to walk and jog around her private lake that was located behind her house. At this point, she still hadn't seen Keefer.

Where is this man hiding? She walked over to the intercom system and buzzed for him. She was certain that the all-call would not wake up Justin because he could sleep through almost anything. They had even had to place his alarm clock across the room from his bed because he would either ignore it or just turn it off and keep right on sleeping.

Surprisingly, she didn't get a response from the all-call on the intercom system. *That's strange. Where could he be? I know he's not exercising, because he likes going to the gym in the evening.* She quickly walked back upstairs to check the other six bedrooms; no Keefer. Just about running back down the stairs, she looked in the mini-master, guest suite, the living room, the dining room, the den and then proceeded to walk to the basement. *Maybe he is working on something down there.* Keefer was nowhere to be found. *What's really going on, did he decide to run early this morning rather than waiting until this evening?* Slowly walking back up the stairs, she walked back into the kitchen to finish her carrot juice. She reached for her cell phone that was on a chair cushion to dial his number. As she punched in the sixth digit, she heard the key in the front door.

Briskly, she walked out from the kitchen into the foyer. Staring at her was a red-eyed, weary looking man wearing the same clothes he had on the previous morning.

Stunned, Ginger sternly addressed him. "No, the hell you are not coming in at five, fifty-five in the morning! Have you lost your mind? What's wrong with you?" She was livid and hurt beyond words as she physically started trembling. Ginger had assumed that because she was tired, she didn't hear his trifling behind come in. Now she realized that she didn't hear him because he had not come home. Before he could answer, she continued, "If you think you are going to disrespect me, my son and our home like this, you had better get another thought. Whoever you've been with, you can just go back to her, because you are no longer wanted here!" she snapped with much attitude.

Keefer raised his hand and said, "Ginger, I can't deal with this right now. Let me get some sleep first." He tried to stumble up the stairs.

"Sleep! No Keefer, I will not let my son see this. You cannot stay here!" As she shoved him backwards, he lost his balance, falling onto her polished hard wood floor.

"Where am I supposed to go?" he stammered.

"I really don't care where you go, but you can't stay here! I thought you were in the house and you are out all damn night, doing God knows what and you think you can come home like this is normal. No, no, and hell to the no! This is not the Graham home that you grew up in! Man, you've got the wrong one!" Keefer's father had been a drunk, gambler, and a playboy who stayed out in the streets when Keefer was a little boy. His mother had put up with it; however, Ginger wasn't having it.

As she got near him again as he struggled to get on his feet, she caught a whiff of the alcohol on his breath. She knew he could not drive in that condition. *I wonder how he made it home,* she thought to herself. *Well, that's not my problem, but I don't want him to have an accident and die or kill somebody else.*

She blew her breath and said, "Call Jim and have him pick you up; you're out of here!" Jim was his best friend who happened to work in the county hospital's emergency room. Dr. Jim Berkeley had seen and treated enough bullet and stab wounds, as well as car wrecks in his career. He also had plenty of war stories to share from when he was a medic for the Marine Corp. After twenty years in the military, he retired and had accepted the position as an ER doctor.

Keefer pulled out his cell phone from his pocket and struggled to find Jim's number in the contact list. Snatching the phone from him, Ginger found the number and dialed it. When Jim sleepily answered the phone, she said, "Good morning Jim, this is Ginger. If you don't come and pick up Keefer, it's going to get real ugly over here. Right now he is an embarrassment to me and I don't want my son to see this disgrace of a man." After saying that mouthful, she started crying.

"What's wrong Ginger? What has he done?" Jim had sat up in the bed and his wife Karen was mouthing the question, 'Who's on the phone?' as she rubbed her drowsy eyes while glancing at the clock. Karen knew this was Jim's off day from the hospital and only hoped they were not calling for him to come in to work.

"He's drunk, and he stayed out all damn night. Just come get him or I swear I may snap on him. I won't be responsible for what happens. This is absolutely too much!" She aggressively wiped the tears from her face, angry at herself that her emotions were all tied up to a man that didn't have the sense to treat her right.

He heard the seriousness in her voice and responded appropriately. "Okay, I'm getting up now and I'll be right over. Ginger, please don't do anything that you will regret."

"Well, you had better get over here quick or it's looking like it's going to be a bad day for your buddy." She hung up the phone and turned back to him.

Keefer looked at Ginger's angry face and wondered what had her so infuriated. Strangely, in his inebriated condition he was not fully aware of what had her so angry.

Shouting, she said to him, "Keefer, you gave me an STD! You had better be glad that it's something curable! Get out, get out now!" She screamed like a crazy woman; she had never acted like this before.

*An STD; h*e though back to his recent liaisons and instantly knew who had probably given him the problem.

Brownie Baby and crew! *I'll have to butter Ginger up.* With a surprised look on his face he said, "Ginger please, be reasonable. I can't drive like this." He motioned to his body and then continued. "It's a miracle that I made it home. I'm sorry baby. This will never happen again. I'm sick of the way I'm living. I don't want to lose you or Justin. I love both of you more than life itself." He was pleading with a pitiful look on his face.

"Well you damn sure should have thought about that when you didn't come home last night. Your lies aren't going to work this time. This STD is my proof that you've been cheating. You were sneaky with it before, but now to stay out all night, I don't have to wonder anymore. This is low, even for you! I'm not having it! I refuse to live like this! Get out! Get out now before one of us gets hurt. Wait on the porch for Jim! I can't look at you another second!"

"What STD?" He nervously stalled for time. *What do I have?* He inwardly reflected realizing he'd really messed things up this time. *I wonder who else I infected.*

"You've been dealing with trash Keefer! Thanks to you I'll be seeing my doctor tomorrow to treat gonorrhea! You nasty bastard; get out of *my* house, now!"

"Gonorrhea, get out of *your* house? What are you talking about?" He still didn't realize how fed up she really was. His inebriated condition made it difficult for him to understand what she had clearly said.

"I'll show you better than I can tell you!" She abruptly turned around and raced up the winding staircase, literally ran to her second floor master bedroom doors, threw them open and ran to the nightstand. She then started trembling as she reached for her 38 special that she had purchased for protection. *This is crazy. Girl, what are you going to do?* She inwardly questioned herself as she whirled around to march out the double doors. She kept moving forward, despite knowing violence was not the way to deal with his infidelity.

While standing at the top of the stairs, she called his name in a crazed, eerie voice that he hardly recognized.

"KEEFER, I would advise you to get the hell out of *my* house while you can!"

Intoxicated and barely standing in the two story foyer, he was about to respond when he turned around and looked up at her. To his astonishment, Ginger was pointing a pistol at him. He blinked his eyes and looked closer. Yep, it was a gun. "Ginger, what..."

"Get out now and you won't ever have to worry about me calling to ask where you are, who you're with, or what time you're getting home. It's over! You get out of here now before my finger slips and a bullet finds its way into your wicked heart!"

"I've never heard you talk like this..." he gasped.

"That may be true, because you've taken things to a different level! You're a dog; an STD – are you kidding me, Keefer? I advise you to get to stepping because I can't stand the sight of you. You've broken my heart for the last time."

Through slurred speech he said, "But Baby, where am I going? My place is here with you." He really looked quite pathetic.

Ginger yelled, "You should have thought about that before now!"

"But Ginger, I do love you. I need help. Please don't do this."

"You're right, you do need help - psychiatric help, and if you stay in here another minute, you'll need either an ambulance or an undertaker. It's your choice. Do you hear what I'm saying?"

"No, Ginger, what are you saying?" Now, he was genuinely frightened. *What happened to sweet amiable Ginger?* He wistfully thought to himself.

As a sudden image of her doctor's report flashed in her mind, Ginger moved to an irrational state of consciousness. Abruptly, she was through talking. Ginger didn't say another word but cocked the trigger. Keefer had taken her over the edge. Their roller coaster relationship and the emotional trauma he was taking her through simply made her snap. Civility and lucid thinking went right out the window along with his breach of integrity.

Ginger thought, *Hell, what do I have to lose? How dare he cheat and subject me to a foul STD? What was that woman's name who cut the sucker's penis off? Whatever! Here goes nothing.* Raising her arm and then slightly lowering it, she aimed the weapon and shot toward his groin.

Hearing the terrifying sound of the trigger pulled, he grasped the door frame while trying to maintain his balance and hold his liquor. As if in slow motion, he turned his drunken body to leave the residence; however, the substances in his system hindered his desired, rapid movement. Unfortunately, he was not quick enough. His fear caused him to be frozen in the foyer, frightened to the point of defecation as he attempted to leave the home and family he loved.

With his shrieked sound of agony, Ginger pulled the trigger again, this time aiming for his chest. She surmised *He broke my heart; maybe I can literally shatter his.* What was this loony, violent presence dominating her spirit? Fortunately for Keefer, her aim was off and she grazed his shoulder.

Ginger noticed blood as it suddenly flowed from his body as he quickly fell down to the ground. He actually looked weird stretched partially in the residence, the other half of his frame stretched across the threshold of the grand double doors.

Ginger rushed down the stairs with the gun still raised, looking down at Keefer as he was lain out in the doorway. A creepy smirk crossed her face; she seemed to enjoy seeing him in obvious pain.

Suddenly, panic gripped Keefer's heart as he heard Ginger's swift movements as she descended the stairs and walked crossed the beautiful marble foyer directly towards him.

With strength he didn't know he had, Keefer dragged his aching body forward onto the massive stone, front porch. He quickly stretched his long arms over his head attempting to grasp the twisted iron railing to pull himself to his feet. Frightened, he thought, *I've got to get away from Gin before she kills me. What is she thinking? Better yet, what was I thinking? I must have been out of my mind to have unprotected sex with those hookers!*

That was the problem. Neither of the two was using the good sense the Lord gave them.

He weakly muttered, "Ginger, please don't..."

"Ain't too proud to beg...," a song from the sixties echoed in the recess of his mind. He was at her mercy.

Unfortunately, the sweet Ginger that he knew had checked out. She was all the way over the edge. Too much drama can make you want to kill!

Chapter 16

Ginger felt driven to madness as she was standing about two feet from Keefer; she lowered the gun and was about to pull the trigger again when she heard a car come to a screeching halt in her driveway.

"GINGER, DON'T!" Suddenly, she snapped out of the crazed mentality that she was operating in and looked at Jim who had jumped out of his car and was running toward them. "No Ginger, you don't want to do this!"

Ginger looked from Keefer, who was rolling on the ground whom she could now hear groaning, and his best friend Jim who looked shell-shocked.

Blood oozed from Keefer's pants and his shoulder and for a fleeting moment, she wanted to drop to her knees to console the foolish man that she loved. She thought to herself, *What have I done? Did I actually shoot him?*

With a voice of authority, Jim said, "GINGER, GIVE ME THE GUN!" He slowly walked over to her. His Marine Corp training proved useful as he took control of the situation. Jim could see that Keefer's wounds were not life threatening. He wanted to make sure the distressed woman that he truly didn't recognize right now, didn't change Keefer's status by pumping more bullets into him.

Sighing loudly, Ginger abruptly let the pistol that she tightly grasped over Keefer's frame pivot downward as if swinging from her trigger finger in earnest surrender.

Jim grabbed the weapon and quickly placed it in his pocket. He momentarily held her as she collapsed in his arms sobbing. She was angry as a starving lion, but relieved at the same time that it was over. After a few seconds, Jim released her and gently pushed her back away from him so that he could render aid to his hurt friend. They were still standing on the vast stone front porch.

"Ginger, go back in the house. I'll take care of Keefer and get him to the hospital." As he spoke to her, he was glad they lived in a secluded estate which would allow for anonymity. He glanced over his shoulder; as he suspected, the trees and heavy brush that surrounded the substantial property isolated it from outsiders. He was confident that there had been no witnesses. *I don't know what I will say at the hospital. This is a mess. My best friend is down and his sensible wife is the perpetrator. This situation would make good television if it weren't so pathetic.*

Silent and obedient, Ginger turned to reenter the home. She was shocked that she had actually pulled the trigger. *It serves him right; I told him not to mess with me. I am not Betty Graham!* Betty Graham was Keefer's mother who had tolerated all sorts of foolishness from her husband until the day he died.

"The devil is crazy! I bet he'll think twice before staying out all night on me again! I'm not the one; he should have asked somebody!" She spoke with attitude at first and then, she became emotional as tears filled her eyes. Not wanting to feel weak, she brushed the back of her hand over her eyes and ran her hand through her hair. Walking over to the family room, she flopped down into the over-stuffed recliner and closed her eyes. *What has our marriage come to that we*

128

*are casually passing out STDs and bullets like its normal? I
know we're better than this!*

After reflecting for about thirty minutes, *Ginger* got up
and walked over to the garage, grabbed some bleach and
liquid cleaning solution from the shelf and proceeded to the
deep sink that stood basically unused in the corner. Once her
bucket was filled, she picked up the coiled water hose and
walked over to the control panel near the smaller door. After
pressing the button for the automatic door opener, she waited
as the door ascended. Placing the bulky weight of the hose
down, she took the other end and connected it to the outside
nozzle. Turning on the water, she allowed it to spatter on the
grass and walkway as she lazily walked over to the front
porch. As she power sprayed the blood from the porch, she
shook her head in despair. Satisfied that it looked normal,
she went back inside to get another cleaning solution to wash
the marble floor in the foyer before Justin could see it.

As she finished wiping up the blood and sterilizing the
area, she heard Justin's door open upstairs. "Good morning
Mom. What was all of that noise?"

She wanted to say, *You're just now realizing there was a
problem?* Instead she said, "What noise? You must have
been dreaming." But in her head she thought, *This boy can
sleep through anything. We had a civil war right under his
nose and he doesn't know a thing. Good. It was 'grown
folks' business anyway, as Big Momma would have said!*

"Okay Mom, I'm going back to bed." With that, Justin
turned around and went back to his room.

* * *

Outside, after covering his seat with a large, thick cloth,
Jim struggled to lift Keefer into his car's back seat. He could

tell his buddy was in tremendous pain, but fortunately he was alert.

Jim huffed and puffed until Keefer was sprawled on the back seat. Jim found a stuffed animal in the trunk to place under his head. "Hold on man, I'm going to get you to the hospital."

"NO, NO, NO! PLEASE, DON'T TAKE ME TO THE HOSPITAL! He yelled. It's my fault. She snapped, man. I shouldn't have stayed out. You know what to do for me. If you take me to the hospital, they'll call the police. What would you say to them?"

"Keefer, are you sure?" Jim asked, simply perplexed.

"Yes, I'm sure. Take me to your house. This is embarrassing and I really don't want Ginger to be arrested." Though drunk, Keefer was finally making some sense.

Reluctantly, Jim drove to his home, not knowing how he would explain everything to his wife.

When they arrived at Jim's house, to his relief, his wife Karen had left for work. She assumed that Ginger and Keefer had just argued and that Ginger was angry. Of course she would never have thought her friend would actually pull out a gun and shoot him. *Good, she does not need to know this; the fewer people who know the better.*

"Okay Keefer, this is not going to feel good, but I'll take care of you."

"I know I'm in good hands Jim. Fix me up." Keefer winced and groaned from the pain of Jim moving him. Jim stood him up and assisted him into the house through a back entrance.

Good this is hard wood instead of carpet. Blood is nearly impossible to get out of carpet, he found himself thinking. As they navigated through the house to Jim's basement, they left a telling trail of blood on the floor. He stretched Keefer out on a long, sturdy-looking table that was

130

in their basement and put on a pot of water to boil. He then rushed to the restroom to scrub his hands. He hurried back up the stairs to gather some towels, medical supplies, a scalpel, anesthesia, and other needed items. He retrieved his medical bag that he kept stocked for emergencies. Although prepared, he never thought he would need to use it for a friend's domestic matter. Jim carefully administered the local anesthesia in order to treat his friend.

As he examined Keefer, he noticed that there was a flesh wound in his shoulder that fortunately had really just grazed his skin. The other wound was more complicated. It had landed in his buttocks of all places. *Hell, I wonder if she was aiming for his stuff and he turned just in time.* Despite the seriousness of the matter, he smiled when he realized what must have happened. When everything was over, he made a point that he would have to tease his friend on how lucky he was that his private part was not blown off.

"What's so funny man? I'm in pain here." Keefer was not tickled at all.

"I know man. I'll have to share with you later what I was thinking about. Trust me, you would not appreciate it right now. Man, be quiet now and let me treat you."

"I just don't see what's so funny when I'm sitting here with bullet holes all over my body."

"Keefer, believe me, it could be much worse. Let's talk later. You wouldn't want me to leave lead in you now would you? Now, turn over man." As Keefer turned over, Jim couldn't help but smile again. Jim thought, *Man, Ginger is Karen's friend, so, no matter how tempting a woman may be, don't you even think of cheating on Karen!* He admonished himself, and just shook his head as he dislodged the bullet from Keefer's swollen derrière.

Chapter 17

Dr. Jim Berkeley glanced at his best friend Keefer Graham, who was now his patient. Keefer was the seemingly professional, cool and collected family man that he played golf with once a week at a local country club. He was also the gentleman he observed in church twice a week sitting with his wife and step-son looking like he adored the very site of her, and the idea of a happy family. They faithfully attended both the Sunday morning service and the Wednesday night Bible study, even more regularly than he did. *They always seemed to attentively absorb the messages that Pastor so eloquently teaches, but clearly Keefer is just living a double life. Ginger is a beautiful woman who works hard, and loves Keefer. What more could he want? This is crazy! Keefer is too old to be staying out all night like a young playboy who doesn't have a care in the world. Who is he, really? What would make Ginger angry or hurt enough to literally shoot him?* Keefer was resting after his good doctor/friend had hooked him up with an old-fashioned "house call" after his wife had released her pinned up frustration and shot him. *Good the wounds were not life threatening – superficial flesh wounds; however, injuries nonetheless. I hope I never get so crazy to test Karen's tolerance level. Besides, I played around enough to last a lifetime in my younger, single days. I've got sense now, and I know cheating on Karen would be just foolishness. Nobody is worth losing my family. I'll have to talk to my friend when he wakes up.*

* * *

"Hey buddy, how are you feeling?" Jim asked Keefer as he noticed him waking up. He had medicated Keefer so that he could get some needed rest.

"I feel like crap to be perfectly honest. What time is it anyway?" Keefer yawned and looked at his wrist that was void of his watch.

"It's about seven and you've been sleeping all day. You should be well-rested."

"Where's my cell phone? I need to call Ginger."

"You may want to give her a day or two to process everything that has happened between you."

Keefer insisted, "No, I need to talk to her now... Where's my phone man?"

"Hold up playa' - I'll get your phone." Jim walked out of the room and returned with the cell phone.

While dialing, Keefer thought about Ginger, Beverly and the street women. He didn't have long to think because Ginger's phone was turned off. Dejectedly, he left a message and reached for the remote to turn on the television to ESPN.

He chided himself, *Man you had better make some decisions soon before you lose out on Ginger and Beverly. Well, it's not much to think about. I love my wife, but I know I like being with Beverly too, at least sometimes. Why can't things be simple where I could have them both? What am I thinking? That would never work.*

Chapter 18

As Keefer recovered from his injuries, he had time to reflect on his actions. Ginger was not taking his calls at home, her cell phone or at her retail clothing store. Once he had waited outside her business door until closing, but when she spotted him, she threatened to call the police. *As far as I can tell, she hasn't hired a lawyer. Maybe there's still time to make things right with her. I know.....*

Keefer turned toward his computer to look up the number for a local florist. While dialing the number, he simultaneously retrieved his credit card from his tri-fold wallet.

"Yes, I would like to place two orders for red, long-stemmed roses." There was a pause as he heard the clerk take out the order forms.

"Okay, who is the first order for and what would you like the card to say?"

"I need a dozen, long stemmed red roses sent to a very special lady, Mrs. Ginger Graham. The card should read, 'I love you and I miss you.' The salutation should say, 'Your husband, Keefer.' Now the second dozen should read... Well, never mind. That will be it. Thank you." He proceeded to give the address for the delivery and his credit card information. Before hanging up the phone, he said, "On second thought, make it three dozen premium roses with baby's breath." When the clerk mentioned the additional amount of money, Keefer said, "No problem, thanks again."

As soon as he heard the dial tone on his office phone, he quickly looked up another florist's name, dialed the number and proceeded to place another order. Once during his actual single days, Keefer had patronized one florist and trusted them to deliver a dozen roses each for Valentine's Day to two different women. The incompetent salesperson had mixed up the cards and their messages to the wrong addresses. Keefer was royally busted and he had learned from that experience to use separate florist shops.

Keefer uttered to the wind, "I've got to keep my 'playa' card intact!" Suddenly, he laughed, quite amused with his own self-imposed title.

Once he placed the call to the next florist, he said, "Yes, I would like to send one dozen, long stemmed yellow roses to a friend." He waited while the clerk, identified as Rochelle, pulled the form.

Rochelle said, "What is the recipient's name and address and what would you like the card to say?"

Keefer gave the pertinent delivery information and then he unashamedly exclaimed, "Let's see...ah...let it say, 'Darling Beverly, I can't wait to see you later this week! This is just a little something for my baby until then...' make sure you add the ellipses at the end." The clerk quoted the price and after giving the saleswoman his name and credit card number, the woman said, "Yes, I have it just like you want it. They'll be delivered tomorrow. Can I help you with anything else Mr. Graham?"

"No, that will be just fine."

"Sir, we appreciate your business."

"Thank you too. Have a good night." Keefer hung up the telephone feeling really full of himself. He had the nerve to honestly declare his sincere attempt to reconcile with his wife Ginger while at the same time he was still very actively continuing the relationship with Beverly, his longtime mistress on the side.

Seriously, some men never learn. Even after being shot, Keefer still wanted his cake, pie, and cobbler; he was content being a womanizer. Unfortunately, he was split in his mind loving a wife, lusting after another woman, and indulging in the forbidden casual connections with women of the night.

All I have to do is wine and dine these sorry women a little and I'll have them both eating out of my hand in no time. Surprisingly, Ginger is playing hard to get...but I'll get her. I know what makes her smile. I know what turns her on. She's going to love the long-stemmed roses. I can get just about anything I want from her after sending long stemmed roses. No, this time that may not be enough. What else can I get for her?

Keefer rubbed his head as he earnestly thought about what Ginger would like. Suddenly, a million dollar idea popped into his mind. '*A girl's best friend;'* Diamonds- *what woman can resist diamonds...? I know Ginger can't. That's it! She could always use new jewelry in her ears or on her wrist!*

Smiling, he continued contemplating his smooth moves to woe Ginger back into his arms. He really did miss her although when he was in her good graces and they were together, he wasn't satisfied to have the love of his life; he wanted her and others too. Keefer definitely had conflicted loyalties. He reflected, *Let me go to the mall and pick out something special for my wife.*

It took about twenty minutes for him to get to the mall. He found a parking space and strutted into the Jared's jewelry store. A woman hostess greeted him and said, "Someone will be right with you."

"Okay." He responded to the hostess. While waiting for a salesperson, Keefer scanned the brightly lit cases that glistened with sparkling diamond rings, bracelets, necklaces, and earrings.

He continued to browse the showcases. After about five minutes, a man came to help him.

"Hello, my name is Jeffery. What's your name and how may I help you today?"

"I'm Mr. Graham. Let me see your one caret diamond earrings."

"Sir, would that be one caret total weight or one caret per earlobe?"

"One caret for each ear and make sure that they are your highest quality diamonds. She really does deserve the best."

"Yes, I'm sure she does." After viewing the vast selection, Keefer made a decision. As an afterthought, he told the salesman to separately wrap a tiny, clustered-diamond heart necklace that hung from a thin chain.

Before leaving the mall he visited a specialty gift wrapping shop and had the two caret earrings beautifully wrapped in fancy layered boxes. He designated that the earrings be hand delivered by courier service to Ginger's retail clothing store. Earlier, he had dropped the inexpensive heart necklace into his pocket with the intention of giving it to Beverly the next time he visited her. Little did Beverly realize she came second in his priorities in every way. Ginger had his name, the mansion, the joint bank account privileges, the credit cards, the life insurance policy designation, and even the prime make-up gift. Beverly only had what energy, money and time that Keefer had left over. He had just spent thousands on Ginger's gift, and literally less than a "Benjamin Franklin" on Beverly's. Quiet as it's kept; second string is never as valued as number one picks.

Chapter 19

The next day, Ginger was in the rear of her retail clothing store assisting a loyal customer, when she heard the door chime. She assumed it was another customer. Instead, a man came in with a shoe-sized box in his hand. Brea, Ginger's sales assistant, addressed the man. "May I help you?"

"Yes you may. I have a delivery for a Mrs. Ginger Graham. Are you Mrs. Graham?"

"No, I'm not, but..." she stammered.

He quickly asked, "Is she here today?"

"Well, yes she is, but I can sign for her, if that's okay."

"No, I'm sorry madam; this is a special delivery for Mrs. Graham. I need to see a photo ID before I can leave it. All I can say, it must be a special gift."

Brea sighed and replied, "Well alright then, I'll get her for you." Brea rushed to the back of the shop near the beautifully decorated, oversized dressing rooms where she had seen Ginger walking moments earlier. Her movements toward Ginger made her look up. Brea motioned for Ginger to come toward her. When they reached each other, she excitedly said, "Ginger, you have a package in the front that I can't sign for. I wonder what it is."

"Really, well thank you Brea."

"You're welcome." Brea answered, "I'll go assist the other customers." She pivoted around and went back to the sales floor.

Ginger turned toward her customer who was entering the dressing room foyer and said, "Mrs. Fortune, I'll be right back to help you." Excusing herself, Ginger walked to the front of the store where the man was patiently waiting for her.

"Good morning Mrs. Graham. I have a special delivery just for you!"

"Hello, where do I sign?" She reached for his pen.

"Actually, I need to see your identification. Apparently, it's a really special package."

"Okay, I'll be right back." Ginger went to her office, retrieved her ID and took it to show the courier service worker. He showed her where to put her 'John Hancock' and after she signed the ledger, she thanked him. Ginger walked behind the counter and grabbed a box cutter to open the outer box. Once it was opened, there was a beautifully wrapped red, faux suede box inside sealed with a multi-colored ribbon that looked too pretty to disturb. Tilting her head to the side, she arched her brow and smiled while she hunched up her shoulders. She quickly untied the ribbon and lifted the lid. To her surprise, there was another colorful, ribbed box tied with more elaborate ribbon. Ginger smiled again, shrugged her shoulders and opened that box to find a third fancy box. After unwrapping it, she couldn't do anything but exhale when she saw the signature black box inside. Opening it, she was pleased and impressed by the brilliance of the perfect pair of sparkling diamond earrings. The light reflected from them like a thousand sun rays. When Ginger lifted up the miniature case, she noticed a card under it that read, 'Our love is as solid as these diamonds. Please forgive me...; Keefer.'

139

"Humph," she sighed. She then whispered, "Solid as diamonds? Is that so, Keefer?"

"What did you say Ginger?" Brea hurried to her side in time to see the beautiful gift. "Ohhhh! Ginger, they are gorgeous! And, 'He went to Jared's,' Brea used her index and middle fingers on both hands to simulate quotation marks in the air as she mentioned the line from the jewelry chain's commercials. "I wish I had a good man like you, who would send me rocks like that just because. Let me see them!" She leaned over to get a better view.

"Thank you Brea. They are lovely, aren't they?" She then reassured her by saying, "You'll have a good husband one day." *And, I wish I had what you are assuming I have. You would be shocked to know that Keefer is a dog who mainly buys expensive gifts when he has royally messed up!* Ginger thought to herself. She made sure to keep her private life separate from her working relationship with her young employees.

"I hope so. Let me get back to work." Brea was smiling from ear to ear as if she had weighted, sparkling "rocks" to place in her own ears.

When her employee was far enough away so that she could not hear her, Ginger said, "Everything is not always what it seems. I'm going to wear these earrings because I deserve them, but it will take more than jewelry to get me back." Her words said one thing, but the gesture did tug at her heart.

Ginger took the pretty boxes to her office, placed them on the desk and walked to her private restroom to get some alcohol and a cotton ball to clean the earring posts. After cleaning the earrings, she carefully placed them in her ears screwing the backs up to her lobes. Glancing in the mirror, she turned her head from side to side admiring the radiance of Keefer's selection. She thought to herself, *these are beautiful...maybe, just maybe...*

"No, what am I thinking? I can't go on like this. Something has got to change." She left her office softly singing the lyrics from a Jennifer Lopez song "Don't be fooled by the rocks that I got, I'm still Ginger from the block." Back on the sales floor, she greeted customers with a genuine smile as she moved to re-rack clothes.

Ginger heard the buzzer indicating that a customer needed assistance in the dressing room. Walking to the area, she noticed that the handicap fitting room was occupied. An oversized designer handbag was on the floor which Ginger knew belonged to Mrs. Fortune.

Mrs. Fortune was in the dressing room happily trying on clothes while humming a tune that Ginger didn't recognize.

"Mrs. Fortune, I'm so sorry. How may I help you?"

"It's certainly alright Ginger. I just need your help zipping up this beautiful after-five dress. My arthritis is cutting up today; otherwise, I could zip it up myself. I have a charity event scheduled for next Saturday evening. This dress would be perfect!"

"Yes, Mrs. Fortune, you know I don't mind at all. Let me get that for you." When Ginger finished and straightened the flow of the material, she stood back and commented, "You look stunning in that dress! I believe it has your name on it."

"I believe it does too." As the two of them admired the gown, the customer eyed herself in the floor length tri-wall, mirrored room. The bodice of the dress was designed with stripped pleats of taffeta that crisscrossed to lift and hug her bust, revealing a slight hint of cleavage. Underneath the bust line, silk fabric was stretched and gathered to one side at the waist which gave an illusionary slimming effect. The bottom of the dress was a shimmering flow of silk that created an upside-down V-shape at the knee in the front, and full gathering of material swished in the back. With a fancy up hairdo, appropriate heels and sparkling jewelry, Mrs. Fortune would certainly turn heads.

Finally satisfied she said, "Please unzip me and wrap it up along with those two suits and the blouses that are hanging on the hook. I simply love coming here. I always find the perfect outfits!"

"Yes madam, we aim to please." Ginger warmly smiled as she cheerfully carried her customer's selections to the counter to write up the ticket and ring up the sale.

As Mrs. Fortune signed her credit card receipt, she said, "I love my clothes. I'll see you the next time. Have a good day."

Ginger was also pleased with the lucrative sale. "I'm so happy you are pleased. Thank you Mrs. Fortune and please hurry back. Have a great day!" As long as her customers were happy, Ginger was ecstatic-all the way to the bank!

Chapter 20

After locking up the shop, Ginger headed toward the market to pick up some long grain rice, shrimp, crab legs, oysters, andouille sausage, okra, onions, gumbo file' seasoning, and other secret ingredients so that she could make some of her signature, Louisiana style gumbo for dinner. It was a big undertaking after working all day, but it was what she had a taste for. She also grabbed some special cheeses, nuts and other fresh fruits and vegetables just to have them on hand. She had made a promise to herself that she would start cooking and eating healthier, modeling for her son Justin the way to stay fit and disease free.

After leaving the market, she drove over to the dry cleaners to pick up her clothes and then headed home. About ten minutes from home, her cell phone started ringing. Glancing down, Ginger noted that it was Justin. *My big baby!* With her hands free device, she answered, "Hi baby; how was your day at school?"

"It was cool, what about your day at the shop? Was the register ringing all day like printing new money?"

"We had a great day son, thanks for asking. Do you have a lot of homework?" She paused to allow a man to ease into the flow of traffic ahead of her.

"You know my teachers piled it on today. Each one acts as if she is my only teacher. They assign reading chapters, regular work, reports and projects. I feel like I'm already in college!" He blew his breath into the phone in frustration hoping his mother was going to side with him. He should have known better.

"What your wonderful teachers are attempting to do is to get you ready for college because that's where you're headed. You're in honors and advanced placement classes because you can handle it, and you need to be challenged. It's going to help make a man out of you."

"Yeah, yeah, Mom, that's what you're always telling me- It's just that I'm tired. Plus, you know I have swim practice. I was just calling you to get a little sympathy. Whose side are you on anyway?" There was a hint of happy in his voice despite his attempt to sound betrayed by her support of his teachers.

"You know I'm always on your side, but the right side takes precedence over your feelings. Toughen up, and get to practice before you're marked late. You know Coach Frisk does not allow late participants." Coach Frisk was a retired Marine and he was as tough as nails. He preached that if he allowed the team members to arrive to practice late, they might assume that they could arrive to a swim meet late. And, he didn't accept excuses.

"Okay Mom. I'll talk to you when you pick me up. By the way, what's for dinner?"

"Dinner will be one of your favorites – Gumbo!"

"Don't you need my help to clean all of the shrimp? I can miss practice today."

"Good try, but I'll manage. Now go to practice son. I'll see you later."

"Okay Mom, see you later."

* * *

Ginger opened the door to the sound of Sterling the cockatiel chirping and her dog Pepper's happy grunt as she jumped up from her dog bed. Pepper's tail was wagging with excitement as she made her way to the foyer to greet Ginger. Pepper was not only happy to see her; she was also ready to go outside.

Well, at least someone is happy to see me! Ginger thought to herself. She dropped her purse in the leather recliner and stopped to deposit her keys inside.

"Come on girl, want to go out?" Pepper started doing her doggie dance twirling around and around in a circle with anticipation of going out. She also was enjoying the attention from her owner. "Okay girl, let's get your leash on…hold up…Pepper you need to get out more – all of this excitement over a stroll with me." Her enthusiastic pull of the leather strap almost echoed her agreement as if to say, 'I thought you would never get home; let's go woman!' *Dogs have the most unique way of communicating without saying a word.* Ginger thought, while allowing Pepper to lead the way to her favorite spot past her Japanese garden which was centered by a beautiful red Japanese maple tree. After Pepper finished her business, Ginger scooped it up into the designated plastic bag, tied the knot and tossed it in a wrought iron garbage can.

Turning toward the gorgeous garden, Ginger decided to sit under the red tree and enjoy a few moments of fresh air and wind blowing through her hair before going back inside the house to prepare the Gumbo.

After about forty-five minutes she stood up and faced Pepper who looked as if to say, 'No lady, we just got out here. I've been cooped up all day while you've been only the Lord knows where. I'm staying outside, thank you very

145

much.' When Ginger pulled on Pepper's leash, she resisted and started rolling in the grass having a good time.

"You had better come on Miss Pepper; you don't have three pounds of shrimp to clean and a whole list of spicy ingredients to blend together to create a masterpiece. I've already promised Justin that seafood gumbo will be on the table and I intend to do just that."

Pepper looked up at her as if to say, 'So, it's not like you're going to give me any of the gumbo!' She tried to stand her ground, but Ginger pulled the leash again and said, "Come on, Pepper!" The canine shook off the loose grass that she had just rolled in and strutted in the direction of the deck.

Once inside, Pepper raced to her water bowl and drank it like clear Kool-Aid had been substituted instead of plain water. After she had her fill of the needed liquid, she strutted over to her elevated princess bed, circled her steps about three or four times, and then stretched out. She blew her breath like she had worked a job, and looked at Ginger with an attitude about having to come back inside.

Ignoring the elephant in the room- her diva pooch, Ginger went into the hall restroom and washed her hands. She then walked over to the den, grabbed the remote control and turned on the television. Opting for the local news, Ginger was motionless when she heard the report of the missing Griffin, Georgia woman.

The anchor woman said, "Elsie Mae Coats has been missing for 14 days and it gets more and more difficult to expect a positive outcome the longer this Griffin native is gone. Her family remains optimistic that she will be found alive." The camera then moved to a field reporter who had the latest updates on the woman's background recent developments, and some footage of interviews with family and church members.

146

"That's so sad. I hope they find the woman alive; but, where could she be? If she's okay, she should contact her family members. That's such a strange situation." Ginger's words were interrupted by another tragic announcement by the reporter. She reported that the missing woman's sister was on her way to join a search crew, but tragically she was involved in a serious automobile accident. The sister, Pauline Howard, was the mother of twin daughters and she was currently in a drug induced coma. Mrs. Howard's condition was listed as serious, but stable by the hospital staff and family members who were interviewed.

"When it rains, it pours." Ginger quoted from an old, popular salt advertisement. "Those poor people are really going through...I wish I could help out, see what I could find out. That's a lot for one family to handle. I just wonder...what's really going on in that case? According to the interviews with neighbors and family members, the woman seems like a nice "girl next door," clean cut, church member with a close knit family. I overheard a conversation at the beauty shop that Elsie Mae Coates was not who she appeared to be. It's rumored that the woman may have a shady past or maybe it's something going on now. Could that be why she's missing? I don't know, but what I do know is that if I don't start turning pots in my gourmet kitchen, we won't be eating gumbo or anything else because it's getting late and I'm tired!"

Though Ginger was "home alone," she was carrying on a full conversation with herself, captivated with the Elsie Mae Coates case. One thing was for sure, the woman had to be somewhere. Ginger just hoped she was still alive.

Chapter 21

Dazed and woozy, the woman sat on the side of the bed to clear her head. She attempted to focus on the fan blades that constantly swirled above her. It was an interestingly shaped lighting fixture; the blades looked like palm tree leaves. The room felt heated because the sun rays beamed into the room with the tenacity of a bulldog, unrelenting in its quest to be noticed. She stretched and tried to stand up. Instead, the swimming in her head hindered her from maintaining a vertical position. *My head feels terrible. What did they give me? Now, the last thing I remember is being picked up in a large black Ford Expedition with tinted windows. Uncle Chance said we were going to see three of his friends, but who were all of those people...all of those men. There were way more than three men. Oh no, they all had a turn with me...what have I gotten myself into?* She leaned back on the pillows and tried to collect her thoughts. *What in the world have I become. My God; I'm a paid whore!*

I feel so dirty. I feel so empty inside. How do I get out of this place? I've got to wash up! I feel so filthy. I need a shower! I need a shower, do you hear me! I need to wash all of those nasty hands from off my body! The woman thought she was shouting to the top of her lungs, but actually she hadn't said one word. Mentally, she was screaming to the enemy of unreasonable actions, trying to make sense of a deplorable state of being. Suddenly, she started trembling and weeping, feeling an anxiety attack that was threatening to unnerve her senses.

Out of desperation, she lunged forward only to fall to the floor bumping her head on the nightstand. "Ouch!" she cried as she went down. To her dismay, nobody came to her rescue. She struggled to get on her feet and finally gave up. She already felt dizzy and now her head was throbbing from the small bump forming right under her fingers that rubbed the sore spot. *My head is killing me, oh, my head. What's this swirling in my head?* "Whew..." She blew dry breath through her parched lips, abruptly feeling very thirsty.

Unexpectedly, she heard the door to the room as it was opened. She turned toward the sound of rushing footsteps approaching her. Her blurry eyesight prevented her from identifying their exact features, but she could tell they were foreign men as they spoke in broken English with a strange accent. Although she could not see all of the details, a woman in the hallway later recounted that the men had curly, black hair, olive colored skin, and they were muscularly built. One stood about six foot two and the other was about five foot nine. They both were dressed in khaki colored slacks, black loafers, and black golf shirts as if they were in some sort of uniform.

"Get up! Get up at once!" Six foot two barked, "You have a special repeat client who has flown in for an important meeting. I promised him a good time, and he requested you by name. Get up I say!"

The woman glared at him in her best infuriated scowl hoping to send him to another girl's room. The reality of her situation was starting to come back to her. In her inebriated condition, she started seeing fragments of memories flash into present day scenes of occurrences. To her, it was starting to feel like sheer madness.

Thoughts raced in her mind, *Back to the vehicle...; it was parked diagonal to my house with the engine still running. Before seeing the vehicle, I remember quickly packing my bag while Uncle Chance persisted on rushing me to get ready as soon as I had come in from the movie date with Blake Baker...; Blake didn't understand why I was in such a hurry to get back home that night. If he knew, he would probably hate my guts!* Elsie Mae was alive. Unfortunately, the scandalous rumors that were being spread around town about her were true.

In all reality, her date night with Blake had ended early, at only ten o'clock. She had promised her uncle that she would satisfy the sexual fantasies of his three buddies like she had done for other customers so many times before. Chance had revealed to her that it would be a little different this time without telling her what the difference would be. She just knew that Uncle Chance didn't play when it came to making his "paper." Every girl in his group knew the conditions under which she worked and gladly submitted to his rules. Besides, Chance bought them beautiful clothes, jewelry, perfume, and shoes and they were always treated to special hair styles and they had frequent health checkups.

With her Uncle Chance breathing down her neck, she had immediately walked into the house, and threw her sexy dresses, booty shorts and skirts, halter tops and a few casual clothes into her bag. Chance had placed his arm on her shoulder and ushered her out the front door like she had stolen something. Walking the short distance to the sports utility vehicle, a man had appeared out of nowhere to open the passenger side door for her to enter. She had noted that a foreigner was driving the SUV. When she stepped up on the running board and glanced around the darkened automobile, she noticed that there were three other women inside.

As she boarded, the driver yelled at her, "Hurry up! We've already lost time waiting on you! It's twelve minutes after ten!"

"I'm sorry; I got ready as fast as I could." Feeling embarrassed, she quickly took her seat and leaned back against the headrest. Elsie Mae recognized two of the young women from previous jobs. One was a new face. She hadn't noticed before, but now she saw an immensely frightened young girl crouched in the corner of the back row. After making momentary eye contact, the little girl quickly looked away to stare out the tinted window.

The tiny, young girl named Mia, nicknamed Tot was later revealed to be a fourteen year old baby. Mia had been sold into the underworld of child prostitution at a premium price. Who would ever guess that this sort of transaction would go on in the great United States of America? Her innocence would be lost for a price. It was a shameful deal negotiated between her parents and a third party envoi. The leader, Chance, would not be implicated because he was careful to use other people to do his dirty work. This kind of double-dealing, child exploitation and trafficking was propagated despite the nation's inclination to bury its head in the prodigal sand and ignore the sin, and bankrupted moral decay that threatens to destroy it.

A foreign business man was scheduled to arrive in Alabama to attend a conference. He had paid a hefty price to share a couple of hours with a young virgin girl. Mia's mother had explained to her that her participation was not only necessary to their family's survival, but she also made the child believe that her involvement had something to do with the security of the nation. What a ridiculous lie and horrible burden to place on an innocent and impressionable child. Although Mia didn't understand her mother's deceitful explanation, she was a daughter that wanted to please her parents. Mia felt that if going with these strange people was her obligation as the oldest child, then duty to family and country was a high honor for her to oblige. Shame on her parents, shame on the lustful business man; hell, shame on all who would allow such filthy practices to coexist with decency and civility!

Mia's mother had told her another lie about the need to feed, clothe and medicate the family's ailing grandparents after the girl had run to her crying when her father told her she had to go away. The girl had screamed, "Mommy, please don't make me go, I'll be good, I'll care for Grandmamma, I'll help keep the house clean, please, please, don't send me away!"

Insincerely, the mother had consoled the girl the best way that she knew how; but, at the same time, she was a willing participant to the destruction of an innocent mind, a gentle spirit and a loving heart. The deception was told with such convincing words that Mia assumed she would go back home after the very rich man had his way with her. Little did she know that this 'one time deal' was a well-rehearsed lie. Mia's parents didn't mention to her that they probably would never see her again. As the old folks used to say, "A lie don't care who tells it!" It wasn't proper English, but it was a country saying. Baby girl was in for a rude awakening; a nasty world of drunken men with probing hands and lustful intents. It was an ugly side of reality that most people never experience and even fewer realize existed. Third world countries were not the only civilizations with shady, backward brothels located in obscure towns that made plenty of dirty money on the backs of stolen innocence.

Before Elsie Mae and the others realized it, the van they were traveling in had crossed over into the state of Alabama to complete the desecrated deeds.

Elsie Mae was abruptly moved from her reminiscent state of mind of how she arrived at this place, back to her presence in the sunny room. She heard the angry voice of the strange man. "Did you hear what I said? I need you to get up at once, take a shower and prepare yourself for our respectable client!"

Elsie Mae thought, *Respectable? Hardly!* Apparently, she didn't move fast enough. Suddenly, she found herself snatched up from the floor and literally dragged to the shower where she felt her clothes ripped from her body. She tried to cover her breasts, but felt the impatient shove of the man's rough knuckles knocking her hands away.

He angrily growled, "Now wash up!" He tossed a face towel her way as she felt the sting of the cold water hit her face like an icy snowball. After a couple of minutes of cold water to wake her up, she felt the pleasant drenching of the multiple jets pulsate warm water against her aching body as she slowly washed herself. Elsie Mae stumbled several times, placing her left hand against the shower wall for support. As she exited the shower stall, she unexpectedly felt the presence of a gentle woman who appeared and helped her dry off as she was led back towards the bed. The unnamed woman started rubbing oils and lotions on Elsie Mae's body knowing that she was unable to do it for herself. Afterwards, the woman sprayed sensual smelling perfume on her neck, wrists, behind her ears and knees, and on her ankles.

"I just want to sleep, please let me get some sleep!" Elsie Mae begged. The woman looked sympathetic, but she didn't say a word. She didn't have to because unfortunately, the harsh man was near them again and he quickly answered Elsie Mae's plea.

"You'll sleep after you've finished your job and not a minute before!" He hissed.

How will I ever survive this ordeal? Elsie Mae thought to herself as the woman gave her some unknown pills, bottled water, and a mug filled with strong, black coffee.

Finally the man commanded Elsie Mae, "You had better sober up, because the client will be ready for you in two hours!"

I'm not ready to see anyone...It was all fun when I first started tricking, but now it's torment...This has got to end. I think I've been drugged! What more do they want from me-my life? Although she made good money, Elsie Mae was beginning to want out of the sleazy prostitution lifestyle. She felt trapped and worried that she was in too deep; that she knew too much...way too much to simply walk away. The saddest thing about it was that the men, who were controlling her mixed up life, including her uncle, knew that she was at their mercy. Unfortunately, she was equally bound to silence and illicit acts.

Elsie Mae kept her job as a housekeeper by day, several times per week, and devoutly attended church to maintain her duplicitous life. She actually had her family, friends, church members, and neighbors totally deceived by her phony pious demeanor. The truth was that Elsie Mae Coates was a thorough housekeeper by day, hooker by night – two very contrasting roles lived by a double minded woman.

Whatever the combination was between the medicine and the coffee, Elsie Mae was sobered in record time. Her heart felt like it was racing, which she assumed was the side effects of the medicine. Her mind was perplexed from the heavy weight of it all; however, she mechanically serviced her client while crying inside. Elsie Mae performed her whorish role as if her very life depended on it. If her pimp's threats were to be believed, a lot was 'riding' on a job well done; because at the end of the night, she just wanted to go home. She didn't know it, but this would not be just one night to work her sexual magic. It would be a night season that would negatively affect her for a lifetime.

* * *

Elsie Mae's Uncle Chance stood in the corner of his private, executive courtyard counting his stacks of bills with his back to the shrubbery and his face focused on the huge positive bottom line from this latest venture. The van would usually carry the women across the state line to go into Alabama, Florida, the Carolinas or Mississippi, for them to do sorted, illegal acts. Then the vehicle would be driven back to Georgia. This time his girls would be gone for an indefinite period of time. Chance had started marketing his goods on the Internet and business had never been better. Most of the young women he acquired had been run-a-ways; forgotten or disowned by family members who had long-since washed their hands of the wayward and defiant, wild natured teens. For some reason, these families didn't approach the local law enforcement agency's Missing and Exploited Children's task forces to find their daughters who had gone astray. Chance assumed that all of his latest rejected, cast-a-ways fell into that category. However, he had underestimated the strength of the Coats family and the tenacity and determination of Chief Spurring and the officers of the Griffin Police Department. The chief's perseverance and commitment to finding Elsie Mae would eventually aggravate the seedy world of hookers, pimps, and their foul customers.

While sitting there adding up his money, the last words of Elsie Mae now ran through his mind. She had said, "Uncle Chance, I'm glad you take such good care of us. What time are we leaving in order to get back in time for Big Bethel's church service tomorrow?"

He had calmly replied, "You probably won't make that service, Baby Girl. Maybe some time in the future."

"Okay Chance, whatever you say." Elsie Mae didn't call him uncle around other people. She had leaned back her head, and had decided to relax. Little did she realize it at the time, she wouldn't warm the pews of the Big Bethel AME sanctuary for a very long time.

For a moment, Chance felt a little guilt because he had not revealed to his girls the planned length of their stay. He realized that they would probably start talking to employers, family, and friends which could jeopardize the secrecy of the illicit business. If caught, he could possibly face a felony charge. It was not only an illegal prostitution organization, but he was also crossing state lines to manage the operation. Chance also could not risk the possible revelation of his prominent clientele which not only included rich business men, but politicians, celebrities, entrepreneurs, professional athletes, and their referred associates. These customers paid dearly for a secret liaison with expensive ladies of the night. Therefore, what the women didn't know ahead of time was better for all involved. Chance might have been shady, but he was no fool.

* * *

Once Elsie Mae had completed her job, all she wanted was some fresh air, something cold to drink and some much needed sleep. From the indoor garden loft level, she descended the short flight of stairs into the lobby and then

156

stepped outside to enjoy the night atmosphere outside the hotel. It was a humid evening and there were many people who had her same idea. She moved through the various groups of friends, families and couples towards the Japanese garden admiring the beauty of the huge courtyard. Strolling over to a wrought iron bench to briefly sit down, she took several deep breaths and closed her eyes. While reflecting on her present life, she looked ahead for a better day. Elsie Mae imagined being in the Bahamas sitting under a fruit tree, sipping on a mixed drink while taking in the fresh smell of the ocean water. After what seemed like only a few minutes of dreaming, but actually was an hour; she stood up to go back inside the building.

Climbing the stairs, Elsie Mae entered the luxuriously remodeled lobby of the Swiss owned hotel. Every place she looked was laced with luxury. In the middle of the lobby was an enormous and beautiful floral spray, centered on a cherry wood round table standing on bear-claw feet. The table was polished, shining like new silver dollars. The front desk was made of cherry wood accented with a marble inlay through its middle on the front and on top of the counter. The front desk staff wore beige uniforms with brass nametags. All of them were friendly and very professional. Elsie Mae often wondered if they knew what was really going on at the south end of the top floor.

There was a beautiful waterfall at the end of the massive lobby that was surrounded by hundreds of tropical plants and flowers. Benches were strategically placed throughout the oasis to ensure that there was ample seating for the guests. Glancing into the ceiling, Elsie Mae noticed a masterful oil mural of angels, clouds, trumpets, violins and an assortment of birds. Before she knew it, she exclaimed to nobody in particular, "Wow...that is an amazing painting!"

157

"Yes, it is." A man with a warm, handsome face turned toward her and extended his hand to shake hers. He said, "I'm Byron Camp, and I'm here on business. What's your name?"

"My name is Gina; nice to meet you." While stating her alias, she started walking away from the man. He looked friendly enough, but Chance had a rule about setting up all of the customers to ensure his girls stayed safe.

"What's your hurry sweetheart?" He probed.

"Sorry, I have an appointment." She stated quickening her pace to escape the man's curious pursuit.

"I bet you do." He muttered as he turned around to watch the large fish that swam at the bottom of the waterfall.

Elsie Mae briskly walked to the elevators which were buffed brass and pressed the button for the upper levels. Various people entered and exited the moving compartment. By the time she reached her floor, she was the only occupant. She exited the elevator and walked to the wood podium to give her special bar-coded identification card to the female attendant. The older woman scanned the card to ensure its authenticity. She then used a hand-held radio to alert the other male employee further down the hall to use the special key to engage a different elevator that went to the executive VIP floor.

Once on the VIP floor, she quickly walked to the end of the hallway, opened her suite door and jogged to the restroom. She turned on the shower, quickly undressed and stepped into the stream of water. After bathing, she exited the restroom, walked to the sofa and turned on the television.

About two hours after Elsie Mae returned to her two-bedroom suite, she heard the door open. She thought, *These people never think about knocking...I may be a whore, but I deserve some privacy!* To Elsie Mae's surprise, the same mean-spirited guy who had man-handled her earlier, walked inside holding the hand of the young girl who they had nick-named Tot. She looked traumatized, but she refused to cry in front of the man. Elsie Mae remembered that Mia told her that her parents had told her to make them proud and be a big girl. The child quickly walked across the living room with a determined countenance, but her eyes told the real story of her internal devastation. It was gut-retching to watch her brave display of normalcy.

"Elsie Mae, take care of the girl until someone else comes up here. We've been pretty busy tonight." With that last command, Chance's employee turned and left the suite.

Elsie Mae walked over to the second bedroom where Mia had pushed up the door, but not completely closed it. At first she didn't know where the girl was hiding.

"Tot, are you okay?" Elsie Mae could only imagine how distraught the girl must be feeling. It was an understatement. Within a few minutes, Elsie Mae heard the overwhelming howls that echoed from the bathroom. Racing to the door, she turned the knob to find it locked.

Knocking, she repeated, "Tot, are you okay?" A stupid question now since she could hear the gut-retching sobs growing louder. "Let me in, Tot. I can help you. I promise I won't do anything to hurt you."

After a few minutes of repeated requests for the child to open the door, Elsie Mae heard the crying getting closer to where she was standing.

Mia opened the door and Elsie Mae immediately felt sorry for the child. The expensive make-up they had used on her baby face was ruined. Elsie Mae noticed that Mia's eyes were blood-shot as she literally collapsed in her embrace. She lifted Mia up and carried her to the sofa where she consoled her and allowed her to weep until she finally fell asleep. About three hours later, the woman that had assisted Elsie Mae earlier came to get the girl. The woman silently led and half carried Mia into the bathroom, placed her on the animal fur rug and ran some bubbly bath water. She gently washed the girl, brushed her hair and eventually placed her in the bed. The woman never opened her mouth, but Elsie Mae could see a stream of tears flow down the woman's face. This was too much for either of them to swallow. Chance had taken the business to an all-time low. Elsie Mae made up her mind that she had to get away; somehow, some way and she was determined to take Mia with her.

Exasperated, Elsie Mae said, "This is too much to process!" She made the statement without expecting the woman to reply. As expected, the woman shook her head and silently walked out of the suite while wiping tears from her eyes.

* * *

The compassionate woman returned in the morning, walked straight to the bedroom where Mia was sleeping and tried to open the door, but it was locked. The woman then knocked on the door, but there was no response. She banged on the door louder and said, "Mia, please open the door; this is Elizabeth. I promise I will not hurt you."

Mia timidly replied, "Please...I don't want to come out there right now. May I get some more sleep?"

"No, I'm sorry. Mr. Chance gave clear instructions for me to come get you. We are going shopping to buy you many beautiful clothes and shoes. He also said we can get the game system he promised you, several different games and many other wonderful things!" Elisabeth explained.

Hesitantly, Mia came to the door, opened it and peeked out. The young girl appeared to be relieved that there were no other people, notably men, with Elizabeth. After sighing in relief she asked, "We're going shopping for me?" A smile tugged at her mouth at the thought of getting new clothes, toys and even a game system. She never had access to electronic game systems or new clothes at home. There never seemed to be enough money to make the regular living conditions bearable; much less have extra funds for the fun things in life. Before leaving home, her parents had told her about the possible gifts. Now their conversation came back to her mind with the discussion about shopping at the mall.

"Yes Mia, Mr. Chance said this trip to the mall will be special just for you!" Elizabeth said, making the shopping spree appear to be the result of Mr. Chance's thoughtfulness. This was a ploy that he used with all of his new "girls" to convince them that he was on their side and that he really cared for them. They had all been tricked into the web of deceit, skillfully spun by a pimp who was in the position to entrap them for a lifetime.

"Yeah!!!" Mia exclaimed. The poor child had no idea what her parents had gotten her into. She was momentarily ecstatic about the plans for the day as she thought about the electronic games she would soon play. *Marsha always had the latest game system and the newest games too. Wait until she sees me!* Mia thought, not realizing that she would not see her friend again. The sexually abused girl had no idea that it would be a long time, if ever, before she would see anyone that she knew.

"Now child, hurry and get ready. We don't want to keep the nice driver waiting." Elizabeth said.

From the sofa, Elsie Mae watched the scene unfold and it made her want to vomit because Mia was a child. As an adult, she knew what she was getting into when her Uncle Chance had explained his illegal business venture that he was planning to start. He had asked her first to be part of his "staff." Chance was very persuasive as he explained the lucrative possibilities; therefore, she made the decision to join his clan of women even though it went against her morals and her family oriented background. Unfortunately, Mia's choice was made for her by dysfunctional parents.

"Okay. I'll get ready. It won't take me long to get dressed. All I have to do is wash my face and brush my teeth since I had a nice bath last night. Can I wear jeans?"

"That will be fine my dear. I'll wait right outside the door." Elizabeth replied.

Though the fresh memories of her rape were still in her mind, Mia didn't have the maturity to understand that Mr. Chance was responsible for it all. He made sure that he steered clear of the daily duties which might even include roughing up a stubborn subordinate. He always wanted to appear to be the good guy. Unfortunately for the teenagers and the women, his strategy worked. They all loved him.

The soreness Mia was currently experiencing and the excruciating pain she had felt between her legs the night before under the weight of the strange talking man suddenly flooded her mind; and she trembled at the chilling memory. As she reached in the closet for her jeans, she suddenly experienced a jolt of pain in her private area that made her whimper and tilt over to steady herself. As she recovered, she heard someone approach the doorway.

Concerned, Elsie Mae asked, "Mia, are you alright?"

"I'm just fine." The girl mumbled, but her eyes told a different story. Mia thought to herself, *I promised Mommy and Daddy that I would be a brave girl and do everything that they tell me to do. Mommy didn't tell me that it would hurt this bad. I can't tell anyone because they will think I can't do the job. I've got to be strong. Grow up and stop that whining Mia! You are better than a big cry baby!*

"Okay Mia; let me know if you need anything. Do you hear me? A rapper named T.I. had a song with the line, 'You can have whatever you like.' Well, you my little Tot can

162

have whatever you want from me. If you ever have a problem or need anything, just find me. I'll make it happen." Elsie Mae then reached to give Mia a hug and the poor child hesitated, unsure of what to do. *Did I see her shrink up as if afraid of me? This is an awful situation? What can I do? I don't want to abandon my Uncle Chance, but I can't keep living like this. And now they have this fourteen year old baby doing the unthinkable. She's even distrustful of me. Let me reach out to her again.*

"Mia, come here; I'll never hurt you. That's a promise. Do you hear me? I'll never cause you any pain." Then Elsie Mae thought to herself, *You don't know it right now, but I'm going to figure out a way to make sure you get out of this before it ruins your life forever. I made the crazy choice to start tricking; unfortunately, your decision, sweet Tot, was made for you and that's not right!*

"Okay Elsie Mae, I believe you." With a look of relief on her face, Mia fell into Elsie Mae's arms and cried for a few minutes until Elizabeth came back for her.

"Child, we've got to go. What's taking you so long?"

"I'm sending her out now, Elizabeth." Elsie Mae said, and then she whispered to Mia, "Have a good time Tot. I'll see you when you get back."

"Okay Elsie Mae; thank you for your help." Mia was excited about going shopping. Even though she was a young girl who was being forced to do grown folk acts, she skipped out of the door laughing, like a normal, happy child.

* * *

Mia came back from her mall excursion loaded down with bags from various stores in the mall. Elizabeth was right behind her with plastic bags holding four new pair of shoes, and clothes. There was a smile on Mia's face even though

163

sadness rested in her eyes. Joy and sadness, two very conflicting emotions were competing to take over her mind. Unfortunately, madness doesn't discriminate because of age.

Earlier that day during breakfast, Mia had burst into tears because the sausage was almost gone in the buffet pan and her waffle had burned. Then, she was laughing as she left to go out shopping. Elizabeth later said that she broke down in tears as they passed by a family eating lunch together in the mall's food court. Elizabeth said they had to sit down in a chair outside a restaurant in order to allow Mia to calm down. Elizabeth reported that Mia said to her, 'My parents used to take me and my sisters and brothers to the mall. Sometimes we didn't have money to shop, but we would split a whole pizza. Daddy would say he wasn't hungry and he would smile and watch us eat. I think he was hungry, but he only had enough money for one pizza. We didn't go out to eat that often, but it was fun when we did. I really miss my family. When do you think I can see them?'

Elizabeth said that she comforted the girl and assured her that she would soon see her family. "Elsie Mae, I hated to lie to the child. I really don't know if she's ever going home, but I couldn't tell her that!"

"I know what you mean, Elizabeth."

Elsie Mae reflected, *Why would we subject an innocent baby to this twisted lifestyle? Uncle Chance doesn't care that this business is illegal; we all know that and we are equally guilty. Now, he's willingly contributing to the delinquency of a vulnerable little girl. This is too much! God, how can I escape with little Mia? There must be a safe way out. Where can I go for help? Who would even care about me now?* Suddenly, Elsie Mae felt dirty and depressed. The weight of her decisions and the possible consequences such as diseases and arrest were overwhelming thoughts that she really didn't want to think about. After Mia and Elizabeth left to eat in the hotel's restaurant, Elsie Mae whispered, "I wonder how long Uncle Chance will keep Mia. This is a risky business. I guess some people will do anything for dirty money."

Chapter 22

Chief Bruce Spurring walked into his office feeling refreshed after sleeping for five restful hours. His wife Sandy had called to say she wanted to meet with him for dinner Friday night, and he was hopeful that she wanted to work on reconciling their marriage.

She is a terrific wife and the house isn't worth a flip without her. I've lost fourteen pounds and the plants are all wilted; hell, I don't know what I'm doing. Maybe they need watering. I wonder has anything credible come in about the Elsie Mae Coats investigation. Dead or alive, she has to be somewhere – maybe she's hidden in plain sight. This case is quite bizarre. It gets crazier by the day. Now Ben is in jail trying to make bail while claiming that she's a hooker. How does he know that with such certainty unless he has been with her? Or, he may have seen her walk on the street. But, we've swept through all of the known beats and whore houses that are documented and she was not a part of any of them. I checked her record and it's clean. This is strange. I've got to get to the bottom of it. Maybe today will be the day!

As Chief Spurring approached his office which was located towards the back of the precinct, he tossed his hat on the top hook of the coat rack and rushed to the restroom.

I just used the restroom before coming to work. What's wrong with me? He could almost hear his estranged wife's voice echoing in the recesses of his mind saying, 'Baby, you need to go get a checkup.' When he would vehemently protest, she would say, 'If not for you, go get one for me. I need to know that you are okay. I feel wonderful, but I still get my annual physical including my mammogram. Bruce, despite what you may think, you are still human!'

'Well of course I'm human, but I don't have time to sit up in a doctor's office all day with perpetrators running rampant!' he would retort.

'Baby, you won't catch one criminal if you are in the hospital. Please make an appointment, or do you want me to make it for you?' Faithful Sandy would always offer.

'I can do it myself, thank you.' Chief would snap, aggravated that she kept asking him.

"Maybe I should make an appointment. As much as I dread the doctor's office, I would absolutely hate the undertaker's mortuary. I'll make the appointment today, for me and for Sandy." He looked up the number and made the call breathing a sigh of relief when the date he requested was available.

* * *

Chief Spurring had dealt with countless criminals and many cases involving petty theft, bad checks, breaking and entering, drugs, domestic violence, drunken pedestrians, spousal abuse, and the occasional murder, but he never questioned his ability to handle anything. For some reason, he was nervous about this doctor's visit. *All I know is that I constantly have to use the restroom. Something has got to be wrong with me.*

It was the morning of his physical and he decided to call his wife Sandy for morale support. *She'll probably fuss a few minutes asking what took so long for me to make the appointment.* For some reason, he felt funny discussing his symptoms with her. It had been awhile since they had seen one another. He truly loved his wife and felt that they needed to put their marriage back on track. They were scheduled to have dinner together on the weekend and he wanted to share the news of his doctor's appointment with her knowing how concerned she had been about him.

Seeing his number in the LED window on her cell phone, Sandy said, "Hello, Bruce, how are you doing?" Sandy spoke with a pleasant voice.

"I'm better now that I hear your voice, Sweetie. How are you?" Chief thought, *Good ole faithful Sandy. She is always there for me. Why couldn't I be the husband she deserves? When I get her back, I'll spend the quality time with her that I need to in order for us to be close again.*

"To be perfectly honest with you Bruce, I'm looking forward to seeing you. I've really missed you even though you were not home that much anyway. I guess I had gotten used to being alone. Now that we are separated, I don't like not seeing you at all. I know your career is important to you, I just want you to make our life together just as important. Bruce, what are we going to do about us?"

"Sweetie, let's talk about it over dinner, okay. I promise I'll listen to everything you want to tell me."

"Okay dear, this weekend." Sandy was smiling thinking about seeing her husband.

"Sandy, thank you…uh, for putting up with me and, guess what?" He waited while making a false drum roll with his mouth.

"What is it?" Sandy could not imagine what his news was.

"I finally made a doctor's appointment for a physical."
He sighed like a huge weight had just been lifted off his
shoulders.

"Yes! Bruce Baby, you've made me soooo happy today.
That's the best news I've had in a long time. When are you
going?"

"Today and I wanted you to know. Well, Sandy I'll talk
to you a little later tonight. I'll let you know what the doctor
says. Thanks for pushing me. I could still hear your voice
encouraging me to go. Have a good day, Sweetie."

"You too honey. Now, call me tonight." Sandy was
smiling from ear to ear.

"Okay, out." Chief was a retired military police officer
and the town's police chief. The law enforcement lingo came
natural even when he was speaking to his wife.

"Bye Baby," Sandy said. She was beside herself with
joy that her words had helped convince her husband to
finally go to the doctor. Sandy reflected; *Miracles never
cease.*

Chief Spurring leaned back in his office chair amazed at
how easy the conversation had gone. Sandy had not even
fussed or mentioned that she had harped on the same tune for
three years; not one mumbling word. That w*oman; when I
think she's going to argue, she says nothing and when I think
I'm in the clear, I get a mouth full. It may not always be easy
being married to her; but it would be better than living
without her. Maybe I'll never figure her out, but it will be fun
trying again!*

* * *

Chief went to the doctor's office and gave blood and
urine for all of the standard urine and blood panel tests. He
discussed his family's medical history and was subjected to

the normal male examinations. After the doctor finished the examination, he mentioned that the Chief's prostate was swollen and that he needed to run further tests. He also explained the various health concerns that the swelling could indicate.

"No problem Doc. Just let me know what to do."

"We'll call you once we get the lab results. If there are no problems, great, otherwise, we'll go from there. It was good seeing you Chief; however, don't wait three years before coming back. I need to see you at least once a year for an annual physical." The doctor withdrew his glasses from his eyes and placed them in his chest pocket.

"Yeah, yeah Doc, I hear it enough from Sandy. I'll do better."

"Okay. Now you can get dressed. Take care Chief, hopefully, everything is okay. We'll notify you if there is a problem or concern." The doctor placed his pen in his opposite breast pocket and walked out of the exam room.

Chief Spurring got dressed and went to work feeling good to be out of the doctor's office; however, he couldn't help being worried about his lab results.

Chapter 23

Friday could not come fast enough for Chief Spurring; not only was he technically going to be off from work on the weekend, but he was planning on taking his estranged wife Sandy to dinner. Of course, he was hoping that it would turn into dinner and a "private movie" with his sweet lady. *Man, I've missed her! I've got to bring it tonight. I know, let me send her some roses today just because.*

Chief leaned over and pressed the buzzer for his secretary, Maritza. When she answered he said, "Good morning and happy Friday to you Maritza. Please look up the number to a florist for me."

"Do you have a preference as to which florist, Chief?" Maritza was worth her weight in gold. She helped Chief Spurring stay organized and she ensured that the daily routines and procedures of the office flowed as smoothly as possible.

"It doesn't matter, just get me a number and I would like some strong black coffee. Do we have donuts today? I've got a sweet tooth that won't wait."

"Yes Chief Spurring, you know I picked up a dozen Krispy Kreme donuts this morning. You ask me every day if we have them. One day I'm just going to pick up fruit and see how you like those apples and oranges for a change. You know we all need to start eating healthier anyway." Maritza stood so that she could start preparing his coffee.

"Yeah, yeah, I hear enough from Sandy, the doctor and now you. Maritza, get off my back and bring me my sweets!"

"I'm coming with it Chief – I just wanted to throw in my 'two cents' worth of advice. I'm not studn' you." Maritza said. It is Southern slang for not thinking about you. "I'm working on my figure; I plan to have thirty pounds off by the end of the summer."

"You can do it girl! Go for it. That means there will be an extra donut for me, right?" Good ole Chief always has a comment or two for good measure.

"No, I'm eating the donut today and I'll work harder on the treadmill after work. Maybe tomorrow I'll resist. It would be better if you would fund fruit and perhaps yogurt instead of these fat pills every day!" Maritza loved Krispy Kreme donuts- maybe too much.

"You've got a point which I'll consider another year. Where you at, girl?" Chief let proper English escape him half of the time while in the office. He periodically joked that you can just be yourself among friends. At press conferences though, he made sure to project a professional image and spoke using the appropriate grammar.

"You are a mess Chief Spurring." Maritza hung up the phone, washed her hands and walked to the break room. While preparing her boss's coffee and grabbing the two glazed donuts from the box, she paused to watch the newest update on the Elsie Mae Coats' missing person case. She softly muttered, "Wow, I wonder what has happened to that woman. I heard again in the beauty shop that she was a freaky little something, not "the girl next door" that has been portrayed. I remember that wacko informant said out right that the woman is a whore. Go figure!"

172

"Maritza, are you talking to yourself again?" Officer Bill Minor said. He had walked into the break room without Maritza noticing him.

"Well, the old folks used to say you're not crazy as long as you don't start answering yourself. Hell, I'm trying to figure out what happened to that Elsie Mae Coats lady. Do you know yet, but you're just not telling the press?"

"Actually, we have some leads, but no cigar yet. I'll keep you posted though." Officer Minor grabbed a cup and filled it with steeping hot coffee. After blowing on it, he took a few sips and then commented, "Great cup of coffee Maritza. Thanks for doing such an excellent job."

"Yeah, yeah, compliments in cash please!" Maritza liked joking with her coworkers and the other officers. She really did love working there.

"I know. We could all use a raise. Have a good day." He turned and left the break room to start his day.

"You do the same." Maritza replied.

In his office, Chief Spurring turned his attention to a Daily Briefing Report to determine what the most pressing issues were in order to task his deputies with assignments.

When Maritza reached the Chief's office with the goods, she noticed he was very engrossed into something he was reading so she stepped back to exit when he saw her.

"Come on in, besides, I need what you have in your hands."

"Yes, I aim to please. Have you heard anything credible on the Elsie Mae Coats case?" Maritza walked into his office with a huge mug of strong black coffee which she placed on a coaster on his desk, and sat the saucer with the donuts beside the mug. She also placed an index card near his telephone with the phone numbers of two florists as he had requested.

173

"You're the best Maritza. No, not yet, but I feel like we're getting close to a break. Just call it 'officer intuition' – I know what I know!"

"If anyone can crack the case Chief, it's you. You get my vote even before the next election. I'll be down the hall when you need me." Maritza knew it was not a matter of if, but when he would need her to do something.

Before she could make it back to her seat, her intercom buzzer went off again. *I knew it...he can't live without me for five minutes.*

"Yes Chief?" She waited for his urgent need this time.

"Maritza, please get me the number to that new restaurant called Southern something. It's got a second name to it. Ah...you know the one I mean, don't you?"

"Yes, the new place is called Southern Specialties Restaurant. I haven't been there yet, but I was told by some friends that it's an excellent place, good food, nice music, lovely ambience and excellent service. It sounds like a special place." Maritza immediately turned to her computer screen to Google the additional information.

"Thanks." He continued to read his report.

Chief Spurring had heard good comments from a couple of his deputies about the new bistro in town. He thought that it would be a good place to wine and dine Sandy. Chief had heard that the food was delicious, the décor was fancy, and that it had exceptional service. There was even an article in the *Griffin News* that said Southern Specialties was an upscale restaurant and the kind of business that Griffin needed to boost its economy and to help enhance the attractiveness of the dining options for the citizens.

Southern Specialties added a wonderful addition to the culture of the area too. Of course, when each guest is seated he is given the menu to review, but after the guest makes the selection, the menu carte du jour is removed. Directly after that, a different person who assists the server does a unique thing. At the appropriate time the server's assistant brings a tiny bowl of warm sudsy water and a warm towel to each guest and positions them to the right front of the guest so that he can wash his hands. The idea behind it is that many people have touched the menu and your hands need sanitizing before eating your meal.

Chief called the first florist on the card and ordered two dozen long stemmed peach-colored roses for delivery that afternoon to Sandy. "Have the card say, 'To my beautiful wife Sandy, Love Bruce.' Do you have that?" He then gave the pertinent information for payment and Sandy's address. *I should have given her roses more than I did and said the loving things she deserves to hear on a more regular basis. God, if you allow me to win Sandy back, I'll love her right. I won't neglect her or take her for granted this time.*

Some lessons are learned late, but at least it didn't seem to be too late for the Spurring marriage.

* * *

Sandy was working diligently in her home office on her third novel. The publisher had given her an extension on the deadline for the final draft of the new detective thriller. As she was making the finishing touches on the final chapter, the doorbell rang. She thought, *I wonder who that could be.* Pulling her glasses from her face, she placed them on her executive braided wood trim desk and pushed back to get up. *Ah, let me first save these changes before I walk away. I learned my lesson the hard way on that one.* Smiling, she walked through the hallway toward the door and hurried when the bell rang again. "Okay, I'm coming."

She reached the door, peeked outside and was stunned to see the vast array of gorgeous roses and baby's breath set in a very fancy peach-colored, squared ceramic vase with shimmering gold running through it.

"I have a delivery for Mrs. Sandy Spurring."

"I'm Sandy. Oh, those roses are magnificent!" She read the card and beaming with joy, she noted Bruce's effort to do something nice for her. *What a surprise...*

"Well, if you will just sign right here."

Sandy signed the form and said, "Thank you." She closed the door and walked to the living room. Removing the lovely silk floral arrangement from the coffee table, she placed the bountiful bouquet in the center and stood back to admire it. "These are beautiful, and they smell wonderful too."

Walking back to the kitchen, she picked up the cordless phone from its base and dialed Bruce's cell number. On ring number five he picked up.

"Hello Sugar, how are you today? Are you as excited about tonight as I am?" He silently wondered if the delivery had been made. He didn't have to wonder long because Sandy immediately started showing her appreciation.

"Bruce, the flowers are simply gorgeous! Thank you so much. I love them and they smell so good!"

"I'm glad you like them. I'm really looking forward to seeing you tonight. I'll pick you up at six. We have a reservation for seven. Will that work for you?"

"That's perfect. I'm busy working on the book, but that gives me plenty of time to work, keep my hair appointment, relax and get ready. Bruce, I can't wait to see you too. I love you, bye."

"I love you too. See you tonight." Bruce hung up the phone feeling good. He definitely had earned a few extra points by sending her the roses.

Chapter 24

Chief Bruce Spurring arrived at Sandy's townhome at exactly six in the evening. He was looking dapper in his black slacks, grey shirt and striped grey, black and white tie. His outfit was complete with black wing-tip shoes that were polished to perfection. He sprayed some breath fresher in his mouth and exited the car feeling and smelling good with Chrome cologne spayed on his chest. He took a deep breath before ringing the bell.

Sandy opened the door and looked simply radiant in a one-side, off the shoulder, black wrap dress with black open-toe stiletto heels and a small clutch purse to complete her look. Her hair was freshly done in a curly up-do and her makeup was flawless. Sandy had Georgia-tanned skin, blond hair, brown eyes and a petite frame. She stepped back and motioned for him to enter the foyer.

"Sandy, you look beautiful!" He reached for her and grabbed her waist, pulling her body into his for a warm embrace. Brushing his lips against hers, he released her momentarily and then plunged into a passionate French kiss. He thrust his tongue into her mouth probing it, tasting her sweetness. Bruce sucked on her bottom lip and briefly wondered whether they would make it to the reservation for dinner. She happily kissed him back and suddenly rubbed his back with the tenderness he remembered all too well.

Then she whispered into his ear, "Down Big Boy, I'm hungry. Let's go to dinner. By the way, where are we going?"

"Wow, girl, you know how to get me going. Dinner is a surprise. I hope you've never been there before."

"Really, a surprise Bruce, okay then, let me put up my puppy."

"A puppy, you've got to be kidding me! I thought you always said a puppy would remind you of having two husbands and that you didn't want to have to pick up any more mess than you had to. What happened to that, Sugar?"

"Well, let's just say that I had a change of heart. Topaz is so much company for me. Are you jealous?"

"No, as long as the second husband has four legs instead of two, we're fine. Where is the little fellow anyway?" Bruce winked at her.

"I'll let you see him when we get back if that's okay. I don't want us to be late for our reservation." She quickly walked away to another room to put Topaz in a kennel.

When she returned, she eased her hand on his arm to lead him out of the doorway.

"Right you are Sandy, as always. We don't want to be late. I'd say you are a keeper!"

"Sure you're right!" She turned to lock the door and they walked to the car. He opened her door feeling like a school boy out for a first date instead of with his wife of twenty years. *The Lord still works miracles,* he happily thought. He quickly walked around to his side of the car, as she leaned over to open his door. He got in, buckled up, and adjusted his radio to a smooth jazz station. They enjoyed the music as they rode to the restaurant, smiling and talking like there had been no marital separation.

When they arrived at their destination, he checked the time and realized that they had about ten minutes to spare. They both unbuckled their seatbelts and as he turned to open his door, he paused to say, "Girl, I'm so glad to see you. It's been a long time you know." He winked at her and placed his hand on her bare knee, gently rubbing it. She placed her hand over his and savored the tender moment.

"Bruce, it's good to be out with you. Let's enjoy the evening. I know we promised we'd discuss our problems tonight, but we could really talk about our issues another time. I just want to relax and enjoy you and me, together again without the drama of discussing past conflicts and disappointments. Would that be okay with you?"

"Absolutely, Sandy; whatever makes you happy is what I want to do tonight. You know that old saying, 'If momma ain't happy, nobody's happy!' And Sweetie, you are my woman. When we get back together, everything is going to be different—better than you can imagine. I realize all of the mistakes I made, and how I basically neglected you. I assumed you would always be there; waiting for me to come home no matter what time I finished a job. I'm really sorry."

Sandy suddenly leaned over and placed her index finger over his lips indicating that she had heard enough. "Baby, we'll talk, let's just appreciate this time together and do whatever grown folks like to do; okay?" With that statement made, she leaned closer to him and planted a sweet kiss on his lips, this time allowing her tongue to search for his. He kissed her back and when they awkwardly embraced, because of the armrest between them, they both laughed.

"Five minutes to spare dear, let's eat." Bruce exited the car and opened her door. Stretching out his hand he grabbed hers and watched admirably as her five foot, four inch frame gracefully exited the car. He thought to himself, *Look at her beautiful hair, brown bedroom eyes and tanned skin. She's a knockout!* "Girl, and to think I almost let you get away!"

"Bruce, I'm not going anywhere. You're stuck with me."

"Amen to that!" He was thrilled to hear her say that.

There was complimentary valet parking and Bruce gave the driver his spare key. They walked across the beautiful stone entranceway to the huge, wooden double doors in front of the Southern Specialties Restaurant.

Upon entering the atrium, they could hear wonderful dinner music. An attractive and friendly hostess immediately greeted them, took their name and found it on the reservation list, and beckoned for them to follow her. She led them to a cozy corner table that had a linen tablecloth and a live flower arrangement. The focal point of the impressive room was a baby grand piano. As they took their seats, they noticed that a thin, middle aged man skillfully played the ivory keys.

"Wow, this is a beautiful place. Look at those custom drapes and the crown molding." Suddenly, Sandy sighed and exclaimed, "Bruce the ceiling is fabulous!"

He hadn't looked up at the ceiling because he was so focused on Sandy's beauty in front of him. Glancing upward to see what had her so enthralled; he could appreciate what she meant. There was a gorgeous mural of clouds, birds, and stringed instruments in an alcove shaped ceiling surrounded by a circular polished brass perimeter. In the very center of the ceiling was a magnificent chandelier which sparkled with such opulence that it was breathtaking.

"Good choice, right?" You couldn't tell him a thing now. He knew Sandy well enough to know she was very pleased with how the evening was going.

"It absolutely has a wonderful atmosphere. I hope the food is as good as the décor." As she said that remark, the waiter approached them with the fancy menus which were gold with a thick braided rope draped through the middle.

"Good evening, welcome to the Southern Specialties Restaurant of Griffin, Georgia. We are delighted that you are here. The specials tonight are grilled salmon with honey-lemon marinade, trout almandine, chicken masala in wine sauce, shrimp creole, and chicken piccata. I'll allow you time to peruse the menu. May I start you with cocktails and an appetizer?"

"How about a bottle of Pinot Noir wine and some fried calamari with marinara sauce; Sandy, will that be okay to start?" Bruce was in his element with his wife.

"That sounds great, Bruce." *Order on Baby,* she thought to herself.

The waiter quickly scribbled down the request, then said, "And for your meal Mrs. Spurring?"

Impressed that he would call her by name, Sandy tilted her head and said, "Please come back to me. There are so many wonderful choices."

"Certainly." Turning his attention to Bruce he said, "What will your selection be Mr. Spurring?"

"Well, I think I'll have the grilled salmon with honey-lemon marinade, asparagus and garlic mashed potatoes." He passed his menu to the server.

"Are you ready, Mrs. Spurring?" Patiently waiting as he noticed her scanning the many choices, he then asked, "Do you have any questions about the menu?"

"No, I've decided on the shrimp creole, green beans and Cesar salad. I would also like a Cherry Coke, please."

He reached for her menu and said, "I'll place your orders. Janette will now serve you."

A young woman approached their table wearing a uniform similar to the waiter's, black pants, a black vest and a white shirt. She had a tray on her arms and gracefully presented a tiny bowl of warm sudsy water which she positioned to the right front of the Spurring's place settings.

"What's that for?" Bruce asked a little confused.

"Sir, it's to clean your hands. It's a European idea that once the menus have been touched by other guests, your hands should be sanitized before you consume your meal." As they dipped their hands in the liquid, she then presented a warm linen and cotton towel for them to dry their hands. Once they were finished, she stated, "Your meals will be out shortly. Enjoy your evening and again, we appreciate you choosing Southern Specialties Restaurant for your dining." With that, she turned to leave them alone to listen to the pianist make the ivory keys dance.

"Well alright then!" Sandy was smiling from ear to ear. She thought, *My man is definitely a class act!*

"Yes Baby, it's a new day in the Spurring home."

They talked and ate until they were full and satisfied. The restaurant and the dining experience were all that they had heard it would be, and so much more. Before they left the facility, the manager came over to greet them.

"Hello, I'm the manager, Cameron Castleton. Was everything to your satisfaction tonight?"

"Everything was wonderful!" She chimed. "The food was delicious and this restaurant is simply beautiful. We'll definitely be back."

"I concur with my wife. We'll be back."

"Great, we're happy that you are pleased. Have a great evening." The manager then walked to the next table.

They left the restaurant and drove to a dinner club that had a dance floor. Chief ordered more wine and they danced until it was about two in the morning.

"Are you ready to go home honey?" He inquired.

"Yes I am, and I want you to go with me." She smiled, winked, and gave him an expression that he understood. The night was far from over.

* * *

On the way to Sandy's townhome, Bruce slipped in an Elton John CD and they bobbed their heads and sang to "Benny and the Jets," "Lucy in the Sky with Diamonds," and "Don't Go Breaking My Heart." Once they arrived at her place she sat and waited for him to open her door. She then led him inside. As they entered, the puppy started yelping because he was happy to know she was home.

"Bruce, take Topaz out and let him use the training mat."

"Okay dear. He's cute. What kind of dog is this?"

"He's a Silky Yorkshire Terrier. I love him Bruce. How would you feel about me bringing a dog to the house?"

"No problem as long as he has health insurance and a caretaker to pick up his mess." Leave it to Chief to keep the humor alive.

"Man, a caretaker? Your hands and mine will be just fine, right?"

He just grunted and shook his head.

"Give him some food and fresh water too, honey." Sandy could have done it, but she was testing him to see how he would react to her simple requests. She mentally noted that he truly didn't seem to mind.

After doggie duty, she suggested by motioning with her index finger that he follow her to the bedroom. He had never seen this part of her place because when she suddenly moved out, they were not communicating very well.

"Baby, let's take a shower together. Are you game?" *Go on now Sandy Spurring, romance your man.*

"You know I am." *You better go boy...* he thought to himself.

They embraced each other warmly and started kissing. He gently turned her around and caressed her back. Smoothly, he eased the zipper down on her dress, used his finger to expose her other shoulder and worked the dress over her hips. She had a black lace bra on with matching bikini panties. While kissing her, he unhooked her bra and tossed it over to the chair that was near her bed. He relished the look of her exposed breast suddenly missing his two special friends. He lovingly embraced one with his hand while placing his mouth on the other. Sandy moaned while he gently licked, kissed and sucked on her nipple. He felt it harden as he transitioned to the other one. After a few minutes, she stepped out of her panties as he quickly undressed.

Without a word spoken, they moved to the shower, turned on the water and kissed and caressed each other while waiting for the water to get hot.

Sandy grabbed two wash cloths, a bar of soap, and some foaming body wash. She opened the shower door, stepping inside while gently pulling him with her. They romantically washed each other with soap and body wash using a bath sponge. While they cleansed their bodies, they enjoyed the pulsating spray of the elongated shower heads. Once out of the shower, they dried each other off, walked over to her bed, pulled down the cover and then she gently pushed him down. Grabbing oil from her nightstand drawer, she lovingly rubbed him down and then herself.

"Let me do that, honey." He said.

"Okay, Baby." She lay down to be pampered by her husband.

Skillfully, Bruce started kissing her at her ankles slowly working his way up her leg, then her thighs, pausing in the middle; he touched her clitoris, and used his fingers to probe her insides. He continued to kiss her all over her body and again let his mouth enjoy the fruit of her breasts. They passionately made love like it was the very first time.

Bruce fell asleep with Sandy's head on his chest. He woke up in the middle of the night thinking, *Thank you Jesus; I know there is a God!*

Chief and his wife had pleasantly reconnected.

Chapter 25

Joseph Howard sat on the side of his wife's bed with his head bowed down as he prayed for her recovery. *God you know I haven't been the best Christian, but I want to rededicate my life to you now. My wife is unconscious and I need her to get better. I don't know how to raise girls by myself. I love my wife and I need her healed, whole and fully functioning, in Jesus' name.*

The doctor came in directly after he finished his prayer to inform him that all of Pauline's vital signs showed some improvement, but she was not out of the woods yet. The good thing was that she was no longer listed as critical, but stable. He hoped that she could be moved to a regular room within the week.

"Thank the Lord! And, Doc, I appreciate everything you have done for my wife. Everyone has been so professional and nice."

"Sir, we're here for you. I really believe your wife is going to be fine. She's young and otherwise healthy, and she has improved. Have a good day." The doctor left after reassuring him.

Joseph sat back down and started flipping the channels on the television when he heard the name Elsie Mae Coats, his sister-in-law.

The reporter said, "There are still no new leads in the case of missing Griffin housekeeper, Elsie Mae Coats. There were reports of sightings, but none have been confirmed. Reporting from the Griffin Police Department, I'm Ryan Younger."

"I hope to have some promising news about Elsie Mae to share with Pauline when she wakes up." He whispered.

After sitting with his head back for a while, Joseph dozed off; apparently he was tired from the many nights toughing it out in a hospital chair instead of going home. One of his sisters, who happened to be a stay-at-home mom, had volunteered to keep their daughters in the evenings and take them to daycare every morning until Pauline improved.

When an abrupt noise sounded, Joseph woke up in a startled panic. Turning to his wife's bed, he noticed it empty. *Where's Pauline? Oh my God, has she gotten worse?* Rushing out to the hallway, he nearly sprinted to the nurse's station. "My – wife – Pauline – Howard - is – not – in – her – room!" He was nearly out of breath.

"Let me check; yes, Mrs. Howard has been taken for some tests. That's all I can tell right now. We'll keep you informed as soon as we know the results."

"Thank you." Joseph walked down the hall to the waiting room to make a few calls. He checked on the twins and chatted with his sister; he was hoping that the girls were not too much for her. She had her own toddler to care for. She quickly put his mind at ease. "Everything is going well. Just take care of yourself and keep the faith big brother." He also called two of his other siblings, one of whom was a preacher. He wanted to request extra prayers for Pauline's swift recovery.

Joseph returned to his makeshift bed in the chair pulling the thin blanket around his neck. Miserably, he thought to himself, *I wonder will this crook ever leave my aching neck,* as he rubbed the painful spot. Sighing, he punched the pillow and eventually fell asleep.

Early the next morning, Joseph awakened while it was still dark outside. Straining to see the time on the clock hanging on the wall, he realized it was 3:45 a.m. Slouched down in the jumbo seat, he sat up and noticed that Pauline was right there, sleeping soundly. It was hard to tell in the dark, but there appeared to be fewer tubes and less machinery attached to her. He assumed that to be a good thing as he thanked God and drifted back to sleep.

The sun was extra bright that morning as he walked down the hall toward the cafeteria to grab some breakfast. Pauline was still sedated, but the doctor had come by to examine her and gave him a positive report that her condition had greatly improved. Some tubes and machines had indeed been removed, and her prognosis was good. He had an additional zeal today because his twins were being well cared for and he was assured that the love of his life, Pauline was expected to fully recover. His prayers had been answered.

I just wish I could give her some promising news about her sister Elsie Mae when she wakes up. Where are you Elsie Mae Coats? God, just like you've blessed us to hold on to Pauline, we also need Elsie Mae. And God, I've heard some horrible rumors about Elsie Mae; even if they are true, we still love her and want her home. Pauline would be devastated to lose her now. Please bring her back to us, in Jesus' name, Amen.

Joseph didn't know it at the time, but his prayers would soon be answered again. Many times in life, our breakthrough is right around the corner, so we've got to hold on until we see the change come.

Chapter 26

Elsie Mae sat in the bedroom of her hotel suite contemplating her next move. She was determined to get away from the madness that had become her life. She thought *I miss my family and my friends. Uncle Chance won't let me call home, go home or question why we are still here. Let's see...; it's been at least three weeks. Mr. and Mrs. Bennett probably think I just abandoned my job. I didn't like cleaning someone's house anyway but I would have wanted to at least give them some kind of notice. This is a mess!*

"Elsie Mae...Elsie Mae...Oh Elsie Mae!" Mia was standing in front of Elsie Mae trying to get her attention. Elsie Mae seemed to be a million miles away daydreaming, and didn't notice Mia standing near her.

Suddenly, Elsie Mae heard a noise and the wave of a little hand in front of her. The sound and the movement made her jump and snap out of her pensive state.

"Oh, I'm sorry Mia. What's going on girl?" Elsie Mae wondered, *How long was I sitting there ignoring her? This situation is making me crazy.*

"Mr. Chance said the man I worked with a few nights ago wants to see me again. You told me that if I needed something to come see you. I don't want to work with him

189

ever again. He was nice to me, but he made me hurt down there." Mia's eyes suddenly filled with tears as she looked at Elsie Mae, expecting her to have all of the answers.

I did tell this baby that I would help her. What do I say to her now? How will I get away without totally betraying Uncle Chance? Well, why would I care about him? I love him because he is my uncle, but this is more than I can handle. This is a child who needs to be with her parents, but her parents are the ones who basically sold their precious baby into this crazy world. No, they don't deserve her at all. Some other couple would have to adopt Tot. She can't go back to those insane people. What parents in their right mind would sell their child? Where will I go? Who can I call?

I can't really contact anyone; Uncle Chance would probably beat me. He may even try to kill me. I know he is nuts and does not play when it comes to the big money he makes in this business. Maybe I'll just take my money and try to buy Mia and me bus tickets to go back home. I believe on the bus no records are kept of passengers. That's what I'll do!

"When did Mr. Chance say you had to work with the man again?" Elsie Mae needed to know how much time she had to work her plan.

"At ten tonight; Ms. Elizabeth said she would be here at seven to help me get ready for him. Please don't make me do it again. I know I promised to work hard and make my mother and father proud, but I just can't do it again. I'm still hurting from the other night." Mia started trembling now from the memory of her ordeal. "Please don't make me do it; please Elsie Mae, you promised to help me."

"Don't worry Mia. I will help you. You've got to trust me though. When I tell you to come with me, don't ask any questions, just come with me. Do you understand me?"

"Yes." Mia took the back of her hand and wiped her eyes.

"And Mia, you can't talk to anyone, not even Ms. Elizabeth about me helping you. She is a really nice woman with a good heart, but she works for Mr. Chance. Her loyalties are with Mr. Chance. She is not your friend. If you want to make it to a safe place, don't say a word to anyone. Can you promise me that you will let this be our little secret?"

"I promise Elsie Mae. I won't tell anyone."

"If you tell someone, anyone, Mr. Chance will be very angry. This is very important, okay?"

"Okay; I understand."

Abruptly, the door to the suite opened. Speaking of the devil, Chance walked in.

"Elsie Mae, Elizabeth will be here at seven to get the kid ready for another job with Rich Boy. If she needs any help, make sure she has whatever she wants. I'll see you later tonight."

"Okay Mr. Chance, I'll make sure she's straight." Elsie Mae lied right through her teeth. She planned to be long gone by the time they came for Mia.

* * *

After an early dinner with all of the girls in the hotel's restaurant, Elsie Mae decided to make her getaway. She told Mia to come with her, explaining to the other girls that Tot, as the girl was fondly called, had an important "date."

Some of them nodded their heads and others winked at Elsie Mae. They didn't appear to be the least bit concerned for the young girl, like Elsie Mae was. Perhaps they just did not feel comfortable discussing the situation because all of them were intimidated by Chance and his possibly brutal

191

retaliation for anyone who crossed him. And if you voiced your opinion, you couldn't be sure if someone would tell on you. Everyone wanted to be seen as a team player.

Elsie Mae thought, *Surely, some of these women understand that it is not only illegal, but also dead wrong to involve an innocent child with this foolishness. I can't be the only one with a sliver of morality left. I may be a whore, but I'm no child abuser. This is abuse if I've ever seen or heard about abuse. Bless little Mia's heart, she honestly thinks that being with her parents would be a good thing. They are the very ones who got her mixed up in this twisted dilemma. They sold their child for a fat check! Who does that? They don't deserve her in their life. I don't know how I'm going to pull this off, but I've got to at least try to get her away. I'm tired of living this way myself, but even if I don't make it out of tricking, I'm determined to set this baby free.*

"Snap out of it, trick!" The mean foreigner that had man-handled Elsie Mae before, named Louie, was speaking to her in a very rude manner. A patron at a table two over from theirs looked offended by his hostile tone.

Suddenly, Elsie Mae's attention was brought back to where she was - in a five star Birmingham, Alabama hotel with a host of prostitutes who were determined to ignore the elephant in the room - a minor who was being pimped out like a willing adult woman.

"Are you talking to me?" Elsie Mae sometimes forgot that it was not common knowledge among the women or the hired help that she was the pimp's niece.

"Yes I am! Do you have a problem with it?" he barked at her without regard to her feelings or of the apparent classy atmosphere they were in.

Elsie Mae thought about what she was planning to do that evening and she didn't want to bring attention to herself or a reprimand from her Uncle Chance, so she humbled

192

herself and said, "I'm sorry, I was preoccupied. What do you need Mr. Louie?" She used wisdom and spoke respectfully so that he would leave her alone.

"That's better!" He hissed while bucking his eyes at her. "Elizabeth will not be available until later so I'll need you to make sure Mia is bathed and dolled up until Elizabeth can come and approve her appearance. Make it happen!" He seemed to be happy that the good little whore recognized her place under his authority. What a jerk!

"No problem." Elsie Mae immediately thought, *That's just perfect for my escape. Mia and I will be alone.*

"Come on Mia, we need to get busy," she announced this in front of everybody while holding her breath that the child would remember that she wanted to help her. Apparently, nobody had gotten wind of the plot to go back to Georgia.

Mia waved goodbye to the others in the group and took Elsie Mae by the hand. They quickly walked to the elevator as if in preparation for the set up "date" with the business man. Little did the others realize it, Elsie Mae planned to be on a bus heading home. She didn't know what she would do once she got there because her Uncle Chance knew where to find her. She just knew that she was on a mission to save Mia. It was the right thing to do.

They went into the suite and Elsie Mae quickly packed a small duffle bag with her most treasured belongings. She then helped Mia pick the items that she just didn't want to leave behind and they exited the suite, trying not to look too suspicious. Elsie Mae anxiously rode the elevator not knowing how to calm her nerves. Though afraid of being caught, she had to at least try to get the girl away.

Elsie Mae and Mia made it to the lobby without running into any of the other women or any of Chance's staff. Elsie Mae had already counted her money and knew that she had about three hundred dollars which would more than cover the bus tickets.

Miraculously, they not only made it to the main lobby, but through the massive atrium with Elsie Mae constantly, but discreetly looking over her shoulders.

When they made it outside, she figured they were home free. Flagging down a taxi, they got inside and told the man that they wanted to go to the closest bus station. He said okay and drove them there without incident.

Once in the bus station, Elsie Mae told Mia to sit on an end seat that was near the ticket desk and watch the bags. Since the pieces they chose were small, they were not planning to place them underneath the bus, but they were going to carry them on board with them. The bus would be leaving in one hour and thirty-five minutes.

Elsie Mae was starting to calm down when Mia made an announcement. "I'm sleepy Elsie Mae; do you think I can take a nap before we leave?"

"Sure child; take a nap. Just lay your head on my shoulder."

"Okay, thank you Elsie Mae. And, thank you for taking me back to my mommy and daddy.

Bless her little naïve heart! I wouldn't turn her back over to those sick people if I had to raise her myself. The minute we cross over into Georgia and I get home, I'm going to call Child Protective Services and report everything but my Uncle Chance's name. I can't betray him, but I can't let this madness continue. However, Elsie Mae could not share with the poor child the depravity of her parents. That would be too much for the child to understand, and certainly not her place to do.

Verbally, she just concurred with the girl to put her mind at ease. "Okay Tot, I know they will be glad to see you too." Sometimes you can't tell everything you know.

Within minutes the young girl was asleep. Elsie Mae had just started to relax and opened up a magazine to read until time to board the bus.

After about an hour, an announcement was made that it was time to board their bus. She looked at her watch to check the time and glanced back at the article she was reading. Suddenly, Elsie Mae felt a violent jolt of her arm.

"What the…." She looked up and was just about to curse somebody out when she found herself looking into the eyes of evil Louie! He was on her right side and her Uncle Chance was also there, glaring at her with the wicked stance of an enemy, not the love of a relative.

Since they were in a public place, Chance guarded his choice of words knowing strangers were listening. "What do you think you're doing? Where in the hell do you think you are going with that girl?"

Elsie Mae immediately looked down, unable to answer him. She knew there would be hell to pay once they got back to the hotel; she just didn't know how horrific the assault would be.

Chapter 27

Evil Louie held Elsie Mae's arm in a brutal grip. He roughly moved her through the crowd of people that watched them walk toward the vestibule. Once outside, the cool air felt good on Elsie Mae's face despite the overwhelming anxiety she felt contemplating her probable punishment.

Mia was oblivious to what just happened. She seemed happy to see Mr. Chance because he was the man responsible for all of the toys, clothes, shoes, the video gaming system and games that were given to her. Mia was a naïve child, therefore, she didn't make the connection that he was a big part of the problem. Chance preferred it that way. Unfortunately, Mia was about to see a different side of him. It was his dark side- one rarely seen by any of the women.

Chance held Mia's left hand while she carried her bag and stuffed animal in her other arm. She didn't look the least bit worried or disappointed. Ironically, his presence made her relax. Mia was too young to realize the demons operating within him; believing his duplicity, assuming he was a good man. What a deceptive mask he wore, hiding his depraved character.

"Elsie Mae..." Mia started to ask her something, but since she didn't know what the child was going to say, she discreetly indicated for Mia to be quiet by raising her index finger to her mouth. Elsie Mae knew Chance was furious and she didn't want to add fuel to the fire.

Mia thought, *I wonder what's wrong with Elsie Mae. Mr. Chance doesn't look too happy. I guess I can't go home yet. I want to see my mommy. I thought I could do the job, but Mommy didn't tell me that it would hurt this bad. I want to see my Mom!*

Elsie Mae's body stiffened as soon as Chance's driver pulled the shiny black Navigator with the extra dark tinted windows around the corner. Until that moment, there was a crowd of witnesses all around her, staring at the scene. When the vehicle pulled up to the curb, Chance and Mia got in behind the passenger seat. Elsie Mae was roughly pushed into the third row where evil Louie sat beside her.

As soon as the vehicle pulled away from the curb, Elsie Mae felt the force of the first blow upside her head. Evil Louie punched her repeatedly on her head, jaw, arms, and chest. Elsie Mae released blood-curling screams from the horrible assault.

Mia immediately started crying and pleading with Chance saying, "Mr. Chance, please make him stop! Please don't blame Elsie Mae. It's my fault...I wanted to go see my Mommy. Please make him stop! I'll do the job! I'll do it! I just wanted to see my family!"

Chance sat motionless with a blank expression, seemingly unconcerned about Elsie Mae's plight or the whimpering and pleas of the young girl. After about a minute, Chance raised his right hand which apparently was evil Louie's signal to stop the abusive attack. Elsie Mae rubbed the throbbing on the side of her head as she wiped a small stream of blood that oozed from her nose. Although Elsie Mae was weeping bitterly, she thought, *These brutal blows are not going to stop me! I'm going to find a way to get Mia out of this mess. I chose crazy, she didn't have a choice. God, if you'll help me get this child out of this nightmare, I promise eventually, I'll change my ways. I've got to save her from this abuse, and you've got to save me from myself!*

* * *

When they got back to the hotel, the driver went to a service entrance in the rear of the building. Obviously, they had called ahead and had the connections to get an emergency exit door opened from the inside.

Evil Louie walked Mia into the building and Chance stayed behind to yell at Elsie Mae.

"Haven't I given you everything you could ever want? Why would you betray me like this? I don't believe you! I give you my best clients and I don't even work you as hard as the others! You are my niece – my flesh and blood and you do this! How low can you go? You disrespected me in front of my staff! If you weren't my niece, I would've beaten you myself. You know how much I detest a traitor! You'll regret this Elsie Mae! And, I'm not through with you!" With each declaration, she shrunk lower in the car's seat, uncertain if he would strike her anyway for good measure.

"ELSIE MAE, WHAT DO YOU HAVE TO SAY FOR YOURSELF?" Chance yelled at her and looked like he would hit her any minute. The veins in his neck seemed to pop out, his eyes were bucked, and he was breathing hard.

Feeling ashamed for betraying him, and afraid of his wrath if she said the wrong thing, Elsie Mae chose not to answer him verbally. She simply looked down and just shook her head from side to side in a silent reply as tears rolled down her face. Elsie Mae really didn't have anything to say. What could she say that he would approve of? Her eye was sore and she could feel it swelling. Elsie Mae figured it was black from her beating. She sadly thought, *It will probably take a long time for my skin to heal.*

At Chance's signal, the driver opened the car door and the two occupants swiftly exited without saying a word. Silently, they walked into the hotel and proceeded to his suite where he continued his rant about loyalty and her breach of his trust.

Suddenly, Chance moved toward Elsie Mae with a clenched fist to strike her. Just before making contact, he backed away and said, "Get out of my sight! I'll deal with you later!" He then moved from the living room of his suite to the bedroom, dismissing Elsie Mae with his harsh words and a disgusted wave of his hand. Although Chance had ordered her beating, now he detached himself from the reality of it: he rationalized that he hadn't personally hit Elsie Mae. His twisted love for her as an uncle outweighed the anger he now felt toward her as her boss.

* * *

Elsie Mae quickly walked out of the foyer of her Uncle Chance's VIP suite aching both physically and emotionally. He had made some comments that broke her heart. As soon as his door closed, she began crying a sea of tears. Not wanting to appear weak, Elsie Mae swiftly walked through the hallway to her corner suite. Once safely inside, she was doubled-over with pain from her beating and regret – about getting caught. By the time Elsie Mae had been released from Chance's suite and back in hers, Mia was already gone. Looking at her watch, Elsie Mae realized that it was a little too early for her to already be with the client. She thought, *I wonder where they've taken her. Maybe the "date" time changed.*

Mia was being forced to entertain and fulfill the deplorable, lustful fantasies of a rich foreign man. In this country he would be called a pedophile, but in his country he was just called privileged. This organized ring of a pimp, hookers and their clients were willingly contributing to the delinquency of a minor. Elsie Mae had seen enough. She had made a promise to Mia and her effort had backfired. Though her battered body was suffering behind her attempt to escape and recue the young girl, she was still determined to try something else – anything to set the girl free.

Elsie Mae reflected, *Uncle Chance said he's not finished with me...I wonder what else he's going to do? It doesn't matter; I'm going to figure out how to escape! I've been tricking for over four years. Eventually, I want a husband and children. How will I ever have a normal family, living like this? It's time for a change. No, Uncle Chance, you won't have me to pimp out much longer. I've got a new attitude and it doesn't include living this lifestyle. I'm tired of just existing! I want to enjoy my life. Enough is enough.*

Elsie Mae wondered, *How did Uncle Chance find where we were? Does he know people at the bus station? Did he have me followed? I've never seen him so enraged, at least not directed at me! He could kill me the next time. Would he do that? What am I going to do? I'm determined to get Mia out of this insanity. Let me think...*

* * *

While Elsie Mae was contemplating her next move, her uncle Chance was down the hall handling his illicit business. Grabbing his cell phone, he dialed a number tapping a pen on his desk mat while waiting for an answer.

"Hello Mr. Chance. How may I assist you?" The member of the hotel's security staff had Chance's cell number saved in his phone's contact list.

"Come to my suite within the next ten minutes." Chance directed.

"Yes, I'll be right up." The security guard muttered a few words to a fellow co-worker asking him to watch his group of monitor screens in the sophisticated security station. He then checked his watch, waited a few minutes, and then proceeded to meet his unofficial boss.

When the guy reached Chance's suite and thumped the coded three knocks – pause – one knock routine, Chance's assistant opened the door and lead the uniformed man through the plush suite, to the oversized desk near the window with the picturesque view.

Chance said, "Man, thanks for looking out for me. She would have gotten away if you were not so diligent. Not only did you notice them leaving, you followed them. Keep up the good work!"

"You are welcome." The man silently hoped for a decent payment for his efforts. He didn't have to wait long and he wasn't disappointed.

Chance ended the meeting by placing five crisp one hundred dollar bills into the man's hand affirming his approval with his actions.

The man's eyes widened as he said, "Thank you Mr. Chance. You know I'll keep an eye out for the girls." The man was all smiles, quite pleased with his side hustle. The money was substantially more than his daily pay from his job; not bad for being a snitch! Clearly, the man had a renewed incentive to be an observant spy.

Arrogantly, Chance said, "No problem, and, there's plenty more for a job well done." Chance was the master manipulator; ladies of the night, flunkies, abusers, and spies, were all being controlled by a crooked, criminal leader. As he had reminded Elsie Mae, he literally had extra sets of eyes in the least expected places.

Chapter 28

The next day in Georgia was extremely busy in Ginger's clothing store. She had advertised a twenty percent discount off all price tags that were over a month old in the local newspaper and the bargain hunters were excited to shop for deals. Ginger, Brea and another part-time worker were "earning their keep" that day.

Around noon, the crowd was near the capacity limit that the fire marshal had imposed and Ginger did her best to get the tickets written and the people checked out as quickly as possible. She had a smile on her face just contemplating what her gross sales would be. *I should have gone into this business sooner. I would have if I'd known how lucrative it would be.*

At about twelve-forty the chime on the door sounded and a florist truck arrived. A woman walked in and asked for Mrs. Ginger Graham. Ginger had just finished writing up a ticket and thanking the customer. Upon hearing her name, she glanced up to see the delivery woman smile.

"I'm Ginger, are those for me?" It really was an odd question because the woman had just asked for her.

"Yes madam they are, and they are beautiful! I just need for you to sign this form and I'll be out of your way."

While the woman was talking, Ginger was already making her way to the front of the shop to accept the massive bouquet of red roses, baby's breath, fern and eucalyptus sprigs which were strategically arrayed in an intricate design. She noted that the beautiful ceramic vase would be a perfect complement to her foyer credenza.

Even though Ginger didn't need to read the card because she knew who the flowers were from, she did. The roses were from Keefer and the card read, 'I love you and I miss you; your husband, Keefer.'

"Look at you Ginger! You've got to start sharing your secrets of how to get and keep a man! Wow! Diamond earrings on one day and how many, looks like two dozen roses plus a designer arrangement, the next day! You've got it going on Boss Lady." Brea was beside herself.

"Well, I wouldn't say all of that, but that is a gorgeous arrangement. Thank you, Brea." Ginger turned to place the rose bouquet in the center of a large table that had trinkets for sale on it.

One of the customers commented, "Wow; that is a stunning flower arrangement, and it was so sweet of him. I haven't received roses or any other flowers from my old man in at least five years- the unromantic bum!"

Every woman that was close enough to hear the comment started laughing and adding her two-cent's worth to the pity party of neglected wives and girlfriends.

One said, "Yeah, it's been so long for me that if he brought some home tonight, I'd think he cheated or something. He used to send flowers to my job and home, but all of that stopped once we got married. Ain't that about nothing?"

A middle aged lady with the finesse of an actress said, "Well ladies, I guess I just got used to being the rose of the house, because my husband forgets my birthday and anniversary now. Unless I make a stink about it, he sits on his butt and assumes I'll always be there. However, it's okay because I get to use the credit card anytime I want too. These clothes will just have to be my bouquet of flowers. That's it ladies, new clothes and shoes last longer anyway!" She was quite amused herself as she placed the credit card on the counter to pay for her three suits, one dress, and four skirts.

A young twenty-something woman holding a skirt and sweater while waiting to check out had looked down at what she could afford and commented, "It must be nice because everybody ain't able." High fives went up.

"An older woman finally broke the stream of disappointed rhetoric by saying, "My Ernie always brings me a single rose every Sunday morning with my coffee and the Sunday newspaper. He always says, 'It may be just one, but it represents that you are the only one for me.' Yes, ladies, the good Lord broke the mold when he made my Ernie." The woman smiled as she reflected on her awesome husband.

Ginger thought, *If Brea only knew the truth of what I'm dealing with. These are the surprise gifts of a guilty man who is trying to come back home. The card says, 'your husband, Keefer.' He's too busy trying to connect with every other woman he meets. I know he's trying, but is his effort sincere, or is he just playing games? It's hard to tell.*

Well, this is a gorgeous arrangement. New diamond earrings in my ears, now a two dozen, designer floral arrangement. Keefer is really trying to make it up to me. Should I let him have another chance? Am I crazy for even thinking about it? Or, am I a glutton for punishment? Sadly, I'm just a fool in love with a man that's a lunatic! Let me call my therapist before I end up on the news. Ginger actually called and made an appointment for the following week; nothing was available before then.

"Marriage is for grown folks, not immature imposters! I probably should get the hell on with my life!"

Chapter 29

Chief Spurring received a call from his doctor's office asking him to come back in for some tests. They had identified the reason for his constant urination. He had a condition called benign prostatic hyperplasia which is the swelling of the prostate. The doctor wanted to examine him again and also tell him about treatment options. And, like his family, he was borderline diabetic. The doctor advised him to lose about fifty pounds, drink more water and start power walking at least four times a week. All of the suggestions and advice seemed pretty reasonable to Chief Spurring. He left the office feeling at peace that he had gone to the doctor and at least he now knew the state of his health. *I thank the Lord for a good wife. Even though I was a complete jerk about taking care of myself, she refused to allow my bad attitude to cause her to care any less. That's my Sandy! I'll have to share my health update with her later. I wonder would she want to go to lunch today. Let me just give her a call.*

Dialing her phone number, he reminisced about their recent night together; dinner, dancing, and love making into the night. "I've got to get my wife back home so we can always enjoy each other's company, not just once in a while."

"Hi Bruce, how are you today?" Sandy was working on her novel, trying hard to finish it by the deadline that the publishing company had set.

"I'm better now that I hear your voice Sandy. Are you real busy today?"

"Well, yes I'm pretty busy trying to finish the book. Actually, I'm proofreading and adding a few lines here and there before submitting it to my agent. What did you have in mind?" Sandy pulled off her eyeglasses and leaned back in her seat. *It is good to take a break from the computer screen,* she thought to herself.

"Well, it's a beautiful day and I want to take you out to lunch. What do you think? Can you take a lunch break?"

Tilting her head, she thought, *It would be nice for a change to get out of the house and dine with my husband. I think I'll take him up on it.*

"Bruce, that sounds like a lovely idea. What time can you go?" She pushed back her plush leather desk chair from the desk and started walking towards her bathroom suite to get ready.

"How about noon, is that good for you? I guess they'll just die at the station when they see me leave for a real lunch."

"Baby, being a writer makes my schedule flexible. Noon is fine. Do you need me to meet you someplace since you are working?" Sandy was always very considerate.

"Baby, that's why they pay me the big bucks; I can take my time when I do go out. You must not realize you're dealing with the Griffin City Police Chief. Woman, recognize who you've got in your corner. In fact, I've got your back, your side and your front covered, if you know what I mean! And no, I'm a gentleman, so therefore, I'll pick you up."

Laughing, she said, "Bruce, you're a mess. I'll be ready, see you then."

"Okay, Baby." Chief was feeling happy. He started whistling as he walked outside of his office door, saw Maritza and told her to have everyone except the officer at the front door to come to the conference room for a meeting. Then he grabbed his folder and strutted down the hall, whistling and feeling like a young man in love.

His secretary Maritza noticed her boss and assumed from his demeanor that he and his wife were working on their marriage. *I just hope they get back together soon. He is so much more pleasant when he's with Mrs. Spurring.*

Sandy pulled a yellow, green and white spaghetti strap sundress out of her closet and reached above her head for the box with her Jimmy Choo crystal encrusted instep sandals. The crystals shimmered cream, yellow, orange and green as the sun hit them. "These are the perfect shoes for this dress, if I do say so myself!" She then stepped in the shower to freshen up for her lunch date.

* * *

Chief Bruce Spurring pulled up to the townhome of his wife feeling good about the likelihood that they would reconcile their relationship. He had learned a lot about her, and, more importantly, had personally grown. He vowed to himself and to her to be a better husband, the second time around with the same good woman.

When Sandy opened the door, she looked as sweet as the taste of peach cobbler, shoulders bare, sporting a cute sundress. His eyes scanned her entire frame and paused at her tiny feet. She was wearing some interesting shoes and her feet were freshly pedicured.

"As always girl, you take my breath away. How are you?" He stepped closer and took her by the hand.

"I'm good, Bruce, and you?" Sandy looked deep into his eyes, in love more today than the day before.

"I'm wonderful, honey. Give me a hug." He pulled her toward him and they tenderly embraced. Taking in her scent, he commented. "You are looking good and smelling good. Sandy, you know I have to go back to work!"

"Man, and so do I; let's go eat Big Boy. There'll be plenty of time for all of that!" She touched his face with her open hand and tenderly planted a kiss on his cheek. "I really do love you, Bruce. I'm glad we're working on us."

"I am too, Sugar." He then embraced her again, quickly kissed her on the forehead and said, "Now Mrs. Spurring, let's go eat!"

"Let's; where are we going this time?" *My man is so classy; I wonder where we're going today.*

"You'll see. I assure you, you'll love it." The Chief was sure she'd enjoy it.

* * *

Chief Spurring had driven his personal car to pick up Sandy for lunch. They laughed and talked on the way and also discussed their daughter Robbie who was in an in-house rehabilitation facility for addiction to drugs and alcohol. Sandy and Chief Spurring were concerned, but they were told that she couldn't have visitors for the first six weeks. It was a tough procedure and meant for the patients to realize the isolation that their loved ones must feel when they are on a selfish high, thinking only of themselves. After about twenty minutes, Chief Spurring pulled up in front of a quaint little Italian restaurant that was once their favorite eating spot.

"Bruce, you remembered! I haven't been here in years. I don't know why, I guess it's because there are so many other places to frequent. This is perfect!"

"Stick with me kiddo, I'll show you things you only dreamed about!" *Yeah, I'm showing her how a man is supposed to treat his woman. I'm lucky she hadn't left me before she did. I was stuck on going to work, eventually coming home, and going to sleep. It probably drove her stir crazy because Sandy loves to stay on the go. I'll just have to make it up to her.*

Sandy had her own reasons to reflect, "*Look at my husband, planning dinners, lunches; sending flowers. He was a good husband. Maybe this separation has made him realize you really can't be totally married to your job when you have a spouse! That only works when you're a single person. I understand he loves his career, but I needed some time and attention too, for crying out-loud! I believe he finally gets it now. He's spending more time with me – the woman, not just being in the house with the cook, house keeper, bill payer, and errand runner. I wanted time alone with him, and, it looks like we now can be on the same page and truly enjoy each other; better late than never.*

When they entered the restaurant, they were greeted by a thirty-something hostess who walked them to a corner table. She placed the menus down and informed them that their server would be right with them.

The server came and Bruce ordered an Italian salad and meat lasagna; Sandy ordered salami mixed Italian salad and veal and eggplant parmesan. The portions were huge and the food tasted delicious.

Sandy said, "That was scrumptious and I have enough left over for my lunch tomorrow. Thanks so much Bruce. This was an excellent choice."

"I'm glad you enjoyed it. They do give you enough for two meals which is a bonus. They have a good crowd at lunch and even more diners at dinner. We'll come again."

"Definitely, Baby; are you ready to go back to work?"

"Yes, it's that time, Sweetheart." Suddenly, Chief received a call from the station. "Yes Maritza, what is it?"

"Sir, you have an important call on the line. It's a woman who says it is an extremely important tip about an exploited little girl. She won't speak to anyone else but you, and, she won't leave her number. I have her on hold. What should I tell her?"

"Give her my cell number and let her know that I'm standing by waiting for her call. If she doesn't like that, mention that I'll be back in the office in one hour. Maritza, call me back either way and let me know."

"Yes Chief." Maritza clicked back over to the woman on the phone, but all she heard was a dial tone; the woman had hung up. Maritza tried to return the call, but she was connected to the hotel switchboard. The operator told her that the call came from a rotating router system and there would be no way to immediately tell which of the six hundred guest suites, regular room phones, or office phones could have made the call.

Dialing his number again, she gave him the news. "We lost her chief; maybe she got spooked."

"Okay Maritza, the first time I go out for lunch in months, I get a possible lead in a case. I'll be back in about thirty-five minutes. Out."

"See you then." Maritza couldn't help wondering what the tip would be. *The woman on the phone sounded really stressed out.*

* * *

212

Simultaneously, across the state line in Alabama, Evil Louie had just walked into the suite where Elsie Mae was. Startled, she abruptly hung up the phone. She had picked up the phone in her hotel suite to call the Griffin city police department. She had finally gotten up the nerve to call for help for Mia, but the Chief was out of the office.

"WHO ARE YOU TRYING TO CALL?" Louie yelled at the top of his lungs.

"I was trying to call Ms. Elizabeth, why do you ask?" Although her nerves were wrecked, Elsie Mae hoped that she sounded believable.

"WOMAN, YOU ARE LYING!" He angrily started walking toward her and then viciously struck her with his fist. She screamed out in pain and fell to the floor.

"MR. CHANCE WILL HURT YOU FOR HITTING ME! IF HE DIDN'T GIVE YOU THE ORDER TO BEAT ME, YOU CAN'T TOUCH ME!" Elsie Mae was not afraid and screamed right back at him.

"You're nothing, but a whore! Come here, it's been a while for me! He started unbuckling his belt and quickly unzipped his pants.

"NO! STOP!" Elsie Mae knew that this was against her Uncle Chance's rules. The staff members were not to touch the women.

He violently grabbed Elsie Mae by her arm, drawing her to him, saying, "Don't fight the feeling, I've seen how you look at me! It's not like this is not what you do!"

"I SAID STOP!" Elsie Mae got strength from some place inside as she struggled with him. He tore off her shirt; buttons flew into the air and down to the floor. "STOP!"

He had Elsie Mae pinned down on the floor when abruptly the suite door opened and the sound of a gun exploded.

Evil Louie grabbed his shoulder and winched in pain.

"WHAT THE HELL DO YOU THINK YOU'RE DOING? YOU KNOW MY RULES! SURELY YOU WERE NOT ABOUT TO TOUCH ONE OF MY GIRLS! AND IF ANY, NOT THIS ONE! SHE'S MY NEICE! THIS TIME, YOU HAVE A FLESH WOUND; THE NEXT TIME IT WILL BE YOUR LIFE IF YOU EVER TOUCH HER AGAIN. DO I MAKE MYSELF CLEAR?"

"Sir, my apologies." Evil Louie got to his feet holding his shoulder as blood seeped through his shirt. With his other hand, he was holding up his pants that he had opened.

Suddenly Elsie Mae yelled, "HE HIT ME IN MY HEAD WITH HIS FIST TOO!"

"WHAT?" Turning to Louie, he said, "IS THAT TRUE, LOUIE?" Chance was past furious!

Louie was too ashamed and afraid to answer Chance. He knew he had really messed up, and didn't open his mouth.

Chance knew the answer by Louie's lack of reply. As he walked pass his boss, Chance struck him with the butt of the pistol up-side his head.

Elsie Mae found herself thinking, 'Oops Up-Side The Head; Oops Up-Side The Head.' She wanted to laugh, but her head was still hurting and the situation was serious any time Uncle Chance had used his gun.

After striking Louie with the butt of the gun, Chance then raised his foot and violently kicked him. Evil Louie fell forward to the floor, bumping his shoulder, he groaned in pain, but quickly recovered and limped out the door.

Elsie Mae thought to herself *I thought I had never seen Uncle Chance so angry when he caught me at the bus station - he is worse now. Evil Louie is lucky Uncle Chance didn't kill him!*

Chance looked at her now with a slither of compassion. "Elsie Mae, if he ever touches you again, I'll kill him. Don't get things twisted though, I'm still angry with you for trying to take Mia away, but I won't let anyone hurt you. Just don't ever cross me again!"

"Yes." Elsie Mae was secretly glad that Chief Spurring wasn't in the office when she called because Evil Louie would have informed Chance about her conversation, if he had overheard it.

"I still love you Elsie Mae, you are my niece, but I can't have traitors in my business family. Do you hear me?"

"Yes, Uncle Chance, I know. May I ask you something?"

"Yes you can, what is it?" Chance was furious with Louie and still upset with Elsie Mae, but she was still his niece, and blood is thicker than water.

"How did you know where to find Mia and me?" Elsie Mae had wanted to ask him that question ever since she had been caught, but she knew that would just make him angrier if she had asked him the exact same day that she was caught.

"Elsie Mae I have eyes in the back of my head and many extra sets everywhere. You of all people should know that by now. Now get dressed and we'll talk later."

She just sadly shook her head and thought, *If what he just said is true, how will I ever get out of this mess? How will I get Mia to safety? I've got to figure out something!*

Chapter 30

The next day, Elsie Mae sat on the sofa in her hotel suite waiting for Elizabeth to come out of the room with Mia. The rich business man was leaving on an afternoon flight and he wanted to spend some more time with Mia before leaving. Elsie Mae was now desperate to help the poor child, but she didn't know what to do next. Her plan to escape had backfired and she was caught red-handed at the bus station with the young girl.

"What am I going to do?" Elsie Mae spoke out loud, but abruptly, she remembered her own questions about whether the suite she stayed in was wired with listening devices, commonly known as bugs. She got quiet deciding to brainstorm inwardly to ensure her thoughts remained just that, reflections of Elsie Mae Coats.

Elsie Mae reasoned, *Could this suite be bugged? How did Uncle Chance really know where to find Mia and me? I asked him how he knew where we were, but I didn't get a straight answer. He warned me that he has 'eyes in the back of his head and many extra sets everywhere.' Scary thought. I wonder who told on me. The other women were all in the restaurant when we left so I don't think it was one of them. Could he have paid off the hotel concierge or the front desk clerks to recognize his girls and to immediately report any suspicious activity to him? All I know is that Uncle Chance was furious with me and I don't want to get on his bad side by pressing my luck in a second escape attempt. Then, when I tried to make a rescue call, I nearly got raped by Evil Louie. This is the epitome of crazy! This morning, Uncle Chance verbally warned me again about his intolerance for disloyal business or family members. I already know how much he really loves his actual relatives. I guess that's what saved my life. What can I do to help Mia without getting caught for a second time?*

Elsie Mae shook her head and continued to consider her options, *Let me think...should I try to make a second call? I've got to hand it to Uncle Chance; that was really smart of him to take our cell phones away from us. This would have already been over if I could have used my cellphone to make a quick call to Chief Spurring for help.*

An alarming image suddenly caught her attention; it was of her mother sitting with her head in her hands concerned about her youngest daughter. Although Elsie Mae didn't talk to her mother every day, she at least checked in with her once or twice a week. This trip was now over two weeks old, and with no calls from Elsie Mae, her mother would recognize that as highly unusual. If nobody else cared, Mrs. Beatrice Coats was definitely worried sick by now. *I bet my voicemail is full too. What is my dad thinking? Both of my parents are probably worried to death. Do I dare try to make another call?*

Out of the blue, she thought, *Oh no, maybe, Uncle Chance has all of the phones and the suites tapped so that he can hear every bit of our conversations? I'll have to be more discreet in what I say to the others.*

She paused for a quick word of silent prayer; *'What can I do Lord? Please help me get Mia to safety.'*

217

Maybe I can take a taxi to a Wal-Mart and get one of the pre-pay phones and try calling the Griffin City Police Station again. But, Uncle Chance says he has 'eyes in the back of his head and extra sets in other places.' I've got to do something. What if I were that little girl? I can't imagine my parents selling me into a lifetime of prostitution – that's just insanity!

While Elsie Mae was in her beautiful hotel suite worried about Mia and contemplating how to help her; she had no idea that Chief Spurring and his staff were investigating her anonymous tip. They earnestly wanted to solve the alleged crime and rescue the endangered child.

* * *

Chief Spurring, Captain Reid, and the Sergeant Hall met in the precinct's conference room to review their daily reports, discuss open cases, and to ascertain the meaning behind the call referencing an alleged exploited young girl. Once their meeting was over, Chief Spurring delegated to Captain Reid to gather the police officers into the station's roll call room.

Chief Spurring and Captain Reid stood in front of the staff next to the first line supervisor, Sergeant Hall who spoke to the police officers. "Now officers, we received a call from an unidentified woman yesterday referencing an alleged, exploited little girl. We have reviewed all of our case data and don't have any record of a missing girl at this time. Maritza said the woman sounded stressed out, and when she placed the lady on hold to call Chief Spurring, just like that, the caller was gone. That's not much to go on, but it is a lead in a possible case."

Officer Minor raised his hand and asked, "Sergeant Hall, do we know the child's name, age or any identifying details on the lead?" He had his small notebook out ready to write notes.

Chief Spurring stepped toward the microphone and spoke up, "Unfortunately, I didn't get to talk to her. All we know right now is that the call came from a fancy hotel in Birmingham, Alabama. We have ordered the phone records to verify which suite the informant was in to make the call. The local police department is working that part for us. We believe it's somehow connected here in Griffin, Georgia, because the woman asked for me by name. We should have the information by this afternoon if their police department is worth its salt."

Sergeant Hall continued, "Minor, I want you to take the lead on this case and report back to me as soon as you hear something."

"Yes." Officer Minor motioned to his partner in a hand gesture that only the two of them understood. Maritza passed a folder to Officer Minor that Chief Spurring had given her earlier with the hotel name and address, phone number, police jurisdiction, fellow officer information, name of the hotel's head security person and the public relations liaison that would be the point of contact during the investigation.

After the meeting was adjourned, Officer Minor went to his cubicle and started making calls to follow-up with the information that he was given. Fortunately, they soon had a break in the case.

* * *

By that afternoon, the Birmingham, Alabama police department had sent a plain-clothed, female undercover officer and backup to the luxury hotel. They were racing against time hoping that the anonymous woman, who called with the tip, was still a guest in the hotel. The particular room where the call originated was part of a block of suites which were registered to a company, Chance Enterprises, Incorporated. A cross reference showed that the company was listed as a professional massage agency based out of Atlanta, Georgia. When Officer Minor read that information, he immediately thought, *I bet they're giving out more than messages, and they are across the state line doing it!*

The undercover female officer was now dressed just like the hotel's housekeepers. She was cautiously walking through the beautiful hallway, headed for the suite that had been identified by the hung up call. For security, she was strapped with a miniature wireless microphone. She was also "packed" with a 9mm standard issued firearm. She braced herself as she reached the designated door.

Tap, tap, tap, went the usual three knocks of the knuckles to get the guest's attention, accompanied by the announcement, "Housekeeping!"

Surprised, Elsie Mae glanced around the room and noted that the suite had already been cleaned. Her first thought was to ignore the sound at the door, but suddenly she remembered that the knocking would continue, and then the maid would let herself in. Elsie Mae decided to reply.

"I didn't request housekeeping. The room is already cleaned." Elsie Mae spoke through the closed door.

"My supervisor mentioned a detail that the normal housekeeper didn't finish. I promise I will not take long."

"Well, I can't imagine what she didn't do because the room looks immaculate." As Elsie Mae was complimenting the appearance of the suite, she had simultaneously opened the door.

The very attractive housekeeper came in pushing a cart which was loaded down with all of the normal cleaning supplies; a stack of freshly laundered, plush beige colored towels, an array of toiletries, shower caps, soaps, beige bath robes and matching house shoes.

Once the woman whose nametag said "Misty" was totally in the suite and the cart had cleared the entranceway, the woman suddenly put her index finger on her lips and flashed a police officer's badge in front of Elsie Mae. She then eased up the uniform blouse to reveal a revolver that sat in a leather holster. She had a smile on her face to ensure the guest she was staring at would realize she was there to help.

Startled, Elsie Mae gasped and quickly recovered to compose herself. The woman then held up a note that said, 'Are you the woman that attempted to call the Griffin City Police Department? We have reason to believe that your suite has been rigged with listening devices- bugs. For your safety, please don't say a word.'

The woman then passed a pen to Elsie Mae who nervously wrote the word, 'Yes' on the pad.

The policewoman wrote, 'What is your name?'

Elsie Mae lied by writing her alias name, 'My name is Gina.' It was the same name that she had used with the stranger in the lobby. Elsie Mae thought it was a cute name so she stuck with it. She was worried that if she gave her real name, her Uncle Chance would somehow find out she was responsible for Mia's escape.

The policewoman scribbled a note on a smaller pad, the name 'Gina,' and then wrote on their mutual spiral notebook, 'Is the young girl that you mentioned who is being exploited, still on the property?'

Elsie Mae wrote, 'Yes.'

The female cop then wrote two questions, 'Where is the girl now? What is the alleged exploitation?'

To that question, Elsie Mae wrote, 'She is in the second bedroom, being prepared to service a very rich client. She's being pimped out as a hooker. It's wrong and I want to help her get free!'

The female officer penned. 'Are you afraid for your safety?'

Elsie Mae emphasized her fear by writing in all caps, 'I'M VERY FRIGHTENED! I DON'T WANT TO BE NAMED IN THIS. I FEAR FOR MY LIFE!"

The woman wrote, 'No problem, I've got you. Don't be afraid. Who is with the girl?'

Elsie Mae wrote back, 'A woman named Elizabeth who seems to be a good person who does a horrible job. She seems bothered by this just like me, but neither of us could do anything. I took a chance to call, but Chief Spurring was not in the office at the time.'

The officer then wrote, 'No problem, madam. You did a brave thing. We are here to help the child. Now, I want you to say out loud, "I'll be back, Elizabeth." Okay?'

"Elizabeth, I'll be right back." Elsie Mae said. She grabbed her purse, and slipped on her sandals to leave the suite. She was feeling more anxious than she ever had in her life.

"Okay Elsie Mae, we're almost ready in here. We'll probably be finished and gone when you get back." Elizabeth said. It was the first time that the Birmingham, Alabama police officer had heard "Elsie Mae" for the informant; she scribbled it down on her little pad and mentally noted the difference in the name the informant mentioned, 'Gina' and the name the perpetrator called her. Since the law enforcement officer was from Alabama, she had no idea that this informant was an assumed missing person from Georgia.

Elsie Mae flinched when Elizabeth called her real name, but she knew that there was nothing that she could do about it. She then quickly left the suite feeling nervous, but also very relieved that her little Mia would be on her way to Georgia soon. Elsie Mae walked down the hallway trying to look carefree and unconcerned, not wanting to trigger any of her Uncle Chance's spies that there was an undercover operation underway.

As Elsie Mae walked away from the suite to the elevator, she thought to herself, *I wonder how the police traced my call to the suite, and what made them determined to follow-up given the scarce information that I left with the police station's secretary? The Lord does answer prayer! Even if I don't get out of this lifestyle right now, I want Mia saved from this fiasco.*

Elsie Mae went to the restaurant to order some brunch. She really wanted to leave the facility, but she thought that her Uncle Chance would suspect her if she did anything out of the ordinary. While ordering her food, she waved at one of Chance's other women who was walking her way.

"Why don't you join me for brunch?" Elsie Mae was no fool. She was trying to establish an alibi for use with her Uncle Chance later, just in case she needed one. The two women sat and ate, chitchatting about the nothingness that had become their way of life.

* * *

The undercover female officer intentionally waited until the door to the occupied second bedroom opened to make her move. She wanted to ensure that the informant 'Gina,' was long gone in case she was being watched. As promised, the female officer ultimately protected Elsie Mae and didn't compromise her identity realizing that pimps were inclined to beat or kill anyone perceived as a snitch.

When the bedroom door opened and the woman identified as Elizabeth and the young girl emerged, the

223

female undercover officer had to fight back the tears that immediately settled in her eyes, because she was a mother of two small girls. The girl standing in front of her was obviously very young, maybe ten to twelve years old, but she had been dressed up to appear at least ten years older, with a grown up hairdo and way too much makeup.

Once they had come completely out into the foyer, the officer said, "Hold up madam, you are under arrest for the sexual trafficking and delinquency of a minor! Put your hands behind your back." Elisabeth and the little girl both looked shocked. Elizabeth quietly turned around and positioned her hands in the right place as if she was accustomed to the handcuffing routine. The young girl started crying in obvious relief. The officer spoke into her invisible microphone, calling for backup. Within minutes, the suite was overrun with other officers to include Officer Minor from the Griffin City Police Department and representatives from the Birmingham, Alabama, Child Protective Services who took care of Mia.

* * *

Later in Georgia, there was a raid at the home of Mia's parents. They were arrested and their parental rights were eventually revoked. Evidence was gathered to support the trade of their oldest daughter for money. The detectives discovered a bank transaction that revealed a one hundred thousand dollar deposit of cash into the couple's checking account which they could not explain away. Further review of the line item withdrawals showed an increase in spending that didn't align itself to the couple's actual financial ability. It showed the sudden purchase of a new car in which they paid in full, multiple expensive jewelry purchases, various mall department store shopping sprees and countless automatic teller machine cash withdrawals. The authorities had enough financial records evidence to charge and eventually convict the parents for the illegal sale of their child. They also had the heartbreaking testimony from the victim, Mia, who was painstakingly interviewed by child psychologists who videoed her testimony so that she would not have the traumatic experience of testifying in court.

Apparently, Evil Louie had bugged the block of suites. Tiny devices were found in the pleated lamp shades, behind the headboards and fancy picture frames. By the time the police department surrounded Chance's suite and gained entry, he was long gone and his quarters had been cleaned of all physical evidence. The investigation later revealed that Chance Enterprises was a bogus company.

Elizabeth was arrested because Mia was found in her custody. It was later revealed that she had once been a prostitute in her younger days and now worked as hired help. The older Elizabeth got, the more she disagreed with the whole business, but she had stayed on because she believed the hype that she was not qualified to do anything else.

After receiving legal consultation, Elizabeth decided to turn state's evidence to secure a reduced charge; and she wanted to be able to sleep at night. Yes, Elizabeth sang like a canary, confirming the child sexual trafficking allegations, but never admitted knowing the head of the organization. Actually, she didn't really know Chance's real name or anything about him. He had been street smart and savvy enough to stay unidentifiable.

Unfortunately, Chance was never arrested for his involvement with taking the child across state lines because nobody had the nerve to identify him or testify against him. He didn't use his legal name on any documents and all of the surveillance footage from security cameras showed a distorted view of him with baseball caps pulled down low on his head, and sunglasses covering his eyes. All the police knew was that a male reserved the suites in what turned out to be a bogus business name using a credit card with Visa logo tied to a now closed and fraudulent account. They also found out through interviewing the front desk and other staff that the white, apparently disguised man, always paid in cash for the block of suites, restaurant meals, bar tabs, room service, spa treatments and any other incidentals. Obviously, he was a clever criminal who left no paper trails.

Chance later confided to Elsie Mae that he would never involve under-aged girls again in any of his business ventures. He said that the risk of federal charges was too great a chance to take. Ironically, Chance never mentioned being sorry for ruining the child's life nor did he ever admit that it was an immoral thing to do.

Regrettably, Elsie Mae remained a part of Chance's group of women. She vowed to one day be free, but for now she continued to live a duplicitous life. Elsie Mae believed that getting out of the business now would tip Chance off that she was the one who had helped the police rescue Mia. She was satisfied that even though she was still in the seedy lifestyle, Mia was now free to live a normal childhood, with her new, loving foster parents who would eventually adopt her. Of course, the state made sure to provide extensive therapy, counseling and other forms of support for Mia's recovery from the sexual exploitation. It would take years, but eventually the dark and traumatic experience faded in the child's mind and she later developed into a well-adjusted, normal young lady. She had a passion to help save children who were exploited like her.

* * *

As the investigation of the missing Griffin woman, Elsie Mae Coats came to a close; Chief Bruce Spurring was glad to inform her family that she was in fact, alive and well, but of course he couldn't say when she would be home. Her case was officially closed because she was no longer missing.

During the sting operation and arrest of Elizabeth, the local Alabama and the Georgia news crews had been tipped off. Television, radio, and printed media news had a field day reporting that the missing domestic helper and assumed 'girl-next-door,' had been allegedly living a double life, deceiving her family, friends and church members.

With cameras rolling, as the group of women left the hotel holding or pulling suit cases behind them, they shielded their faces with printed scarfs, sunglasses and caps in an attempt to hide their identities from the probing reporters and their broadcasting equipment.

As Elsie Mae rounded a corner walking, a reporter shoved a microphone in her face asking, "Excuse me, is it true that you and the rest of these women were engaged in a prostitution ring from Georgia?"

Elsie Mae increased her pace as she exasperatedly replied, "I have no comment!" In her hurry to get away, her headscarf inadvertently fell from her face. Even though she had used extra make-up to hide the evidence of Evil Louie's punches, when the scarf fell, her bruised, but distinctive features were clearly revealed.

With the persistence of a Georgia bulldog's grip on a bone, the Metro Atlanta reporter pressed for answers once her face was accidently exposed. "Hey, you're Elsie Mae Coats who was reported missing from Griffin, Georgia! What would you like to say to your family and neighbors who diligently searched for you for weeks? Surely, you want to clear your name and protect your reputation."

"I said no comment. Now leave me alone!" Elsie Mae started running and quickly climbed into one of the Navigators with the tinted windows. Once all the women were seated, both Evil Louie and the other driver sped away from the curb.

The reporter then turned back to the camera and said, "There you have it folks, two Navigator SUVs with Georgia state tags, allegedly at the center of this bizarre case. One thing is certain, that was the face of the missing Elsie Mae Coats from Griffin, Georgia who was suddenly rushed away! You heard it first with our exclusive; Elsie Mae Coats' reply was 'no comment,' to our questions! We can only imagine that her family is pleased that she is alive. I'm Brent Younger; back to you in the station Ernest."

* * *

Back in Griffin, Georgia, Blake Baker and his mother, Mrs. Baker sat watching the shocking news story. While shaking her head, Mrs. Baker said, "I knew it, that girl ought to be ashamed, living such an appalling lifestyle!" Mrs. Baker emphasized the words, feeling vindicated. She always doubted Blake's favorable opinion of the missing woman.

Embarrassed because he thought he could love Elsie Mae even though he really didn't know her, Blake shook his head and said, "Mother, I really don't want to talk about this right now." He hated that he had been so wrong about Elsie Mae's character. He now knew she definitely was not the kind of girl you would want to take home to meet your mother! Suddenly, lines from a Rick James song raced across his mind. *"She's a very kinky girl; the kind you don't take home to mother...that girl's a freak, she's super freaky..."* He concluded by thinking, *I'm glad I didn't have the chance to pursue her! Mother would have had a cow.*

Mrs. Baker said, "Okay son, we can discuss it another time." She then reclined in her favorite chair and thought to herself, *She didn't have me fooled one bit. She was a nasty girl and I knew the Lord would reveal the truth! It was just a matter of time. Thank you Jesus!*

Chapter 31

Ginger's shop was lucrative and she was satisfied with its success as she reviewed the business receipts for the week. Basically, she was pleased with her life, despite the disappointment of her marital separation. While glancing toward the flowers from Keefer, she smiled and admired the breath-taking arrangement. While reflecting, she started reconsidering her decision to refuse Keefer's advances as she thought, *Should I finally accept his calls, after all, he is still my husband. Why didn't he man up and be a consistently faithful mate? Will he ever grow up and put foolishness aside and be true? His track record says the opposite, and I won't be responsible for what happens if he ever crosses me again. I still can't believe I shot him! I didn't think I had a violent bone in me, but I definitely pulled the trigger. Granted, he pushed me, but I did the unthinkable – I aimed the pistol and just pulled the trigger like I was at target practice. I wonder why he didn't have me arrested. I told him to stop pissing on me and calling it rain. We'll see what happens, but if I take him back, it'll be on my terms; and he had better not mess up!*

Most of her usual customers who came in for the next few days commented on the gorgeous floral arrangement.

Each remark made her smile, shake her head, and utter thanks in agreement.

This was the last day of the additional twenty percent off sale, so the shop was very hectic. At the height of the lunch hour crowd, when all hands were busy, either assisting customers with selections, answering questions, writing up tickets, or cashing out clients – Ginger got the biggest surprise of her adult life.

Ginger's head was down as she wrote the ticket for a huge order from one of her most loyal customers, when the door opened to its standard chime. She wondered why she didn't hear the gentle whish of the door's closing. A small, wooden platform had been placed in the doorway to temporarily keep the door ajar. Suddenly, all Ginger could hear were the gasps of customers, the cheers from Brea and Chloe, and the distant, but majestic sound of a saxophone playing, "Isn't She Lovely" by Stevie Wonder.

Looking up into a cloud of balloons and streamers, Ginger said, "What's going on?" As she asked this question, a man came into the shop playing the saxophone like his life depended on it. Another man followed him and as the music volume was lowered he stood on the platform and announced, "I have a very special delivery for a Mrs. Ginger Davis Graham. Is she here today?"

With guarded excitement, she said, "I'm Ginger, what in the world is going on?"

Every customer in her shop stood spellbound. They were motionless at the clothes racks holding weighed hangers, at the register with credit cards or cash in hand, and some had quickly rushed out of the dressing room to see what had generated all of the noise and excitement.

"Yes, Mrs. Graham, I have an extra special delivery for you, but you'll have to come outside to see it!" He appeared to be thrilled himself, with the prospect of her pending elation.

"Come outside? Sir, I have customers, whatever it is, you'll just have to bring it inside." She then shook her head and wondered what Keefer was up to now; he was the only one in her world with deep enough pockets to orchestrate this level of exhibition to surprise her. She thought, *I wish his follow-through was as good as his initial presentation. He doesn't have to bring me presents; all I really ever wanted was him.* Or so she thought, because she had not seen the gift.

"Mrs. Graham, even Houdini couldn't pull off what you just suggested I do. It's not possible to bring this gift into your shop. With all due respect, please step outside."

Ginger was in the middle of a transaction, so she finished ringing up the woman, thanked her and then called for Brea.

"Brea, I don't know what's going on, but please take the register and I'll be right back." Ginger was trying to contain her enthusiasm, but to be honest, she was getting excited too. The people who had hurried out of the dressing room in clothes which hadn't been paid for walked to the picture window and pressed against the glass to look diagonally down the street. There was a parking lot in the rear of the building full of cars, and limited parking in the front of the building, therefore, Ginger's impromptu entourage of followers chose to walk behind her down the street to see her surprise.

Brea told a lady she was ringing up, "My boss has it going on; she received beautiful, diamond earrings one day, that designer floral arrangement on the table behind you the next day and I can't imagine what gift is so large that it can't be brought into the store! All I know, I want to be just like her when I grow up!" She laughed, in awe of it all.

232

The young woman grumbled, "It must be nice. I'm just happy that some of those people who were in front of me got out of the line to be nosey. Your boss's surprise made my wait shorter!"

Another woman commented, "I ain't mad at her, do you and reap the benefits, is what I say!" Other women made similar comments as they one by one purchased clothes and accessories and then made a right turn outside the clothing shop to check out the happenings down the street.

Finally, a roaring sound came from outside and everyone still in the store knew it was a positive sign.

* * *

When Ginger walked about one hundred and twenty feet down the street, she was stopped dead in her tracks. Parked on the street with a colossal, intricately looped red bow on top and ribbon wrapped underneath and around it, was an automobile. It wasn't just any vehicle; it was her absolute dream car – a Rolls-Royce Phantom 62 with an extended wheelbase, shining like the morning sun. The color was Silver with crème light interior and Bespoke trim. For once in her life, Ginger was speechless. Everyone around her was clapping, laughing, hollering, gesturing, or all of the above. She didn't know what to say. She stood with wide eyes and wobbly legs, shocked to say the least.

The man making the presentation was the owner of the dealership. He later confessed that he had never had anyone to come into his business and do what Keefer had done.

"Mrs. Graham, I present to you a gift from your loving husband Keefer Graham. This Rolls-Royce Phantom 62 'is a timeless interpretation of the modern motor car. It was designed without compromise. It has remarkable luxury and presence' - the perfect combination for a beautiful lady.

Please open up this envelope because Mr. Graham was explicit in his instructions." The man quoted the sales pitch from the company's material verbatim, happy to comply with Keefer's directives.

"Okay." Ginger's hands shook as she slowly opened the thick, beautiful silver envelop that the man handed her.

The sticker from the vehicle's window was neatly folded and she hesitantly opened it. Although she had admired the Rolls-Royce from afar, she had never really priced one because she wasn't in the market for one. Apparently, this vehicle was luxurious and fully loaded because when Ginger saw the bottom line, she almost fainted. The sticker price read, five hundred and sixteen thousand dollars.

Pointing to the figure, she asked, "What? Is this correct?" She barely got out the question, when the man said the final shocker of the day. Meanwhile, she was thinking, *this baby almost cost more than my house*! The home they once shared was grand in its own right; the Rolls-Royce would complement its driveway just fine.

"Yes, Mrs. Graham it is. The biggest surprises are the next documents and there is also another package. Mrs. Graham, be my guest and see what else Mr. Graham has provided for you." With that last statement, he gestured with his hand for her to continue her exploration of the padded envelope.

The next document was a bill of sales with a paid-in-full notation. The final document was the title to the car in calligraphic styled font, all capital letters and bold print, which read, *GINGER DAVIS GRAHAM*. By the time she got to it, she was trembling with tears in her eyes.

He encouraged her by saying, "Yes madam, there will be no notes to pay– ever! Now, please go on Mrs. Graham, there is one more thing inside."

Astonished, she couldn't think of what it could possibly be. Looking further, she saw a velvet silver pouch; inside were the keys and electronic switch.

"Mrs. Graham, please get in your luxury motor car. The photographer is waiting to record this moment and the videographer has been recording all of the action since you were in your shop."

As she walked to the gorgeous luxury car and sat inside, all she could think of was, *I could never turn him down now, he's won me back with diamonds, flowers and the best surprise of all- my dream car, with only my name on the title! Keefer, I've got to hand it to you, you know how to win a woman over!*

He held the door open and closed it once she was inside.

"If all of this was not enough, at his direction, I've placed one more gift in the glove compartment. Please open it Mrs. Graham." The photographer and the videographer were both hovering at the opposite opened door on their job to record her reaction.

As Ginger opened the glove compartment she saw a card and an oblong box inside.

"He has asked that you read the card first, out loud for the video, please!" The car dealer was having too much fun with this. He probably was thinking of the great sale his business had just made and the free publicity because now, there were many spectators standing around admiring the automobile and cramming their necks to see what celebrity or VIP person was inside of it. The people in the crowd assumed that a Rolls-Royce Phantom 62 on deck, a video camera rolling and lights flashing had to mean VIP presence!

Opening the card, she read, "This is but a token of my love for the most beautiful and precious wife a man could ever be blessed with. Please accept these gifts from my heart to yours. Loving you always, Keefer."

Ginger then reached for the box; opening it she sighed at the brilliance of a Le Vian ten caret diamond tennis bracelet which the man placed on her wrist.

Now, she didn't even try to stop the tears as they happily flowed down her face. The crowd clapped and cheered like she was about to give each one of them a ride in her luxury vehicle.

Keefer had outdone himself. The vehicle was hers free and clear; nothing owed to the bank and it was in her name. Ginger could hardly wait to call Keefer and invite him over to show her appreciation. He was a man who had broken down her wall of resistance with wonderful diamond jewelry, long-stemmed roses and a show-stopper, silver Rolls-Royce Phantom 62.

Ginger may have been unaware of it, but perhaps her heart could be bought for the right price.

Chapter 32

Ginger was ready to make the call that deep down she had wanted to do for a few days. In all honesty, she really did love Keefer, she just couldn't put up with his duplicitous ways. During their marriage he had cheated and also given her an STD. That revelation had pushed her over the top emotionally and she snapped one day and shot him. Fortunately, both injuries were braised flesh wounds, nothing serious. How she escaped being a jailbird was a mystery to her. She had made a mental note to ask him about that one day. But today, all she could think about was talking things through and spending some quality time with her husband or her sweet "boo-thang," as she sometimes referred to him when talking to her girlfriends. She decided to call one of her closest friends, named Monica whom she had not talked to recently, before calling to invite him over.

Using her cellular phone to dial her friend, Ginger anxiously waited for her to pick up her phone.

"Hey Ginger, it has been awhile; 'how you doing' girl?" She asked the question in her best talk show host, Wendy Williams' voice and waited for a response.

"I'm good; I just need to talk to you for a few minutes. What are you doing?"

"To be perfectly honest, I just finished reading posts and messages from my Facebook account. Now, I'm about to play a game. What's up girl?"

"Well, you will probably think I'm crazy, but I'm seriously thinking about reconciling with Keefer." She squinted while waiting for Monica's reaction. If anyone would be honest with Ginger, she knew that Monica, who they called "Money" because of her lucrative marketing business and lavish shopping sprees, would be brutally honest with her. Besides, true friends will keep it real with each other.

"Girl, all I can say is you've definitely lost your damn mind. You know that man is crazy! After all he put you through, why would you even consider letting him come back home? Why don't you get your divorce and be rid of his foolishness for good?" Monica didn't hold any punches.

"Why don't you just tell me your true feelings? Don't hold back anything!" Ginger thought to herself, *Why didn't I call someone with a little less bluntness? Or, is this what I need to hear?*

"Honey look, give me and more importantly, yourself three good reasons why you should return to a hellified situation; and yes, I just made up a word—when you don't have to? I know that man is fine, rich and takes care of the bedroom business, but you are not a desperate woman and there are some good men left in the world! You've just got to get out there and find one, or as the Bible says it, let him find you. Either way, you, my friend, have a lot to offer. You don't have to settle for a crazy, double-minded joker that doesn't know what he wants and who apparently doesn't have the mental capacity to recognize the blessing he had in you as his wife! Keefer may not have been officially diagnosed, but from all of the psychology classes that I took in school, I'd stake my master's degree on the fact that

Keefer has a Dissociative Identity Disorder! It used to be called Multiple Personality Disorder. To make it plain girl, the old folks would have just said he's two-faced, but that seems to be too simple for that good brother; Keefer is damn crazy – a lunatic, Ginger! Please don't do it; I feel like you'll live to regret it. Give him his permanent walking papers and get yourself a real man!"

"Money, that was a mouthful! I can see you are very passionate about me moving on, but it's not that simple. You said give you three reasons why I should take him back; and so I have them for you. I love him although as Tina Turner sang it best, 'What's Love Got To Do With It?' Besides that, I miss him and he just rained down some serious make-up gifts Money!"

"Girl, what the hell did he give you that you can't buy yourself? Don't be suckered into that abuse again, no matter what he says or what he buys you. At this point, he should know what he wants in life, but he doesn't. That's sad, if you ask me. He's too old for that womanizing crap!"

"He's been calling me ever since we separated, but I wouldn't take the calls. Then out of the blue, he sent me some very expensive diamond earrings – one caret per earlobe, and they are spectacular! Yes, you're right, I could have bought them, but I didn't, he did. That's not all Money; he sent a simply gorgeous designer, two-dozen- red-rose arrangement to the shop."

"Okay, he royally messed up so he's sending gifts that we both know he can afford to try to buy you back? Ginger, you need a man that will love you right as well as adore your precious son, and one that treats you with the respect and dignity you deserve." Exasperated with her friend, Monica was getting a little impatient with Ginger over this issue because she was totally aware of all of the pain Keefer had caused her.

"Money, you haven't heard the best gift of all. It must mean he loves me." Even if she wasn't desperate, Ginger was sounding a little anxious now trying to justify her renewed faith in Keefer's ability to be straight and on the up and up this time around.

"Gin, are you trying to convince me or yourself? Whatever it is, I assure you, it has a cost attached to it." Monica had that much right.

Ginger emphatically exclaimed, "Wait 'til you hear this girl!" She made a fake drum roll with her mouth and then said, "Monica, he bought me a silver Rolls-Royce Phantom 62, had it delivered to the shop with a saxophone player serenading me, balloons and streamers – big fanfare girl, and a beautiful, LeVian ten caret tennis bracelet was in the glove compartment! The car dealership's owner placed it on my wrist! Girl, Keefer had a photographer and a videographer on deck to record it all. It was a spectacular presentation as only Keefer could pull off. Honey, it was over the top! I felt like singing Beyoncé's song, 'Love on Top' when it was all over!"

"That double minded man may get mad over the least little thing and come back and pick the car up or stop making the payments on it. What would you do then? That would be embarrassing." Monica thought that she had all of the possible bases covered by that last question and comment.

"Are you sitting down Monica?" Ginger couldn't wait to give the clincher to the whole scenario.

"Yes, in fact I am; why do you ask?" *I wonder why she wanted to know if I'm sitting down or not.* Monica was now puzzled.

"One of the best things about his effort to make amends with me was that he walked into the dealership, worked his best deal if I know my man, and paid for the vehicle outright. Who does that?"

"What…! Well, hush my mouth, as my Grandmother would have said, God rest her soul! But Gin, whose name is it in?" *Surely I've got her now!* Monica thought.

"Honey, the title states clear as day, 'Ginger Davis Graham' no monthly notes, no repossessions, straight-up, and no jokes. Is my man serious or what Money?"

"Dang girl, what are you doing to that man?" Monica didn't have anything else negative to say.

"Nothing now, but I'm about to start showing him my appreciation. Maybe we need some marital counseling, but I think he has finally come to his senses. All you really need is a made up mind for it to work. He really sounds sincere this time. Since we are still legally married, I really want to give it one final chance to work. If he blows it this time, I'm done trying. Enough is enough."

"Well, all I have to say is; you mentioned there are no monthly notes, no possible repossessions, and no jokes, but I'll dare say there are plenty of strings attached to that 'superior motor vehicle, designed without compromise!' Are you sure you can handle the emotional strain if he crosses you again?" Monica was already very familiar with the luxury vehicle's motto and she used her two fingers in the air with each hand to make air quotes as she said it, as if Ginger could see her.

"I think you are worrying too much over nothing. Besides, I've never heard of a man who womanizes having that mental disorder you mentioned. I'll have to check that out. Everything is going to be okay. If not, I'll contact a good lawyer. Stop lecturing me and wish me well."

"Bless your love sick, naïve heart. Tell that joker from me that if he hurts you again, he may as well start looking over his shoulders on a daily basis because Jesus is still working on me! I'm not totally delivered; I still have some 'Hood' in me and I won't take it back! I'll beat that playa down over my friend. You know, it's nothing for me to get on a plane, fly somewhere and come back home the same day. Just say the word, and I'll take care of a brother for you if he messes over you again!"

"You are crazy Monica!" Ginger laughed. "I really feel like we'll make it this time. He says he loves me and misses me so why don't we hope for the best. I'll talk to you later, okay."

"Yes, we'll hope for the best, but prepare for the worst. My uncle taught me how to use brass knuckles and I've got a few more tricks up my sleeve. Look, Ginger, I want you to be happy so I really hope I'm wrong; but, fooling around with that husband of yours, I have a feeling you'll be talking to me sooner rather than later! Bye, my friend."

"Bye Big Money and thank you for listening, I guess. I'll talk to you later." Ginger was half glad that she called Monica, but the other half of her now held a hint of doubt that Keefer was ready to give their marriage a serious effort of reconciliation. *One thing is for sure, I can't be married to myself. I hope this man is sincere about me and getting back together. Why sure he is Ginger, why else would he pursue you so long and buy all of those gifts. Of course, he knows what he wants and that's me!*

It was settled in Ginger's mind; therefore, she was convinced and totally excited about bringing their marriage relationship back together.

After hanging up the phone, Monica just shook her head; she had a weird feeling of dread about her close friend Ginger, who was insanely in love with a morally corrupt man. She thought to herself, *I know people can change, but I believe Keefer Graham, will go to his grave both crooked and crazy! Time will tell Monica, time will tell.*

Chapter 33

When Ginger got off the telephone with Monica, she raced to the bathroom suite to examine her eyes. They were dancing with excitement because she assumed that the two caret diamond earrings, the sensational designer floral arrangement, the Le Vian, ten caret tennis bracelet, and the luxury Rolls-Royce Phantom 62 were all representative of the genuine love that Keefer must really feel for her. Why would he bother if it wasn't from the heart?

Picking up her cellular phone, Ginger dialed Keefer's number; on ring three, he answered with the delight in his voice she was hoping to hear. Before she could say a word, he said, "Ginger, honey, how are you today?"

Ginger could hardly contain herself, "Keefer, you know how to woo a sister! You are one bad, old-school player who just mastered the king position in my heart. What am I going to do with you?"

Just grinning he said, "I'm serious about us getting back together girl. You know how frugal I am with the funds–anytime I shell out the cash like I did this week on you Baby, you must know you are extra special to me. I love you Ginger and I wanted you to know that I'm through playing around! That lifestyle is in the past and all I want is you."

"We need to talk face to face Keefer; we also need to attend some good marital counseling. The counselors are not just going to give us good advice, but they will be fair and unbiased. Keefer, they are trained professionals."

"Sweetness, I know what our problem was. It was me and my selfish ways. I loved you then and I still love you now. I just struggled to get past seeing others. Baby, I'm for real when I say I'm ready to give up everyone else, every possible woman I could meet in the future, just to be happy and content with you and only you."

"Keefer Graham, how could I ever trust you again after all of the confusion and drama we went through? I gave up trying. I don't have anything else to give if you are not ready to do this. I can't let you play with my heart like that. I'm too good of a woman to settle for someone who wants me and someone else too. That's why I think—I mean I know-we need to get some intensive counseling to help us through this process."

"Ginger, I give you my word that everything is going to be different this time around. Give me the chance to make things up to you, okay. I promise you will not be sorry. We don't need a strange person listening to our problems, giving advice that we are intelligent enough to figure out on our own. Let's give our love a try - a serious try, this time. I know we'll be able to make it. I'm ready, and I've missed you and Justin terribly. How's he doing?"

He knew the way to take the focus off of the two of them and their dysfunctional relationship was to bring up the apple of her eye - her son Justin.

Beaming with joy at the mention of his name, Ginger momentarily reflected on her beloved son and actually forgot the depth of the drama that Keefer caused them to endure. *Is this man for real or am I crazy for even considering reconciling with him? How do you ever really know a person's heart?* She wondered.

"Ginger, are you still there?" Keefer could only imagine what Ginger was going through. He reflected, *You really did take her to hell and back. I don't know what's really wrong with me. Why do I constantly hurt the main women that have loved me unconditionally? Ginger and Beverly; Ginger is a wonderful wife and a good woman. Why can't I be truly satisfied with her? Why do I insist on seeing other people? If she takes me back, I'll have to do things differently. And, if I cheat with Beverly, I'll have to be extra careful. No man, you can't step out on her again. Are you crazy? But, I don't really want to stop seeing Beverly. She has stuck by me all of these years, believing that one day I'll be hers. Silly woman, I'm not divorcing my wife for her. It's really unfair to Beverly, but, I tell her what she wants to hear and it keeps her coming back for more. Is Beverly that stupid to really believe me, or is she that much in love with me? Makes me wonder because, even I wouldn't wait for me the number of years that she has waited. Crazy as it sounds, I really want them both! I know I love Ginger, but having the love of my life is not enough! I guess I'm just greedy. I like Beverly, and I can't bring myself to stop messing with her! Then, sometimes I want the straight out nasty girls of Hellborn and Lost. I think I've really got a big problem, but who could I share this with? Where would I go for help? Or, do I really need help? I think I'm just being a man! I'm cool; I'm a MAN, like my dad.*

Keefer was having serious thoughts with himself debating if he could be faithful, and if not, the ways he could cheat and get away with it. In the end, he had completely deceived himself into believing that his actions and lifestyle were like his father and perfectly okay. He had concluded that he was just being a MAN! Some people just never change… to their own detriment.

"Ginger, what are you thinking about? I've been calling you for a minute."

"Oh, yes, I'm here. I just don't know Keefer. Come by tonight and we'll talk further. Thank you so much for everything."

"Better than that, let's go to dinner and then we'll talk afterwards. Does that sound good to you?" Keefer was the master mac daddy.

"Okay, Keefer, what time should I be ready?" Ginger was happy, but couldn't shake the funny feeling in her spirit. And, Monica who was always on point when it came to judging a person's character was adamant that Keefer was still up to no good.

"I'll pick you up at seven thirty. Is that good for you?" Keefer was in his element; he had finally broken down the icy wall of her heart.

"Okay, I'll be ready. See you then." Guarded, Ginger didn't offer any sweet salutations. *Let me just have a fun evening and we can talk about the heavy things another time.*

"Okay, Sweetie, I'll see you then. Bye." Keefer was playing it cool. He didn't want to overwhelm her, but in his mind, he was already living with Ginger and Justin. He thought to himself, *It won't be long before I'm living at home again, loving on Ginger and doing what I want to do. I've got to be careful though because she is not the woman to mess over. I got lucky the last time. I would never want to tick her off again. I can't believe she actually shot me! I had pushed her too far. I'll be extra careful now. Well, tonight we'll have dinner, talk, and hopefully, I'll get some loving later tonight once Justin is asleep. Yes, Ginger my dear; you ought to know by now, that you were smart to block my calls and advances because when I lay on the charm, you simply can't resist me!*

You wouldn't be able to tell Keefer that he was not the man God created to be his gift to females at large. He was one conceited guy!

* * *

Keefer came over to the house that he and Ginger once shared feeling very confident that he had spent enough money and done enough to prove to his wife that he had reformed from his playa ways. Pulling up to the driveway, he paused to admire his image in the car's mirror. Getting out of the vehicle, he walked to the front door with a swagger of a sophisticated gentleman.

Since the locks had been changed, he had to ring the bell to the home that he still had to pay the mortgage payments according to the judge's order in their temporary separation agreement. He made the money true enough, but in his mind, it was still kind of crazy not to be able to just let himself in the door. He reflected, *We own the house together and she's still my wife! I hate ringing the bell and waiting to be invited into my own house! This is some bull.*

Keefer, who was looking good and smelling better, had exited his Mercedes 600 series, excited about seeing Ginger again in a romantic kind of way. After receiving all of the lavish and fabulous gifts, Ginger had finally called him.

The door opened and Justin stood back while grinning, looking genuinely happy to see his step-father. "Keefer; man, I'm glad to see you!" Once Keefer was inside the doorway, Justin stepped toward him to give him a quick hug.

"Justin, my boy! You look as if you've grown a couple of inches! How are you doing, son?" After the hug, they slapped hands, both grinning like smiles were for sale.

"I'm good, and you?" Justin was still beaming with joy.
He had really gotten close to his step-father and he truly
missed him.

"I'm better now that your mother is talking to me again.
From your happy, smiling face, it looks like you're glad to
see me. Justin, I've missed you."

"Don't get soft on me!" Justin punched Keefer and then
he said, "Man, me too, Keefer." Now Justin felt a little
awkward; he thought to himself, *Keefer's getting a little too
sentimental.*

"Son, will you put a good word in for me with your
mom?" Keefer was just shameless, calling on a teenager to
vouch for him.

"You know I've got you. I'll just be glad when you
move back in. You were my basketball rival and my Wii
challenger. We've got to make up time Keefer!"

"Okay man, together we can make it happen!" Keefer
knew Ginger loved Justin more than the law allowed; his
opinions mattered to her and she really did want him to have
a positive role model in his life. *I can still be the man Justin
looks up to.*

Who was Keefer trying to convince?

Keefer and Justin walked into the family room and took
a seat, Justin in his normal spot on the leather sectional sofa
and Keefer in his favorite plush recliner.

At the sound of them entering the den, Pepper had
started whimpering with anticipation of a good rub-down
from her other owner. She abandoned her princess bed and
strutted over to Keefer's seat and plopped her head down on
his thigh, nudging her long nose under his hand to get some
affection.

"Hello Pepper, at least Justin and you have missed me. I
can't be all bad." Pepper didn't know what he was saying,
but she licked his hand and appreciated the extra attention he

was giving her. Pepper's tail was wagging a hundred miles an hour; a classic sign of her approval.

"Justin, do you think your mother heard the bell?" With his inflated pride, he wondered why she hadn't rushed down the stairs.

"I'm not sure, but let me call her." He quickly got up and pressed the intercom button saying, "Mom, Keefer's here!" For some reason, Justin always spoke in an extra loud voice on the system. Teenagers!

"Okay Justin, thanks." Ginger replied.

Justin was watching an HBO movie which Keefer joined in on during the brief wait for his wife to come down.

Ginger descended the back staircase looking like a spicy hot mamma. She was dressed in a red pleated dress that hit a few inches above her knees. The bodice was crisscross pleats over the breast and waist revealing a hint of cleavage. Her hair was in a classic straight slick style and her shoes were Jimmy Choo, red and black heeled sandals which showcased her petite, pampered feet.

"Ginger, you look beautiful! Are you ready to go?"

"Thank you Keefer. You look rather GQ yourself. Yes, I'm ready."

Turning to Justin she said, "Justin, I won't be out long, call me if you need to."

"Okay Mom, I'll be fine. Have a good time." Turning to face his mother, Justin stood up and let out a whistle, saying, "Mom, you are the bomb! That's a sweet dress."

"Thank you, Baby. See you when we get back." Ginger didn't realize it, but Keefer had plans of his own.

* * *

They drove to downtown Atlanta for an evening of fine dining. Ginger ate grilled salmon, tossed salad, and a baked potato; Keefer had filet mignon, new potatoes and broccoli. They went dancing afterwards and talked about a host of subjects. When it was time to go, Ginger assumed they would take things slow, and she was fully expecting to go home immediately. Keefer had a very different idea. When he took an expressway different from the one that would lead to her house, she questioned him.

"Keefer, why are you going this way?" Ginger tilted her head and curiously looked at him.

"Let's just go for a nightcap. I'll get you home before you know it." Keefer kept driving in the opposite direction hoping she wouldn't need much convincing. He looked over at his wife and winked. He then stretched out his hand and eased it under her dress, caressing her knee and thigh.

"Keefer don't…" Although she said don't, her tone said, 'Whatever you want to do, do it quickly before I have the good sense to scream NO!' Quiet as it was kept, she wanted him too.

He pulled into his garage and they entered the kitchen pulling off clothes as they walked toward the bedroom. Before they could get there, they christened the den sofa. After that, Keefer grabbed some juice and wine from the fridge, then the needy couple moved to his bedroom and they just got buck wild enjoying each other like married folks do, until her internal mother instinct kicked in and she insisted on being taken home. Ginger would arrive at her home a different woman though; Keefer softly spoke the right words and made love like his life was dependent on his pleasing her. It worked; Keefer had made an indelible impression.

* * *

Keefer continued to court Ginger in the old-fashioned kind of way for another month; he sent flowers, brought candy and cologne and perfume and truly wined and dined her. The whole time Keefer tried to get back with her, he continued to profess his unwavering love and commitment to her and their marriage. After a total of three and one half months of re-dating each other, she allowed Keefer to move back into their lovely mansion.

For the next four months, Keefer was not only a better husband, but he had started participating more with Justin's afterschool activities which made her son thrilled to have a dad in the stands supporting him. This made Ginger totally content and happy that she had made the right decision to reconcile with him. She was content, Justin seemed happy, and Keefer had finally learned his lesson and appeared mature and satisfied as an honest and faithful husband.

Ginger woke up early one morning and leaned on her arm to lovingly look at her man who was still sleeping. She stretched and lazily cast her legs onto the floor, easing her feet into cushioned house slippers. Before moving from the bed, she walked over to her hunk-of-a-man, leaned over and gently kissed his cheek. Keefer stirred slightly, but turned over, apparently in a deep sleep. She thought to herself, *I'm so happy! Just thinking about him gives me a warm feeling all over. He really put it on me last night! Yes, yes, Keefer still got it going on like a young man!* Laughing out loud now as she walked to the huge bathroom suite, she didn't notice that Keefer's eyes blinked at the brilliance of the light from the restroom. She left the door ajar and let her nightgown fall to the chair. Keefer got a glimpse of her ample breast and sculpted abdominal muscles and he was instantly aroused.

As Ginger turned on the shower jets and lathered her towel to start bathing, a Whitney Houston song, "You Give Good Love to Me" came to her mind. She started singing it now; within a couple of minutes with her body covered with an intense lather of essence aroma suds, she heard the shower door open. Keefer was standing there smiling with his penis standing at attention.

"Yes love, I give you good love…" Mannish thang.

"Again baby? I've got to go to work!" Ginger playfully protested while taking her towel and splashing him with suds.

"Ain't nothing wrong with a little early morning loving; come here woman! 'I'm going to close the door, give you what you've been waiting for,' he sang. "I love you Ginger!" Keefer continued to sing the old Teddy Pendergrass song as he made love to her in the shower until she begged to be released. Afterward, they washed again, rinsed off and lovingly towel-dried each other.

After dressing for work, they walked downstairs to the kitchen. While Keefer retrieved the newspaper from the porch, Ginger pulled two mugs from the cabinet and poured two cups of coffee, adding cream and sugar to hers and just cream to his cup. *I'm so glad I bought that programmable coffee maker so that my favorite brew is ready in the morning.*

As he walked into the kitchen, she asked, "Would you like a bagel?"

"Yes, baby, thank you." He sat down and opened the paper to read the sports page.

Minutes later, Ginger sat a bread plate with a toasted and buttered bagel with pineapple favored cream cheese in front of her husband. She slid another one by her chair. Before sitting in her seat, she planted a moist kiss on his lips and said, "Sweetheart, enjoy. If you had not been so romantic this morning, I would have prepared us a full breakfast."

"You were my breakfast today, Honey. I can't think of a better way to start my day. You, plus coffee equals a perfect morning!" He made an Italian Baci gesture by kissing his thumb and index finger. They enjoyed good conversation for about ten minutes before she kissed him goodbye and rushed out of the door.

Ginger was feeling satisfied and left for work with a sense of happy down in her soul. By all appearances, it seemed like it would be a normal day. Keefer had shown her affection and he was fully engaged in mutually satisfying activities and conversation with his girlfriend and wife rolled in one sweet woman. Ginger was beginning to feel comfortable in the relationship again, ecstatic that finally, she felt fulfilled in her marital union. There was peace in the Graham home again.

* * *

"Good morning Brea, how are you today?" Ginger walked through the shop toward her office to put her purse in her desk drawer. She then placed her lunch in the fridge.

"Good morning to you too, Mrs. Graham! How is Justin doing?"

"He's good, thanks for asking." Ginger glanced at the clock and realized they had about thirty minutes before the customers would come in. Business was good and Ginger was thankful for all of her many blessings. She had a thriving business, a good son and finally, a strong marriage. Ginger didn't know it, but her feelings of happiness would be short-lived. Unfortunately, she was experiencing the quiet before the storm.

Chapter 34

Ginger left work wondering what she would prepare for dinner that night. She thought, *maybe we'll just go out for dinner.*

Ginger thought about Keefer and wanted to hear his voice. Pulling out her cell phone, she dialed his number. To her surprise, after five rings, his voice mail came on. The recording would be the only semblance of his voice that she would hear. Leaving a message, 'Hey Baby, I was wondering if you would be interested in taking Justin out to dinner at the new restaurant in town. Give me a call. Talk to you later. Love you!"

She thought it was strange that he didn't answer his phone, but she just assumed he must have been busy. She went to pick up her dry cleaning and then drove home.

As she opened the door, her dog Pepper leapt off of her princess bed and came charging toward her beloved owner. Ginger sat her things down on the foyer credenza and bent down to give Pepper some love. "Well hello Ms. Pepper." The dog's tail was swishing back and forth. When Ginger tried to pull her hand back, the pampered pooch nudged her again with her cold nose, wanting the rubdown to continue. After another few moments, Ginger playfully slapped Pepper on the rump indicating the love fest was over.

Raising back up, Ginger walked to the intercom system and pressed the all call button saying, "Hey Justin, get ready because when Keefer gets home, we'll go out for dinner."

"Whoo, hoo, that's a bet Mom. I'll be downstairs in a minute." He cheerfully responded on the intercom.

"Okay." Ginger turned on the seventy inch television and started watching CNN while waiting for Keefer to come home. A hunger pain raced across her stomach which made her reach for the remote control to press the button to check the time; it was eight forty-five. Ginger thought, *Where could Keefer be this late on a work night? Let me just try calling him again.*

After five rings, Keefer's voice mail recording came back on and again she left a message. 'Keefer, this is Ginger; where are you? Justin and I wanted to go out for dinner, but since it's late, why don't you bring something home. Please give me a call as soon as you can. Talk to you later.'

* * *

After another hour, Justin had given up and asked to go to his best friend's house for an impromptu sleepover. It was a Friday night and both the mothers agreed that it was a great idea. Ginger dropped Justin off at the friend's house. Once she was back in her car she muttered, "Keefer could at least call me back."

Arriving home, she quickly walked Pepper in the backyard making sure to take her cell phone so that she didn't miss any calls.

Once back inside, she again mumbled, "Where is Keefer? At least he could return my call and not have me wondering where he is. That would be the way to show respect and do the right thing! If he didn't act so suspicious, I wouldn't have to question him!" Ginger spoke to the air, as she sat in the den alone. She scanned the television and settled on a Lifetime movie. When the movie ended, Ginger was sleepy and she decided to go upstairs, take a shower and try to get some rest. Before climbing the stairs, she glanced out the guest room window to see if Keefer's car was in the driveway; no sign of him or his car. Ginger was getting frustrated. She kept going over and over in her head his promise: 'I love you Ginger and I wanted you to know that I'm through playing around! That lifestyle is in the past and all I want is you.'

As the night grew later and later, Ginger grew angrier as she began to remember the many promises that Keefer had told her when he was wooing her back into his deceitful web of betrayal. 'Ginger, I give you my word that everything is going to be different this time around. Give me the chance to make things up to you, okay. I promise you will not be sorry.'

Keefer had also said, 'Baby, I'm for real when I say, I'm ready to give up everyone else, every possible woman I could meet in the future, to be happy and content with you and only you.'

As the time on the clock ticked away, Ginger thought about the final proclamation that had convinced her that Keefer had matured and was ready to be a true and faithful husband; 'Let's give our love a try, a serious try, this time. I know we'll be able to make it. I'm ready and, I've missed you and Justin terribly.' Ginger spoke now, "Lies, lies, and more lies!"

Chapter 35

Confused; that state of being is exactly what Ginger felt as she waited for Keefer to come home. While waiting, she obviously had fallen asleep. Abruptly awakened, she noticed that it was 4:30a.m., as she sleepily glanced at the digital clock and slowly stretched across her plush California-king bed to find his side empty. She was simply stunned that her husband would have the audacity to stay out all night just months after drawing her back into his crazy world. She thought, *Knowing him and his fragmented mind, he probably thought he was doing me a favor. No thanks. If I wanted to be alone, I could have stayed by myself!*

With the realization that she was home alone, other than her dog Pepper that quietly slept down the hall; the horrible reality of the situation caused her exhausted body to completely wake up, sit up, and get up. Shaking the shock from her spirit, she wrapped her mind around the revelation that Keefer was cheating again. "No the hell this merry-go-round is not going to be my life again with this double-minded, lying man – not this time. The hell you say…"

She immediately started blowing up his cell number which unsurprised, she noticed he refused to answer.

What am I to do now? I've let this certified lunatic talk me into reconciling with him. What was I smoking? What was I thinking? I should have known that once a fool, always a fool. What did the old folks say? 'Once a cheater – always a cheater!' I thought he had made up his mind to do the right thing! His mind seems so confused that his insanity is making me feel totally discombobulated! How do I explain to my family that I reconnected with a nutcase? They might try to have me committed. Hell, two of us can't be crazy! One of us has to have sense! And my poor son, Justin...he has been so disappointed about all of this drama. It's starting to affect his grades and his behavior in school. Keefer doesn't even care how damaging this is to my son. Justin loves him and he can't understand why Keefer's not home half of the time. What should I tell him? How do I explain that Keefer loves you, but he likes what he's doing in the streets better than being at home living the life of a family man? That would go over like a lead balloon! How selfish could Keefer be? I told him when I met him that I didn't want to bring drama into my son's life and if he was not sure that he wanted a stable and mature, loving, monogamous relationship, that he could keep right on walking. I told him that I was not a desperate woman and that I could take care of myself. I guess some men are never ready to have a family. They are street bred and that's all they know and that's all they want; wild street women, slang talk, cheap liquor and telling lies to cover up their trifling ways. Keefer attends church as much as I do, but the messages are not taking root. Not only hasn't he changed, but he has gotten worse. Ironically, I never would have thought it was possible for him to be a bigger cheater than he was before. He has negatively, outdone himself!

After thinking for what seemed to be an eternity, she said, "I guess it is true what Big Momma used to say, 'You sure can't take a womanizing man and expect him to be a faithful husband. He may mean well when he promises fidelity, but in the end, he is going to be who he is! In time, the real man will show up. Some people will go to their grave just as crooked as a screw and there's nothing you can do about it; for them to change would be too much like right!'

"Big Momma, you were right! I always had the naïve thought that a person would be the best that they could be, and that there is good in everyone. It couldn't have been further from the truth."

"Keefer has proven me wrong. I hate being wrong, but one thing I know, I can't choose for anyone but myself. I'm responsible for me, my life and my choices. And, I don't have the right to mess over anyone else's life. If I don't want a man, it is best to tell him the truth, shame the devil, and move forward with my life. Why pretend to be committed? When your heart is knitted to a mate, you'll have no problem being faithful to him. Life is not so hard to figure out; love who you want to love and leave the rest of the pack alone. Amen walls!" While Ginger was on her soapbox about relationship dysfunction, her husband Keefer was in another part of town, trying to decide on what time he would find his way home.

Chapter 36

For a brief moment, Keefer's recent promises to Ginger flashed through his mind like a series of lines from a Broadway play; believable but not reality. He quickly dismissed them because he had bigger fish to fry. Keefer rubbed the spot where his wedding ring usually rested until that evening when he nonchalantly, removed the white-gold and diamond band and tossed it into his back pocket. Once again, he made a conscience decision to violate his vows and disregard his promises to Ginger. *I'm not really married, I just have a wife! Life can't get better than this for me. I'd rather die than conform to what society thinks I should be; a one woman man. I know I should head home, but I'm going to have too much fun tonight with Beverly to go home now.*

If Keefer could have known what a prophetic possibility of his near death was, he would have made a sound decision and gone home to his family. Unfortunately, rational thinking was secondary to the lust of his deceitful heart.

Keefer had a twisted sense of entitlement though he was now fully aware of what his wife Ginger was capable of when she has been crossed. She had shown she was fairly skilled with a gun and not afraid to use it after lodging two bullets in him. Though the wounds had been basically flesh wounds, using a pistol at all, would normally be reason

260

enough for most men to leave the street life alone and be a true husband. But, Keefer wasn't like most men; he was a bold, ruthless playboy. Now, after finally reconciling with Ginger how did he really have the audacity to betray her again? Did he have a death wish?

He thought to himself, *I've got Ginger right where I want her, happy and satisfied at home, with new diamond studs in her ears, a new vehicle fit for royalty and a sexy loving man next to her–at least most nights. I'm good and these women can't live without me!*

Clearly, Keefer was stuck on Keefer.

* * *

During the day, Keefer repeatedly called Beverly, but to no avail. She was not answering his calls. Although he had left messages, she refused to respond, ignoring him completely. After five failed attempts that day, she finally answered her cell phone.

"What do you want Keefer?" Sounding irritated, she placed her hand on her hip and twisted her mouth with much attitude. Though she was angry with him, she had to admit she wanted to see him too. She reflected, *Maybe I've made him suffer enough. I've really missed him.*

"Bev, how are you girl? I've missed you." Keefer was glad she finally responded. He thought haughtily, *I knew it was just a matter of time; how long could she go without seeing me? She can't resist me.*

"Sure Keefer, tell me anything. You can't assume I'll always be here for you. There are plenty of single men out there that would be ecstatic to have a chance to be with me! You are not the only man knocking on my door!" Beverly rolled her eyes and neck in a ghetto fabulous style.

261

"Bev, you know you're my girl, let me make it up to you tonight. I have a great evening planned and I only want you on my arm! How about it Baby?"

Sighing heavily, she thought a moment, *Should I go out with this man? I love Keefer, but I'm really ready for a man who is completely mine. How can I continue to share him with his wife? I wish I could get rid of her...Maybe she could have a little accident.* Suddenly shaking herself as if cold, she thought, *What am I thinking? I can't do jail time. What should I do? I know I should just leave him alone, but he's just so charming and he's a great lover...*

"Baby, are you still there?" Keefer asked.

Sighing again, she finally said, "Okay Keefer. What time should I be ready?"

"That's my girl; I'll pick you up at seven. You won't be sorry. We'll have a great evening Sweetness. Talk to you later."

"Okay." She hung up the phone and hesitantly walked to her closet to pick something sexy to wear for her 'man.'

* * *

After leaving work, Keefer dialed his girlfriend's number. He had made arrangements to pick her up for a night out.

"Baby, I'm on my way, see you shortly." Keefer was grinning from ear to ear.

She said, "Okay, I'll be ready." Beverly faked being unenthusiastic; in reality she was excited because he always showed her a good time.

Beverly had dressed in a sage green, one shoulder beaded bodice, tight fitting party dress that ended mid-thigh revealing smooth, shimmering skin. She paired it with black sling-back heeled sandals and a slender black clutch purse that hung from her shoulder by a thin black braided cord. She was looking and smelling great, anxious to finally be going out with her man, Keefer Graham. Feeling sassy, she thought, *Finally, my man is spending some quality time with his woman! Watch out Ms. Ginger because Keefer may soon be just my man!*

Technically he wasn't Beverly's man since he was legally married to Ginger. He obviously wasn't committed to his wife, because he insisted on dating Beverly. Emotionally, he was not attached to anyone, but himself. Overall, he was a single man with a marriage license and a player card - both battling to be on top.

When he arrived at Beverly's place, he grabbed the inexpensive clustered heart necklace that he had purchased for her and instead of opening the door with his key, he rang the bell. When she opened the door, surprised that he was standing on the porch waiting, rather than using his key, she winked at him and welcomed his warm embrace and sweet kisses. Pulling away, he said, "I have a little something for you."

He was right, it was just a little after-thought gift. He smiled just thinking about the difference in the two carets of brilliant, solitary diamond earrings that he had purchased for his wife Ginger's ears which were much more expensive than this token for his side chick. He knew Beverly would not know the necklace's worth and he really didn't care if she did.

Bringing his hands down from her shoulder, he retrieved the tiny box from his pocket and said, "This would look good with the cute dress you're wearing. Let me put it on for you."

Opening it she exclaimed, "Ahhh, thanks Keefer, it's pretty." She beamed while he carefully attached the clasp behind her neck.

Beverly was as happy as a kid in a candy store, and Keefer knew he really had the real McCoy at home in Ginger who was intelligent, classy and sophisticated. He reflected, *I knew Beverly would be pleased with that cheap crap. She's not a classy lady, but I like her anyway – at least sometimes.*

"I'm glad you like it, nothing but the best for my girl." Keefer lied right through his teeth. He then said, "Let's go so we can beat some of this traffic. These bands are really great and the atmosphere is reminiscent of our old times together!"

"Okay Keefer, I hope we get some good seats tonight."

"You know me; we have a reserved table right down in the front. Sugar, you are going to enjoy this night from the beginning to the end if you know what I mean." Winking at her, he gently squeezed her hips, hugged her again and after she locked the front door, he grabbed her hand and led her to his fabulous vehicle, opened her door and with a swagger all his own, walked to his side to drive to the event.

* * *

When Keefer and Beverly arrived at the venue, he pulled toward the valet parking and gave his extra key to the attendant. They walked across the brick bridged walkway admiring the trees and artsy waterfall that splashed into the pond below, filled with Koi fish. There were neon lights that accentuated the water and exotic sculptured statues on the manicured lawn.

Momentarily, Keefer paused to admire the various metal structures, but suddenly one in particular caught his eye with its eerie appearance and humanlike out-stretched limbs in a twisted, welcoming stance near the door. It was a weird looking relic.

Keefer looked down at Beverly, but within seconds he saw Ginger's face who he realized was probably at home with Justin, worried about where he could be. Guilt gripped him for a few seconds; however, he blinked and shook himself. In the recesses of his mind, he could almost hear a subtle warning in his spirit, *Go home Keefer – Now!* Unfortunately, he disregarded the wisdom of that inner voice that his mother would have called the Lord's gentle guidance.

Beverly noticed him pausing at the entrance and inquired, "Baby, are you okay? Is something wrong?"

"Everything's fine, Sugar, let's party!" Keefer faked confidence as he once again felt an eerie feeling which he refused to listen to.

Keefer had options; he could have taken Beverly to another place or he could have listened to the fragments of what he had left of integrity, by going home to be a better husband to his wife Ginger. The sheer guarantees of a good time at the club, and the lure of obliged promises of romance at their private after-party at their townhome made him decide to stay and play.

Danger Playhouse Dinner Lounge and Amphitheatre was located on the outskirts of town, which he preferred so that he would not be noticed by anyone. While holding hands, they walked toward the entrance.

Before they crossed the threshold of the building, he noticed two signs that hung under the building's name; one was its' slogan, '*Where you're guaranteed to have a hell-of-a-night...*' The other sign declared, *Warning: Enter at your own risk.* The signs only added to the mystique of the club, and the exhilaration of the forbidden evening.

Inside the building, the lights were dim and the party goers were wall-to-wall deep in the building that had a three hundred occupancy limit. The place was obviously over its limit, but no one seemed to notice or care. The people were either on the dance floor, at the numerous bars drinking it up or lounged at the various sofas and mixed chair arrangements. Too many people were standing on the walls and blocking up the lanes. The fire marshal would have had a cow had he conducted an impromptu inspection.

The handsome and well-groomed emcee had made the necessary announcements about the logistics in the club, the rules against the use of recording devises, and the main attraction, the most popular band in the Southeast region's anticipated performance. The group would be the final live act of the night and excitement was high in the building because they were known to put on a fabulous show.

After all of the other soloists, vocal groups, the jazzy saxophonist, and the comedian were finished with their performances, the lights were dimed while the stage was set for the main attraction. A disk jockey started playing current and old-school tunes, rhythm and blues, rock, and jazz music that soothed the soul. The crowd was delighted and they responded by walking over to the shining, hardwood floor, dancing and socializing while the disco ball rotated, its reflection of lights twinkling against the walls.

Thirty minutes of dancing had passed when the emcee announced that the special group was scheduled to perform in ten minutes. They not only were known for playing wonderful music accompanied by great singers, but they always concluded their segment with an extravagant, hieroglyphic explosive, grand finale.

With excited enthusiasm everyone in the audience partied while waiting to experience the band personally knowing that their engagements were always sold out. After the announcement, the DJ continued to play a wonderful mix of hits until the emcee came again to introduce the band.

The enormous, suburban nightclub still allowed smoking in certain areas and the haze from the nicotine was making Keefer's eyes burn; nevertheless, he was having fun.

He was admiring his long-time interest on the side, Beverly as she did her thing on the dance floor. He was pleased that she had finally started taking his calls again. It had been a slow, up-hill journey back into her arms. After securing his marriage with Ginger and living faithfully for a few, pretentious months, it was time for the master player-player to show back up. Ironically, the "husband" side of Keefer really did love and care for Ginger. His bad-boy side struggled to get a grip on reality in order to commit to his wife permanently; the playboy inside was determined to have its way.

There were two available restaurants for the people to choose from; an elegant bistro that served you at your table and a fast food section that you could order your food and carry it back to your table or chairs that were located around all of the rooms. Keefer had secured the best table in the house directly in front of the stage, and he and Beverly perused the menu to decide on their meal.

The club's fast food short-order cook, Ms. Gladys, regularly fried chicken strips, chicken gizzards and livers, trout and whiting fish and plenty of French fries. There was also a young girl that created smoothies to order. There were three employees who worked as bouncers in case patrons got unruly and for crowd control. There were two more employees; the baker, who specialized in making beautiful deserts and a general manager.

"You are so beautiful Sweetness. Are you enjoying yourself?" Keefer admired his woman on the side while a vague thought of Ginger flashed through his mind. *Ginger is going to be so angry with me. Well, I'll deal with her later.*

"Absolutely, thanks Baby, it's good to be out with you again."

"I know, I feel the same way." After scanning the audience and believing it to be void of anyone familiar to him, he leaned over to kiss Beverly while caressing her shoulder. He didn't realize it, but across the massive room sat one of his employees, Jenna who was out with her boyfriend Jeffery and two other friends. Jenna had spotted him and she was not happy about his behavior at all. Quickly she hit Jeff's arm.

"Hey, Jenna; what's wrong?" Jeffery rubbed the spot where Jenna had struck him. As he noticed the look on her face as she nodded toward the opposite side of the massive room, he thought, *What's going on now?*

"Jeff, that's the same woman Mr. Graham had with him at the bowling alley. He's got some nerve out with her again, disrespecting his wife and family!"

"That's awful." Jeff agreed.

Grabbing her purse from the floor, Jenna dug through the maze of items and produced a camera with an extended lens. She set the switch to date and time-stamp the pictures to secure their authentication. Jenna then flipped off the lens cover, extended the lens automatically and started snapping various pictures of the romancing pair. Jenna thought to herself, *Women are going to have to start sticking together. Maybe Mrs. Graham didn't ask for this type of evidence, however, providing proof for a scorned wife would be satisfying enough. I'll just send these to Mrs. Graham anonymously and she can do whatever she wants to do with them.*

"What are you going to do with those pictures?" Jeff asked.

"Baby, don't ask me any questions, and I won't tell you any lies..." Jenna responded knowing Jeff wouldn't approve of her plan. *He doesn't need to know everything I do.* Jeff just shook his head and continued to enjoy the music.

The group was excellent as they had anticipated. Right before the grand finale, Jenna had to use the restroom. "Jeff, I'll be right back, I've got to go to the ladies' room."

"Right now, Jenna? I hear we shouldn't miss the end of their performance."

"I can't wait! I'll be right back." Jenna pushed her chair back to leave.

"There are a lot of weird people in here, I'll go with you. Hey Ray..." He spoke to a guy at their table, "Save our seats, we'll be right back."

"Sure. No problem." He answered while he placed his hat in Jeff's chair.

As Jeff and Jenna held hands as they made their way to the restrooms that were near the entrance, they weaved in and out of couples and groups of people who were standing along the hallways and huddled beside tables. Jenna reached the door, pushed it open and handled her business. As she washed her hands, she could hear the awesome music; she started hurrying to reenter the main floor. As she exited the door and smiled at Jeff she said, "Okay, my handsome shadow, let's go back inside."

"Let's go, we don't want to miss anything." Jeff grabbed her hand.

The band started its grand finale with a roll of drums, a clanking of symbols, the flashing of lights, white smoke escaping from vents and a host of fire-cracker like blasts. The crowd was going crazy with enthusiasm.

Jeff and Jenna hadn't made it five feet before their steps were interrupted...

Abruptly, they heard what sounded like an explosion. Something had gone terribly wrong. Suddenly men and women started running madly toward the front door, pushing Jeff and Jenna along the way. It turned out that Jenna's ladies' room break had saved their lives. The band's high tech, hieroglyphic equipment had somehow mal-functioned.

As metal strips flew through the air, a large chunk struck Keefer's hand pinning it to Beverly's hand and the table below where they had been holding on to each other. Beverly screamed out in pain as they struggled to release their flesh from the grip of the invading metal. Blood oozed from their injuries as the couple stood up and made their way through the crowd. A piece of wood was hurled toward Beverly's head resulting in an ugly gash above her left eye. Tiny bits of shrapnel had pierced her skin. Her green dress was covered with dirt, sheared glass particles and splotches of blood. Suddenly, as a panicked throng of people rushed their way to exit the club, she and Keefer were separated from each other.

"Keefer, where are you?" Beverly faintly called out as she made her way outside. Moments after saying this, she collapsed onto the sidewalk from the exhaustion of the horrid event, the acute pain from her injuries and shock. She was later picked up and carried to an ambulance.

There had been a stampede of people flooding out of the club grasping bruised and bloody limps. Many people had called 911 and as the ambulances approached, the people with the worse injures were loaded into the vehicles first, and taken to local hospitals.

A nail that protruded from a damaged table had punctured Keefer's leg during the explosion. He limped from the injury as blood seeped out onto his pants. The pain in his limb was excruciating. He applied pressure realizing he was losing a huge amount of blood.

Keefer's mind flashed to the eerie thoughts that he experienced before entering the club; he was sorry now that he hadn't heeded the warnings. He quickly thought of his wife Ginger and wondered how he would explain his predicament. He wasn't concerned about her finding out about Beverly because he didn't know about Jenna's plan to expose him by sending the pictures anonymously. Keefer struggled to keep moving, wanting to get as far from the club as possible. He was eventually picked up by two EMS personnel and taken to a local hospital. Not just morally wrong, this time, cheating had caused Keefer physical harm. Had he been home with his family, he wouldn't have been hurt.

Flames bellowed up to the ceiling as various artifacts melted from the heat of the fire. Eerie screams from patrons echoed throughout the facility. The scene inside was chaotic with the band members and others hurt. Debris was falling from the once beautiful ceiling. Instruments became weapons as they fell apart and spiraled into the air hitting unsuspecting party goers. People screamed from the fear and the pain caused by the flying objects. As the fire spread, the club was quickly emptied by the various workers, from the bouncers to the kitchen staff, helping to lead patrons out of the auditorium into the atrium and out the door into the night air to safety.

The fire department arrived with sirens howling; the uniformed men jumped from the red trucks and grabbed the massive water hoses to begin to fight what was now an intense blaze.

* * *

Once Beverly regained consciousness at the hospital and had a conference with her doctor, she learned that she would recover from her injuries. She also found out that she had a sexually transmitted disease. Keefer had been her only partner. She thought, *An STD? You've got to be kidding me...I'm really through with Keefer, Ginger can have him – he's nasty! I wonder did he also infect her. This is too much!*

I've had enough – This means that he's messing with someone else too because he told me that Ginger is faithful to him, and I know I've been faithful to him. So, that means he's been with someone besides the two of us. That's it! We're done. My heart can't take any more back and forth between the two of us. Now to know there was somebody else. Wait a minute…it could have been more than just another woman. How many other women are in this fiasco? That's over the top! I know I was wrong to mess with a married man, but he must have a sexual addiction. I can't do this anymore. And, I deserve better! I want a man of my own who wants only me!

Reaching over to the drawer that was beside her hospital bed, she turned her cell phone on and texted Keefer. 'Keefer, I hope you are okay from the blast at the club. I am fine. When you get this text message, make sure you really read it and then delete my number. We are through- DONE. It's OVER. You can take your STDs and find someone else to play around with. I deserve better than you are willing to give me. I WANT A FULL TIME MAN. OBVIOUSLY KEEFER, YOU'RE UNAVAILABLE AND INCAPBLE OF BEING FAITHFUL TO ANYONE! GOODBYE, AND THANKS FOR THE MEMORIES.

I could have been all yours,
Beverly

Chapter 37

Keefer woke up to a vision of plain white walls, bleached closet doors and blue and yellow stripped curtains; seeing nothing that was familiar to him.

He focused his eyes on a round wall clock to the time of ten thirty. *It must be morning, but what day is it?* He wondered. Trying to ascertain why he was in this strange place, he sat up in the bed only to feel a sharp pain race across his head. He later found out that he had been in a coma, had undergone surgery and was apparently blessed to be alive.

A registered nurse came in to take his vital signs and administer his medicine. "Good morning Mr. Graham; how are you feeling today?"

"Actually, my head is killing me. Can you give me something?"

"I'll have to check with your doctor; he'll have to approve and write the order for pain medicine."

"Thank you."

"No problem." She left him and before long, Keefer had drifted back to sleep.

After floating in and out of various states of consciousness, Keefer had improved, and now he had been stable for a few days.

Waking up again, he suddenly thought about the events of his last date with Beverly. As the scenes invaded his mind he thought, *I wonder where Beverly is and how is she?* He pulled open the drawer where his cell phone was, turned it on, and noticed several missed calls and text messages. Reading Beverly's text hit him hard. He could tell from her words that his ride with her was over. "Is there no loyalty in this world? Who needs her anyway? Forget Beverly!"

Abruptly, he thought about his wife Ginger and wondered if she knew what had happened to him and who he'd been with at the time of the accident. "No problem Beverly, I still have my wife - faithful Ginger." He placed a call to Ginger, but after five rings, he heard her voicemail. He thought, *That's strange; does she know I'm in this hospital? Why didn't she answer? Maybe she's busy. Maybe she's angry.*

He didn't have to think long. Within an hour, Ginger walked through the door holding a folder and an envelope.

Offering a faint smile, Ginger leaned over to Keefer and gently hugged him. "Good morning Keefer, how are you feeling today?"

I'm better now that you've come through the door. I know I don't look like much in this crappy hospital gown!" Keefer motioned toward his garb.

"No, to be honest, you are not exactly dapper today, but what's most important is your health. Are you okay?"

"I'm good. What's up with you?" Keefer adjusted the volume on the television so that he could hear Ginger.

"Keefer, this may seem like the wrong time to talk about this, but I need to know what you were doing in that club and who were you with?" Unconsciously, Ginger had started tapping the envelope that she held against the folder, and she was not looking like her normally calm, collected self.

274

"Well, what do you mean?" Keefer stalled for time - not exactly sure how to answer Ginger; he assumed that she was generally questioning him with really nothing to dispute his version of events.

"Who went to the club with you the night of the explosion?" Ginger was getting impatient with him as she thought to herself, *You had better not lie to me right now, I'll have a little mercy if you'll just tell me the truth.*

"I went with some of the guys from work." He lied just like he so often did in a sticky situation.

"Really, Keefer, you insult my intelligence. You have the nerve to look me in the face and lie! I'm sick of your foolish games! Take a look at these!" Ginger hissed as she tossed an envelope onto his chest.

Keefer opened the envelope and was stunned to see the mixed array of pictures of him hugged up and lip-locked with Beverly, his chick on the side – at the nightclub! There were shots from various angles as well as frames of them while they were on the dance floor with his hands in a compromised position around her hips and butt.

Feeling vulnerable, he said, "How did you get those pictures? Did you have me followed?" Caught, he tried to divert her attention from the issue at hand – his infidelity. He had the nerve to have an attitude.

"No, I didn't have you followed, but this envelope arrived in the mail yesterday. Somebody thought I should see the photos. You know a picture is worth a thousand words and frankly, I'm glad to know the whole truth."

"Those are old pictures Ginger. They don't prove a thing." The lie easily rolled through Keefer's lips like melted butter on hot popcorn.

"No Keefer, look closer. The pictures are date and time stamped, within minutes of the explosion. Furthermore, you are wearing the new Versace shirt that I gave you for Father's Day. You can't lie your way out of this one!"

"Ginger, I can explain…"

"Who is she Keefer? What's her name? Is she the nasty whore that you caught the STD from?" Though Ginger was very upset, she was keeping her tone down, not wanting to cause a scene, but she was getting angry just thinking about the whole ordeal of being treated at her doctor's office for a foul STD. She raised her finger to imply 'wait a minute.' Ginger then walked over to close the door to his private room and then returned to his bedside raising her eyebrows, waiting for an answer.

Inhaling and then blowing a deep breath, he replied, "Her name is Beverly; and no Ginger, she's not a whore!"

"Then what would you call a woman that sleeps with a married man?" She snapped. *If this man wasn't sick already, I'd hurt him myself. How dare he defend her reputation!* She angrily thought.

"She's my friend, not someone dirty…" Stammering, Keefer didn't know what to say.

"Yeah, she's your 'friend with benefits' who passes out sexually transmitted diseases! Give me a break!"

"She didn't give me anything! It wasn't her!" He raised his voice slightly finding himself offended that she would consider Beverly a whore.

"Then who was it? Or, are you just trying to protect the sleazy woman?" Now Ginger had raised her voice; she was glad that his hospital room was at the end of the hallway.

"It was a street woman, Ginger!" In his quest to defend Beverly, Keefer had blurted out the unthinkable.

"A STREET WOMAN?" she yelled. "Are you telling me that you had sex with a nasty prostitute; a hooker – UNPROTECTED? Keefer, are you saying you did that, and you then came home to me and made love like everything was normal? YOU'VE GOT TO BE KIDDING ME!"

Ginger sighed heavily, and continued. "Do you realize you could have contracted an incurable disease? YOU ARE JUST NASTY, STUPID, AND CRAZY!" Now shouting, Ginger was furious.

With the realization that he had shown his total hand, because he had no intention of telling Ginger about the hookers; Keefer felt he had to come clean in order to possibly save his marriage. "I'm ashamed to say it Ginger, but yes, I'd gotten into some pretty sick stuff. I know you are angry, but we can work through this. I don't want to lose you. I promise this will never happen again. I'll end my relationship with Beverly; I'll get counseling; and I won't see hookers anymore!"

Realizing what he had just admitted to – a habit of frequenting prostitutes, Ginger felt sick to her stomach. Quickly recovering, she said, "Apparently, you regularly slept with hookers... Is that what you're telling me?" She now whispered in shocked disbelief. He was a lower snake than she even realized. She had assumed he had a mistress; now she knew firsthand that he had a host of twisted connections that could possibly kill her. She thought, *He is definitely one crazy man – whom I loved and blindly trusted again! I feel just like a fool.*

He dropped his head and muttered, "Yes Ginger – I'm deeply sorry."

"Sorry? What in the hell were you thinking? You've sunk to an all-time low, even for you!" Ginger suddenly felt nauseous just thinking about him with them – and then him with her. It was overwhelming. She grabbed onto the bed rail to steady herself. Ginger had assumed that he was cheating with someone, but just thinking about her husband with women of the night, made her want to vomit. In fact, she couldn't stand the sight of him much longer.

Keefer dropped his head and again said, "I'm sorry Ginger, but…." When she raised her hand for him to stop, he didn't say another word.

Continuing, Ginger said, "That's okay Keefer, you don't have to break off your relationship with Beverly–she can have you! And, you can lay up with a thousand hookers. I'm done! I just want to know why you would do this to me, and to us."

Raising his head and looking ashamed he said, "Ginger, it was exciting. Being with someone new felt good, but I never meant to hurt you."

"Really? I suppose you thought extra women on the side would help me! Perhaps you figured I would be grateful just to be one of your many sexual partners! You are a very confused and sick man with absolutely no integrity!" With that last statement, she tossed another envelope onto his lap. "Open it up, Keefer!"

"What's this?" As he asked the question, he unfolded the thick packet and realized that he was holding divorce papers in his hands.

"No Ginger, don't do this. Don't break up our family. I'll do whatever you want. We need to talk about this and not race to divorce court."

"*Me* break up our family? This is what you've done!"

"Let's go on a trip so we can talk this over. I'll even go to counseling! Whatever you want Ginger, I'll do it." Keefer pleaded with a distraught expression on his face.

Sarcastically, she said, "Oh, really; now you want to talk and attend counseling? I'm done talking Keefer. I've secured an excellent lawyer and I suggest that you do the same! When you're released from this hospital, don't contact me by phone, letter, text, fax, E-mail, FedEx, Facebook, Twitter, through a friend, in person, via a gift, by a courier service or any other way! Do you hear me, Keefer? WE ARE THROUGH – FINISHED – DONE – OVER!" Ginger yelled. "I'll never let you hurt me again!"

As Ginger noticed the shocked and hurt expression on his face as he opened his mouth to speak again, she quietly tapped her index finger over her mouth to indicate silence. She didn't want to hear any more of his lies or excuses.

Then Ginger said, "Beverly might want to hear what you have to say – and she may also need to go visit her doctor to check for STDs. But, if you have *ANYTHING* further to say to me, you can say it through my lawyer. I'll see you in court!"

Ginger turned around and rushed out of the room. As she entered the hallway, her eyes filled with tears, however, she wouldn't let them flow down her face. She quickly wiped them and walked away from his room. As she briskly walked through the corridors of the hospital towards the elevators, she felt relieved, like she was walking on a cloud.

Once inside the elevator, Ginger took a deep breath and pressed the button that would take her to the first floor. As she walked outside the hospital grounds inhaling the fresh air, she felt free for the first time in years. Ginger mentally promised herself that the weight of an unhappy and unfulfilling relationship would never hold her down again.

Not knowing how she would handle seeing him or the frustration she might feel if he lied again about his proven infidelity, Ginger had hired a friend who was also a licensed chauffeur to take her to the hospital. As she approached her true dream car which was a free and clear gift from Keefer, a Rolls Royce Phantom 62; the driver quickly opened her rear door and held her hand as she stepped inside. Then, after sitting in the driver's seat and buckling in, he said, "Where to Mrs. Graham?"

"Take me to the airport; I'm now free to enjoy a true vacation and dare to live my dreams!" Her suitcases were already in the trunk.

"Yes you are, Mrs. Ginger Davis Graham. And you deserve the best!"

"Thank you Ryan." She replied.

Realizing she needed a break, Ginger had sent Justin to visit his father. Her diva dog Pepper was being pampered at a posh doggie resort.

As the luxury vehicle exited the lot, Ginger pulled off her platinum and diamond wedding ring, dropping it into a pocket in her purse. Glancing at her first class plane ticket, she smiled and pleasantly thought to herself, *I don't need this ring anymore. Besides, I never know who I'll meet in Italy!*